SEE NO
EVIL

Also by Eleanor Taylor Bland

Keep Still
Done Wrong
Gone Quiet
Slow Burn
Dead Time

SEE NO
EVIL

ELEANOR
TAYLOR
BLAND

ST. MARTIN'S PRESS........NEW YORK

Library of Congress Cataloging-in-Publication Data

Bland, Eleanor Taylor,
    See no evil : a Marti MacAlister mystery / Eleanor Taylor Bland.
  —1st ed.
      p.   cm.
    ISBN 0-312-16910-8
    I. Title.
    PS3552.L36534S44   1998
    813'.54—dc21   97-39642
                                                   CIP

First edition: February 1998

10 9 8 7 6 5 4 3 2 1

In memory of Leonard Hogan, "Hero," March 12, 1971–May 5, 1997. We shall always miss you.

ACKNOWLEDGMENTS

My deepest admiration and appreciation to Torren Flink, Executive Director, and the staff at LaCasa: Lake County Council Against Sexual Assault.

A very special thank you to Dr. Gretchen Naff, the Board of Directors, and the faculty of the College of Lake County.

Accolades and applause to Archie Givens Jr., Director, The Givens Foundation for African American Literature, Minneapolis, Minnesota; Mrs. Carol Givens; and the foundation staff.

A toast to Grace, Lee, and Lisa.

To Al Rosenston, Richard Katz, and Mark Agin—Superfans.

For technical assistance, thanks to Michael Beale, paramedic; Marge Beatty; William Fatout; Dr. Charles V. Holmberg; Lt. Hugh Holton, Chicago Police Department; Susan and Todd Little; Sharon D. Johnson; Steve Kalbfleisch; Nathan "Nate the Great" Pangburn; Ed Parnell at Shimer College; Elizabeth Stiles, who is not a witch; and John Zegar, who is a fisherman.

And as always, to Ted Chichak.

SEE NO
EVIL

He entered the house through the back door, using the keys he had stolen. The door clicked shut behind him and he stood there listening, familiar with the sounds of the house when nobody was home, alert for any noise that was different. He had watched them all leave, but a cop lived here. If he got careless, the hunter could become the hunted.

They must have been running late this morning, although they had left on time. Two bowls with little O's floating in milk were still on the table, along with a pumpkin that hadn't been there yesterday, and Indian corn and small gourds.

He stood still, waiting. Once again, several minutes passed before the dog came downstairs. It was the size of a St. Bernard but could have been any of half a dozen breeds. It stood in the doorway to the bright yellow kitchen and gave a quick flick of its tail. When he took the Hershey's Kisses out of his pocket, it came closer.

"Good boy. You remember me. Here, have a treat."

While the dog poked at the silvery paper, he crossed to the window and, looking between the leaves of the hanging plant, estimated the size of the yard again. The distance to the back of the garage, where he could not be seen by the neighbors. The distance to the chain-link fence that bordered another backyard—an easy fence to climb if he had to, and not one barking dog for two blocks.

Almost every house on both streets emptied out by 8:30 in the morning. Only once in the past week had he seen a straggler.

Last Saturday, three houses had had evening visitors, but so far, during the week, guests were rare.

He closed the basement door behind him and made his way down the stairs in the dark, quickly and soundlessly. He turned and walked up as quietly as he had descended. He would have to open the door fast and catch whoever was in the kitchen by surprise. He wanted her. He wanted to catch her alone. He wanted to have a lot of time when he did. He pictured all of them, the two women and three or four kids on the other side of the door. And the dog. He thought it through in every combination of women and children, still unable to decide how to take them all out if he did it downstairs. He would have to kill all of them. If the police figured out who his target was, they would find out who he was.

This was his third time inside the house, although he had made it as far as the yard a few times before and become acquainted with the dog. Now, with his eyes closed, he went from room to room, walking into a wall only once. He visualized each room before opening his eyes and was wrong only about the placement of one chair in the living room. He wouldn't need a flashlight.

He slipped on a pair of latex gloves and kept to the side of the stairs, just as he had seen them do in cop movies, as he went to the second floor. He stopped at the boys' bedroom. This was where he should start. It wouldn't be a problem even if both boys were here. At night, the dog would be in here, too. Yes, he would start here. But if he used the gun, even with a silencer there would be a pop. Would the others recognize the sound? Would they come looking to see what had happened? He didn't want to use a knife or a plastic bag on the boys. He couldn't calculate how long it would take with a bag. It wasn't as quick or as easy as they made it out to be in the movies. The knife would be too messy. Besides, with this many people, he could practice different ways of killing.

The girls' room was next. He picked up Joanna's gym shorts, sweats, and underwear from the floor. He held the clothes to his face and inhaled, becoming erect as he smelled her sweat and a floral cologne. Joanna was so pretty. She was much better looking than her mother, even though they looked a lot alike. Maybe, if there was time . . .

The bureau in the next room was cluttered with jewelry and all kinds of cosmetics and perfume. He picked up a pair of earrings that hadn't been there the day before, yellow birds with bright beads like the beads woven into Sharon's braids. He pocketed them. Junk, all of it. No way anyone would think the inhabitants had interrupted a robbery, not once they came in here.

The cop's room was last. He ignored the unmade bed and the clothes draped over the back of the chair and went to the closet. Today the door was locked. Two days ago, it had been open. The locked box on the shelf, made of such a solid metal that it was almost too heavy to lift, must be where she kept her spare gun, or guns. Too bad he had never learned how to pick locks. He could always use another gun.

He would have to kill the others before she came home, or kill her first. Logic said kill the others and wait for her in the basement. The first light she turned on when she came in was the light in the kitchen. He backed out of the room and went downstairs. He would have to remain calm after he killed them, calm enough to wait and kill her.

At first, his plan was much simpler: just grab her, slit her throat, and have done with it. But now, watching them, walking in the space where they lived, touching the clothing they wore, tasting the food they ate, petting their dog, being able to come and go in their lives just as he pleased . . . now he was truly invisible. He could kill whomever he wanted to, any way that he wanted to, and he wanted to kill them all.

When he returned to the kitchen, the dog stood and looked at him. Curious, maybe, but not suspicious. He collected the candy wrappers and reached for the paper towels to clean a tiny chocolate smear on the floor. The dog—he was almost getting attached to it.

1

Isaac was not superstitious, but when he saw someone float around the yard of that old house in the middle of the night and disappear into thin air, he did wonder if his grandmother was right about "hants." When he woke up in the morning, he took his time folding up the blankets that served as his bed. He hid them in the closet, hoping nobody would steal them, and walked across the empty room to look out the window. The house seemed ordinary enough now, with white curtains hanging at each window, but he could still remember seeing that ghost Friday night, so it must not have been the liquor or the d.t.'s. If his buddy Dare hadn't been gone two or three days now, maybe even four, he would have talked it over with him.

Dare. He reached for the muscatel bottle. Empty. It sure was getting hard to keep enough alcohol on hand. That's probably why he had seen somebody's ghost the other night, and it sure must be why he remembered. Damn shame when a man couldn't get drunk enough to forget he was hallucinating. End of the month and his money was running out. Time Dare showed up with some alcohol. If he didn't get something soon, he really would be seeing things.

They never should have moved here. He knew that as soon as he turned the corner and saw that shopping cart sitting in that vacant lot. He didn't need to be no place where folks kept all their stuff in a shopping cart. Even homeless folk had to have some pride about themselves. Wasn't nothing dignified about pushing no shopping cart around or expecting folks to feel sorry for you or give you a handout.

When the garage next to their old place burned to the ground, the city just came in and tore everything down. Improving the lakefront, they said. Their place was two blocks from the lakefront. Never mind that a man needed a place to live, someplace where he could have some privacy and a little peace and quiet.

This place was too close to civilization. People were living in the house next door, with heat, hot water, electricity and all. Noisy folks, too. Loud music at two in the morning and that damned car with the horn that played that La Cockroach song. No matter that there was a vacant lot on the other side; there weren't no trees, nar' a one. Trees would have been better, lots of trees, but Dare said he hadn't seen no place like the one they'd been staying in, and he'd know, riding a garbage truck and all.

It wasn't like Dare to take off like this. Last time he'd stayed gone, he'd been locked up in jail for disturbing the peace, and the time before that, he was in the hospital because he'd been knocked in the head. Both times, he wasn't gone no four or five days, though. Maybe Dare really had taken sick. Stomach pains had been getting to him for a while now. Maybe Isaac ought to call the hospitals, find him, see how he was. He could go slip him something to drink, just a little something to hold him up until he got better. Isaac picked up the wine bottle, held it up to the light. Not a drop, and he had just seven dollars and another week to be broke.

By the time Isaac made it to Queen Mary's, he was getting the shakes. When his eyes got used to the dark, he looked around. Queenie was at the bar, an itty-bitty old black woman eating a plateful of eggs, bacon, and grits, like she was wanting to get fat. He stepped over the cat litter sprinkled on the floor and held his breath so the smell wouldn't make him want to throw up, too. The place was empty except for a couple of hookers bracing themselves for a long day with a little conversation and some house whiskey.

Isaac sat on a stool and tried to ignore the sweet smell of draft beer that hit him as soon as he got close to the bar. It smelled so good, he could almost taste it. His stomach groaned.

Queenie scooped up some grits and chased them with half a glass of draft. "I ain't seen your friend Dare in four, five days now," she said.

"He run up a tab?" Isaac asked.

"Not yet. But you look like you're about to." Isaac accepted a glass of wine. Queenie replaced it with another, then another as he gulped it down. The burning in his stomach felt good. He could make it for a couple of hours now.

"Cigarette?" Queenie asked, lighting up one for herself.

"Nah, that tobacco'll kill you."

She blew smoke in his face. "This secondhand stuff will, too."

"You ain't seen Dare for maybe five days now?" Had Dare been gone that long? He'd seen him—when? Friday morning, early, before daylight.

"Sure ain't. He come in here with some red Negro. Thursday night, I think it was. They had a few drinks and was gone."

"What red Negro?" Dare had too many friends for Isaac's liking, but he couldn't remember nobody like that. "He have freckles?"

"No, just light-skinned, with them red-looking naps. Boy did have it cut short. Ain't much else you can do with that kind of hair."

Isaac sure couldn't think of nobody he knew of who looked like that. 'Course, knowing Dare, he could have met up with him right outside on the street and took him up on an offer to have a drink.

"Boy's too damned friendly," Isaac said. Dare was known to wander up to Milwaukee or down to Chicago for a day or two if he hooked up with some woman who liked to have a good time. But last week, Dare would have been damned near broke, and he didn't like going nowhere with no money in his pocket, specially not with no female. Isaac accepted one more glass for the road and tried not to think about the tab he was running up.

Wasn't nothing good about getting nothing on credit. Outside, the sun hit him in the face and a cold wind came right through his jacket.

Detective Marti MacAlister negotiated a rutted dirt and gravel road to an unpaved parking area not far from the lake. The body of a young woman had been found there, not far from the old Edison plant. Three squads, an ambulance, and the coroner's station wagon were parked at various angles, along with four civilian cars more precisely aligned. Marti's partner, Matthew "Vik" Jessenovik, got out of their unmarked vehicle. Vik was four inches taller than Marti's five ten. The overcoat he was wearing was belted at the waist and emphasized how thin he was. His face was craggy, with a beaklike nose that was skewed to one side from a break. Vik had a ferocious scowl and almost never smiled. Most adults were intimidated by him, but kids weren't fazed at all. He stood with one hand shading his wiry salt-and-pepper eyebrows as he looked around. This was an industrial area. Chain-link fences surrounded mounds of dirt and sand, stubby trees, scrub and spiky grasses. NO SWIMMING signs warned of dangerous currents, although from where she stood, Marti could see only a large pond-shaped inlet abutting the electric plant and the dunes that obscured her view of Lake Michigan.

"The old coker," Vik said with a nod toward the redbrick plant. "This place has really changed. I can't believe it. This is a real electrical plant, MacAlister. None of that nuclear fusion or whatever they do down the road there." They could see the twin stacks of the nuclear plant in the distance. "This place burns real fuel. See all of those piles of coke?"

They had to drive past the coker to get here. It was several stories high, with three of its eight stacks still operating.

Five civilians stood in a tight circle on the sand near the edge of the pond. As Marti and Vik walked toward them, the lake came into view, gray-blue, with whitecaps and gulls that wheeled and cried overhead. Dr. Cyprian, Marti and Vik's favorite medical examiner, was standing on a footbridge that spanned the inlet separating the pond from the lake. One end of the bridge jutted into the lake; the other crossed to a brief stretch of sand. Cyprian climbed over the railing to stand on the sand. He walked slowly around a circular ridge of boulders several times, then knelt, his back to the wind.

Marti walked with Vik, stood on the metal grating of the bridge, and looked down, surprised by how narrow the inlet was and how shallow the water. The victim looked dry. She was small, lying facedown. Her long black hair was either trapped in the rocky crevices or had been lifted and settled by the wind. Her blue velvet jacket and purple satin slacks were too thin for the weather. The circular pattern of the rocks sheltered the body from sight and from the elements. One of her hands, the color of light coffee, rested palm-up on the sand.

Marti beckoned to a uniform. "Who found her?"

The uniform nodded toward a man sitting in one of the squads with the back doors open. "He called for paramedics. They called us." A fishing pole was propped against the hood of the squad car, next to an overturned bucket and a tackle box.

Marti and Vik trudged back through the sand to talk with the witness.

"I didn't go near . . . didn't touch . . ." he sputtered.

"How long were you here before you saw her?" Marti asked.

"I got here at daybreak. The rocks . . . I didn't see anything. It was the birds. I thought someone had thrown some fish there. That's what got my attention. Then I saw the hair kind of blowing in the wind."

"What time was that?"

"Seven o'clock, seven-thirty."

It was close to nine now. Marti wasn't sure of the work schedule for the Edison plant—if it had two or three eight-hour shifts or eight-hour days.

"Was there much traffic when you came?"

"I came before the traffic," the man said. "I come here a lot. I've been coming for years. I used to come with my old man, then my kids. Now I come alone."

9

"Did you see anything unusual?"

"No."

"Nothing out of the ordinary?"

"Just the birds." He blanched. "Seagulls."

Marti shaded her eyes and looked around. There was nothing, except for a portable lavatory, to encourage anyone to come here.

"Why would anyone fish here?" she asked.

"Salmon," Vik said. "The coho come here this time of year to spawn."

"Isn't it illegal to kill them then?"

"No," Vik said. "You're more likely to catch them afterward, and they die then anyway. Besides, this isn't a local hot spot. How much of an impact on the salmon population can five or six fishermen have?"

Dr. Cyprian made his way up from the rocks. He was a small, slender man with coppery skin and straight black hair. His work was methodical, meticulous, and reliable. "Massive facial and head injuries," he said when he reached them. "She hit those rocks headfirst. The body never touched the water."

"Time?" Marti asked.

"Hard to say. The birds didn't do too much damage, and it's been cold."

Vik kicked at the sand. "How bad is her face?"

Dr. Cyprian shook his head. "We won't ID her that way."

"Can you give us some prints?"

"Since she was never in the water, her hands are intact, with no gloving," Cyprian said. "We'll give you whatever we can as soon as possible."

Vik's eyebrows almost met as he watched Cyprian walk away. "We'll have to canvass the plant workers," he said. "I don't have a clue how many people work there. At least this won't take long." He waved at the trees and sand and makeshift parking lot. "Nobody here but the seagulls and those five idiots over there with their fishing poles. Let's make sure the idiots didn't see anything."

Marti took her camera out of the case and made her way to the body. She shot a roll of color film and then a black-and-white one. As she adjusted the lenses for different shots, she thought about how incongruous this would look when the film was developed: clear, sunny skies, sprays of water as waves crashed against the craggy shore, seagulls overhead, and a woman with long hair, wearing party clothes, dead. Whose mother's child was this? How did she come to these rocks?

Vik came down as soon as she put the camera away. "Our five friendly fishermen didn't know anything was wrong until the uniforms showed up."

"We'll still have to come back," she said.

"Right. And real early, just in case we've got a few before-dawn fishermen as well as the crack-of-dawn rod-and-reel fanatics." He looked down at the body, then shielded his eyes and scanned the lake. "No small craft out there. At least the sailors around here have some sense."

"My father was a fisherman," he said as they headed for the car. "Fished most of the summer. Sometimes he fished here. But never this time of year. Nobody but a damned fool comes out when it gets this cold."

"Didn't you ever go ice fishing, Jessenovik?"

The look he gave her suggested that he had not.

It took the rest of the morning for Marti, Vik, and two other teams to question the first-shift plant workers without causing a major disruption to their work.

When Marti and Vik got back to the precinct, they could hear Slim, one of the Vice detectives who shared their office, whistling before they opened the door. Slim's partner, Cowboy, was sitting with his size-thirteen, hand-tooled western boots propped on his desk and his five-gallon hat cocked back, exposing his wavy blond hair. When Vik raised his eyebrows, Marti gave him a slight turn of her head. If Vik asked them what they were so happy about, they might tell him, and Lincoln Prairie Vice cops didn't lead very exciting lives, at least not compared to Chicago, where Marti had worked for ten years before coming here.

As Marti passed Cowboy's desk, she looked down and saw a drawing of a penis. She looked away.

"You draw that yourself?" Vik asked.

Marti wished she was close enough to elbow him in the ribs.

"Me?" Cowboy said. "Of course not. We had the witness come in and give a description. This is an important piece of evidence. Damned near as good as fingerprints."

"We've got a make on our Halloween wienie wagger," Slim said.

"Not the yo-yo who gets dressed up like a jack-o'-lantern every year and shows little old ladies his 'tongue'?" Vik said.

"You got it."

"Don't tell me that after fifteen years Vice is finally gaining on him. Halloween is still four days away."

"Do you have to encourage them, Jessenovik?" Marti said.

Vik came close to smiling. "I thought for sure you two would get him last year. I mean, hanging out at nursing homes? The man's running out of target populations."

"Jessenovik!"

Slim poured Marti a cup of coffee. "He's beginning to rub off on you, MacAlister," he said. "Be better for the rest of us if a little more of you would rub off on him." Tall, slender, with skin the color of caramel, Slim gave her his most flirtatious grin. The odor of his favorite cologne, Obsession for Men, was almost enough to make her eyes water.

"Does this mean your Halloween stakeout of that college on Sherman is called off?" she asked.

"If it is, I sure hope you don't plan on hanging around here," Vik said.

"This guy is frequenting the off-site campus on Lincoln, too," Slim said. "He's into coeds this year, youth and beauty. Midlife crisis, maybe."

"But we've finally got a make on him." Cowboy held up the artist's rendition of the penis.

"Female officer present," Vik said.

Vik's protest sounded a bit perfunctory. Marti missed the days of Vik's acute indignation at off-color jokes when she was around. She was becoming one of the boys. "Seen one, you've seen them all," she said.

"Aha!" Cowboy said. "Look again, my less-than-observant sleuth."

"At what?"

"A birthmark."

Vik studied the drawing. "It could be a tattoo."

Slim winced. "Man would be a hero, not a villain, if that was the case."

"Who gave you that little tidbit of information?" Vik asked.

"The philosophy instructor," Slim said. "Apparently when our man jumped out of the bushes dressed like a jack-o'-lantern, she thought he looked like a jackass."

"And," Cowboy said, "when he wagged his little wiener, she was not at all impressed with the smiling pumpkin's tongue."

Slim laughed. "She told him he'd better put it back in his pants before she amputated it."

"Typical flasher," Cowboy said, "no ball—"

"Lady present," Vik said, holding up his hand. "So what do you do now? Have a lineup?"

"Actually, we have been considering it," Slim said.

Cowboy chuckled. "It's just a matter of deciding who our honored guests should be."

They were interrupted by a knock on the door.

"Fax," the uniform said.

Vik scanned the sheet of paper and looked at Marti. "We're already getting queries on our Jane Doe."

By the time Isaac walked to the yards where the garbage trucks came in, most folks were going home. It wasn't nowhere near the dump, and the trucks had been emptied, but the stink was so strong, it made him expect to turn around and see Dare. He didn't see anyone Dare rode with, but he asked around anyway. Everyone he asked knew Dare, but none of them had seen him since last week. Isaac was hoping Dare had a locker or someplace where he could have stashed something to drink, but only the regulars had those. Dare was an extra, riding when someone got sick or took a day off. In fact, Dare was an extra because his uncle had worked for the company for thirty-five years before he retired, and he had gotten the foreman to take Dare on.

By the time Isaac asked everyone who would stop to talk with him, including the foreman, when they had last seen Dare, it was almost six o'clock, and in spite of the smell, Isaac's stomach rumbled. He considered whether he seemed sober enough to stop at the church for something to eat. He sure hadn't had enough to drink to feel drunk. Tuesday—the old Catholic church on Eureka. If the old priest was around . . .

The doors opened just before he got there. He stood at the end of the line, then let a Puerto Rican couple with half a dozen kids go ahead of him. When they started jabbering in Spanish, he couldn't understand a word they were saying. They needed to talk like Americans, same as he did. He wondered how long it would take him to learn Spanish if he went to their country. Probably forever. Still, talking so someone couldn't understand what you were saying didn't seem polite.

The round-faced, smiling woman met him at the door. She took a couple of steps back, so he guessed he must smell. The smile sort of froze on her face and her eyes got this "Oh Lord, not him again" look. Isaac caught a whiff of spaghetti sauce. He thought about the salad and warm cheese bread they always served with it, but the woman's face made him turn away.

"Isaac," the priest called when he was halfway down the steps. The old man walked with a limp. "Come and have dinner with me." He was so skinny, he looked as if he was the one who needed something to eat.

They ate upstairs, in a pew near the back of the church. It was an old church, with cracks in the plaster and water stains near the roof, and painted statues, a lot like the church Isaac had gone to as a kid. That priest wasn't so nice, though, and the kids had called Isaac and his brothers and sisters the "dirty Wartons" because they were dirty. "Urchins," one of the nuns said one day, with one of them careful expressions on her face that gave him no clue what she was really saying. "Urchins." He still didn't know what that meant.

"I'll get us some more," the priest said when Isaac sopped up the rest of the sauce with what was left of the bread. He wasn't that hungry, now that he'd eaten something, but he loved spaghetti and cheese bread. The old man had taken just a little food and picked at that, so Isaac knew he wasn't hungry. He didn't want Isaac to have to deal with that uppity woman downstairs. But Isaac knew the old man would give her a look that was like the God of Moses staring at her, and just the thought of it tickled him. Seditty, she was, turning her nose up just because he didn't live where there was running water.

Isaac looked up at the statue of Saint Francis with the bird perched on his hand. Why would a man born rich want to be poor? Did Francis smell? Had he been hungry? And why, for all that he said he would not be, was Isaac still one of them "dirty Wartons"?

"Good man, Saint Francis," the old priest said when he came back. "He had an amazing ability to see."

"Isaac don't never see nothing."

The priest smiled. "Maybe Isaac's already seen too much."

While Isaac ate seconds, the priest poured church wine and a can of soda into paper cups. "So how's it going?" he asked, sipping the soda.

"Can't say." Isaac tried to be mannerly and sip the wine instead of chugalugging it.

"It's getting cold, Isaac. Winter's just about here. Come by after Mass Friday morning, you and Dare."

The sign said there would be a rummage sale in the church basement on Saturday. He and Dare didn't take charity, but there was something different about being treated like a guest and offered the best of what was to be had. "Can't find Dare," Isaac said. "Getting worried. Ain't like him to stay away so long." He hadn't been to confession in thirty years and still told the priest more than he intended to. "Can't even guess where he could have gone to. Ain't nothing been right since they tore our place down."

"Are you getting settled in where you are?"

"Too noisy. Cars driving up and down the street all hours of the night. Noisy folks right next door." He'd thought he'd heard a few shots popping last weekend, but it could have been one of them trucks with the itty-bitty wheels backfiring. Then, of course, there was whatever come out of that window and disappeared in them bushes just like fog. It gave him goose bumps remembering. "Might not be there too much longer. Dare's looking out for some-place else."

The priest poured more wine, and a little soda for himself, and they touched cups. There was no sign of the cross and no prayers and no blessings and none of that Latin, but when their cups met, it reminded Isaac of his grandmother putting her hands on his head.

2

It was almost half past six when he walked into the high school gym. It was an away game, and he had been hung up in traffic as soon as he hit Route 22. The girls' volleyball teams were still warming up, but he had missed most of the practice. The noise already seemed deafening and the game hadn't even begun. Kids were always so damned loud. They couldn't talk unless they yelled, couldn't listen to music unless they turned the volume full blast, couldn't sit in the bleachers unless they stomped their feet. He hated noise. He hated being around kids. Their parents would be just as bad, yelling and catcalling and complaining about the ref calls as if this were a pro game with a championship at stake. He studied the bleachers for a few minutes and didn't see anyone he knew or anyone he thought might recognize him. Even if he did, he had as much right to be here as they did. It would be better, though, if he wasn't noticed, if nobody ever recalled that he had been here.

Joanna was easy to spot. Two of the other girls were as tall as she was, a few were as athletic, but none were as pretty. The Lincoln Prairie uniforms were shorter and tighter than the other team's. The tops were looser, but that only enhanced the bouncing of their breasts as they ran and jumped for the ball. If it wasn't for the exposure of thigh, the soft curve of ass, and the jiggling of breasts, girls' volleyball would be a complete waste as a sport.

He found a seat in a section of the bleachers that seemed inconspicuous, right behind a giggling bunch of girls. Silly, all of them, not ladylike and studious and intelligent like Joanna. And unlike Joanna, underdeveloped. He thought of the pink cotton underpants he had touched just that morning, imagined them silky and still caressing the curves of her body. He imagined the terror in her eyes as he tore them off.

"Excuse me," a woman said. She sounded annoyed. "Sir? Would you please let me pass?"

He clenched his fist and felt like smashing her jaw.

He had to hold his jacket in front of him to hide his erection as he stood up. The whistle blew and the game began. The girls began jiggling and jogging about the court. There were a few distractions, but he never lost sight of Joanna.

Marti checked her watch: 7:15. She should be at her daughter Joanna's game. If it had been just at the high school, she could have slipped out and gone over for a quick half hour, but it was an away game at Stevenson High.

They had an ID on the girl at the beach, and an approximate time of death, sometime yesterday. They didn't have much else. The victim, Ladiya Norris, had lived in Chicago. Nobody was answering the phone. Until they could speak with someone who knew her, there wasn't much they could do. Ladiya had two priors for possession with intent to sell. Both times, she had walked. There was nothing to connect her with Lincoln Prairie, nothing to indicate why she would jump off a narrow, nondescript bridge at a rocky area along the lake where there wasn't any water to jump into. If it hadn't been accidental, or a suicide, there would be enough forensic evidence to be useful, if and when they knew what they were looking for.

"I'll be glad when Halloween's over," Marti said.

"Me, too," Vik agreed. "I hope this flasher is just your ordinary weirdo and not a certified nutcase. He could be getting pretty frustrated right about now."

Over the years, the flasher had become something of a joke around the precinct. Marti didn't think he was funny, but then, this was only her third year on the Lincoln Prairie force. Maybe she hadn't been around long enough.

She tried Ladiya Norris's number again. This time, a woman answered the phone.

"I haven't seen her since Labor Day," the woman said.

"Are you a relative?"

"Her mother."

"We'd like to talk with you as soon as possible," Marti said.

"Lord, what's she gotten herself into now?" Her voice sounded tired, but she agreed to see them right away.

Marti phoned home first.

"You're going to be late," Sharon said. Marti and Sharon had been best friends since kindergarten. Marti's husband, Johnny, had died not long after Sharon got divorced. Now Marti shared Sharon's home and split the expenses. Sharon, a schoolteacher with a daughter six months younger than Joanna, was home after school to watch the girls and Marti's ten-year-old son, Theo. Marti told her she didn't know what time she would be home tonight.

"Well, I want to go out, too," Sharon said. "Joanna and Lisa are fifteen now, and they've both baby-sat before. It seems like they'd be okay here with the boys for a few hours."

Marti had recently become engaged. "The boys" included Mike, the ten-year-old son of her fiancé, Ben Walker. Ben was a paramedic on duty for two twenty-four-hour shifts and off duty for two. Mike stayed at Marti's house when Ben was on duty.

"I need to get out of here for a couple of hours."

Marti chose not to answer, at least not over the phone. Since the divorce, Sharon was alternately celibate for months at a time or dating some Mr. Wonderful who never quite measured up to Sharon's vague and variable expectations. The current Mr. Wonderful seemed to be a lot more demanding than the others. Sharon seemed irritable and disatisfied a lot of the time.

"Look, Sharon, I have to make a quick trip to Chicago to tell a lady her daughter is dead."

"God, Marti, I'm sorry."

"It's okay. I'll get back as soon as I can. We'll work something out about the kids as soon as I get a breather. As soon as this case is over, I promise."

"Marti . . . look, I'll wait until the boys are asleep, and I'll let Mrs. Karcher next door know the girls are here without an adult. And we both have beepers, and ummm . . . Mrs. Karcher is such a night owl. She never misses anything that goes on around here."

"Okay, Sharon, okay." She didn't understand the urgency. No matter how often Sharon saw him, she rarely seemed happy.

Marti checked her watch: 7:35. Joanna should be home in about two hours. She could handle two sleeping ten-year-olds. It wouldn't take that long to interview this woman in Chicago.

"Everything okay?" Vik asked.

"Sure. Let's go." If only she didn't feel so uneasy.

"Your fellow's on duty tonight?"

"Yes." She called the fire station, which was just ten minutes from home, but Ben was out on an ambulance run and she had to settle for leaving a message. Marti took the Kennedy Expressway and exited at Ninety-fifth Street. Vik didn't say much as she drove. He dreaded notifying the family more than she did, even though he seldom did anything more than watch and listen. The address was a quiet street not far from Woodson Library. There was no traffic and no street noise. The sky was hazy and there was a halo around the almost-full moon. The houses were similar but not exactly alike. Chain-link fences marked the property lines; burglar bars guarded the entrances and the first-floor windows. When they knocked at the floor of a tan brick bungalow, almost immediately a woman opened the door the width of a security chain. She had flawless brown skin, a pert upturned nose, and a nervous smile. Marti wondered if the dead woman had resembled her.

"Mrs. Norris?"

"Yes. Are you the police officer who called?" Her voice shook. "Can I see some ID?" Her hand was shaking, too. "This isn't a Chicago badge."

"No ma'am," Marti said. "We're from Lincoln Prairie, not Chicago."

Mrs. Norris hesitated, then led them into the living room. The sofa and chairs were covered in pastel pinks and greens. A collection of teddy bears sat in small wooden rocking chairs and cradles. Books and magazines covered the tables.

"What is it?" Mrs. Norris asked when they were seated. She was wearing a jogging suit and socks. Tennis shoes had been left by the door. She tucked her legs under her and looked from Vik to Marti.

"Ladiya Norris is your daughter?" Marti began.

"Yes."

"I have a daughter, too, Mrs. Norris. I am very sorry to have to come here and tell you this."

The woman hunched her shoulders and hugged herself. She stared at a place somewhere above Marti's head. She knew. All mothers know, even the worst of them. Some sixth sense, Marti thought, but it always surprised her.

"We found a young woman in Lincoln Prairie whom we have identified as Ladiya."

Marti waited, almost holding her breath. There were no tears, no screams. It was so quiet that she could hear the soft hum of the refrigerator.

"What happened?"

"She . . . fell from a bridge."

"Did she . . . Was it . . . ?"

"Quick, yes, very." They always needed to know that there hadn't been any suffering. Marti didn't know how that was possible unless the victims didn't know they were about to be killed. Quick didn't mean much at all, depending on what had preceded it.

"She used to be such a good girl," Mrs. Norris said. "Her father died in Vietnam and I used the benefits to buy this house. I thought we were safe here. I kept her close to home; all through high school, I kept her right here with me. While I was at work, I called. When she went out, she had a curfew. She kept her grades up, went to a junior college, got a job, met a man. . . ." She caught her breath and bit her lower lip. "I just don't know what I did wrong. I protected her too much, maybe. I just don't know.

21

It was as if nothing that ever happened to her in her life before she met Barry Knox meant anything. She moved in with him, did drugs with him. God help me, I don't understand."

"Was she still with Knox the last time you saw her?"

"Oh yes. The love of her life. Everything she lived and breathed for. She looked so . . . tired. I thought maybe things were changing. I was afraid to ask. She came so seldom. I was afraid that if I said the wrong thing, she wouldn't come back at all." Tears glided down her cheeks.

Marti handed her some Kleenex. "Mrs. Norris, did Ladiya know anyone in Lincoln Prairie? An old school friend, girlfriend? Relative?"

"Not as far as I know."

"What did she like to do?"

"Before Knox? Or after?"

"Before."

Mrs. Norris blew her nose. "She did normal things—reading, sewing, theater, movies, concerts, museums. She dated, went out with her girlfriends."

"And after?"

"I don't know. I don't think she did much of anything."

This was just a death investigation, but Marti treated every death as suspicious. Too much time could be lost if she didn't and then it turned out to be homicide. Ladiya was either taken to Lincoln Prairie, dead or alive, or she went there voluntarily. Perhaps she'd had a reason for being there. Marti needed to get a handle on that, just in case. "Do you know of a close friend we could talk to?"

"Her best friend, Shenea, lives right next door. Shenea never met Barry Knox. She's still alive." She put her hands to her face and began sobbing.

"Is there someone I can call for you?"

When her shoulders stopped shaking, Mrs. Norris said, "This will just break their hearts." She dried her eyes, crossed the room, and picked up a telephone. "Momma, it's Deja. Something's happened to Ladiya. Could you and Poppa come over?"

Mrs. Norris made a second phone call, then a few minutes later introduced them to Shenea, who appeared to be in her early twenties. She was already in tears. The two women hugged and cried and patted each other on the back.

"My baby," Mrs. Norris said. "My baby." The younger woman helped her to a chair.

"We're just going to have to get through this, Mama Deja. We're just going to have to do what has to be done." She sat on the floor and leaned against Mrs. Norris's knees.

Mrs. Norris reached out and stroked her hair. "Always fussy about her hair, Ladiya was. We'll have to have Sister Hattie come fix it."

Marti exchanged looks with Vik. Neither of them could tell her that they wouldn't be showing the body.

Marti leaned forward. "When's the last time you talked with Ladiya?" she asked.

"Not in months," Shenea said.

"Do you know of any reason she might have gone to Lincoln Prairie?"

Shenea shook her head.

"What did she like?"

"Music—not dancing so much, just listening. The blues, jazz. At least she used to. It's been a long time since we hung out together. I wanted to see her, but not him." She began crying again.

Mrs. Norris's parents arrived just as Marti and Vik left.

When they returned to the expressway, it was a few minutes past nine. Joanna should be home soon, Marti thought. The boys would go to bed at 9:30. Sharon would have her beeper. Everything was okay. They would be heading toward Lincoln Prairie, even though it might take them another couple of hours to get there. Along with a photograph of Ladiya, who had looked just like her mother, Mrs. Norris gave them the North Side address where she lived with Knox.

Like Mrs. Norris, Knox lived in a nice neighborhood on a quiet street. His house had a wrought-iron fence and burglar bars, too. A beige Cadillac with a wood and leather interior was parked out front.

"Looks like we've caught him at home," Vik said as Marti squeezed the car into a space next to a fire hydrant.

"Marti, suppose—"

"This is Chicago, Vik. They know where the hydrant is."

"So what do they do, flatten the car to get at it?"

"This is Chicago," she repeated, and unsnapped her holster. "And this young lady was doing drugs."

Vik rang the bell. Marti covered him. Someone inside pulled back a little sliding window and said, "Chill, man."

Locks clicked for a few seconds and the door opened. A tall honey-skinned man smiled at them. He was dressed like someone out of *GQ* and hadn't even loosened his tie.

When they flashed their shields, he said, "FBI? Always good to see you. Come on in."

The living room made her think of something out of a British film: maroon wallpaper, dark oak paneling, sturdy furniture, deep-carved, with curved legs, logs crackling in a fireplace. They both declined an offer to sit but insisted that Knox should. "So, where's the lady?" Marti said.

Knox gave them a look that suggested that he didn't understand the question.

"Come on, Knox. Ladiya Norris. About five two, a hundred pounds maybe. That lady. Where is she?"

Knox shrugged. "I haven't seen her in—what?—maybe a couple of weeks now. She said she was going home to momma. You try talking to her?"

"You're sure you haven't seen her in, say, the last forty-eight hours?"

"No ma'am. Hey, what's this all about? Why does the FBI want to talk to her?"

"We're not with the FBI," Vik said.

"Hey, you're not some security guys, are you? Private dicks?"

"Lincon Prairie Police Department," Vik said.

Marti caught a flicker of something in Knox's eyes. Recognition? Concern? She couldn't tell. Knox hadn't asked yet if Ladiya was okay.

"She did live here?" Marti said.

"Yes, ma'am. Until a couple of weeks ago."

"Can we take a look at her room?"

"She took her stuff with her."

"We'd just like to take a look."

"Right," Knox said. "That's all you people ever want to do. By all means, take a look."

Vik stayed in the living room while Marti followed Knox to a large bedroom.

"I'm telling you, there ain't nothing in here," Knox said. "She took everything with her."

"But it's okay to look?"

"Sure. Go ahead." Knox seemed certain she wouldn't find anything incriminating.

Marti found two small rocks of crack cocaine when she unscrewed a lightbulb, but no personal effects that she could identify as possibly belonging to Ladiya Norris.

She weighed the cocaine in one hand and considered Barry Knox. "So, Mr. Knox, you are voluntarily turning in the drugs?"

"I've got no idea of how it got there."

"Of course not," Marti said as she bagged it and put it in her purse.

Back in the living room, Marti looked at Vik and shook her head. "I'm sure we'll be seeing you again, Mr. Knox. Have a good evening."

Outside, a cold wind caught the edges of her scarf and stung her face.

"He didn't ask about her, not once."

"Just male stoicism," Vik said.

They headed for their car. It was almost eleven.

Sharon leaned back against the headrest and closed her eyes. Home, she thought, and with as little fuss as possible. The movie had been almost as boring as the way Phillip's hand kept rubbing her thigh.

"Hungry?" he asked. "I am."

"No."

"How about shrimp?" he asked, as if she was the one who wanted to eat.

"Whatever."

He named a place a half hour's drive away.

"Too far," she said. "I have to go to work tomorrow."

"No calling in sick?"

"No. I'm already on the principal's shit list. I do need my job." She took the easy way out again. She wasn't really having any problems at work.

"Well, then, I suppose we could go someplace closer."

"I need to go home. Get some sleep."

He began stroking the back of her neck.

"I was hoping that this move back to the elementary level would be less stressful for you." His voice, like his hand, was gentle, caressing. "You've been teaching for a long time now. Maybe it's time for a sabbatical, a change of pace for a while. Who knows, you might even discover a new career. Something less demanding, more fulfilling. Something where someone occasionally says thank you and not just more, more. You're such a giving, generous woman, Sharon. And even though you never complain, I can see how this constant take, take, take is wearing you down."

Sharon moved closer.

"You need to be good to yourself. Let me be good to you. We need to see more of each other. We've hardly been together at all this past month, you've been so busy. You almost had to cancel out again tonight."

She had planned to break things off with him tonight, just as she had planned to do the last time she saw him and the time before that. Discussions with Phillip were difficult. He never seemed to hear what she was saying. Like tonight. He was hungry. She doubted that for all the concern he expressed, he had even heard her say that she was not. He'd acknowledged that she had to go to work in the morning, and said that she was probably stressed out, but he was heading for the restaurant, and later, there would be a motel.

She was going to have to stop doing this to herself. Doing what? Choosing losers? Was Phillip a loser? He was charming, affluent, persistent, and great in bed. Maybe she was the loser. She was always telling Marti that *she* wanted too much. If that was true of Marti, what was her problem? Any woman would take one look at Phillip and tell her that she had it all. In fact, when she told two of her friends at work about him, they had been eager to be introduced, if and when Sharon broke things off.

She checked her watch. It was after eleven. Marti hadn't paged her, which meant she wasn't home yet. None of the kids had paged, either, but she didn't like leaving them alone.

"The kids are just fine," Phillip said. "It's not as if you've left four little babies by themselves. You've got two young ladies there who will be going off to college in a couple of years. When you get home, they will all be asleep and just fine. You are always there for them, Sharon, whenever they need you. You're always there for everyone but yourself. This is your time, baby, your time and mine. You worry about work, about home, about kids. Well, I worry about you. Relax, make some time for yourself."

She leaned against his shoulder, without relaxing. Maybe he was right.

By the time they ate and went to a motel, Sharon was yawning. She was sleepy, and she didn't like motels. It was too far to go to his place, and although she thought Marti and everyone else would adjust to the idea of Phillip's being around, just as they had adjusted to Ben, Sharon didn't feel comfortable bringing men home, especially with Marti there. You wouldn't think that with all Marti saw as a cop, she'd be so conservative, but she was. Sharon sighed. She was about to spend another night with clean sheets, dim lights, glasses with paper covers, and a nightstand with a Gideon Bible. So much for romance.

Phillip's hands were persuasive. He always expected more from her than passive sex. By the time she lay back, sweaty and exhausted, she felt like she did after a workout at Women's World. Over and over, Phillip told her how good she was, how good it felt, as he coaxed her into this position or that, prolonging his pleasure. But tonight, as hard as she tried to experience what he did, over and over she felt used and ended up faking an orgasm. Lying against damp, rumpled sheets again, with Phillip content and glistening with perspiration beside her, she decided not to see him anymore. Again. And once again, she wasn't sure why.

Isaac took the blankets out of the closet and pulled them into a corner away from the doors, facing the window. As time passed, he felt sure he hadn't seen anything floating around that window the other night, but just in case, he wasn't going to take any chances on something sneaking up on him. He patted the bottle of church wine that bulged in his pocket and got under the covers. It was so cold, he could almost see his breath. This would keep him warm. The minister at the Presbyterian church tomorrow night wouldn't be so friendly, or as generous, as the priest, but tonight he didn't have to worry about finding a drink.

He half-expected to find Dare already here and waiting for him. Where was he? The priest had called the hospitals, the jail, and the police departments in four towns, but Dare wasn't sick or locked up, at least as far as they could tell. Dare wouldn't just up and leave. They'd been friends ten, twelve years now, ever since they met up in Chicago. Dare had people here, not that he ever saw them, not on purpose anyway. Dare knew his way around here, where to hustle a job or a drink. Maybe, like the priest said, he should talk with Officer Mac. Maybe he would. Maybe he'd wait a few days.

At least folks were quiet around here tonight. It was getting cold. Hell, it had gotten cold already. Maybe that would keep them in, at least for the winter, give him and Dare enough time to find someplace else. Lord, but he hated the winter. And he was too busy looking for Dare to have time to go get some newspaper and cardboard and put it up. This place was too drafty. Dare was supposed to bring home some plywood. 'Course if Dare didn't come back, well, then, he could make it on his own. He had made it on his own for years before he met Dare. Not that he wanted to, but he could. Having Dare coming and going, it was kind of like having a brother again, a brother who liked you. It was almost like having family.

Isaac took the wine out of his pocket and drank enough to keep the nightmares away without emptying the bottle. Suppose Dare had gotten mugged somewhere, gotten knocked unconscious, couldn't tell nobody who he was. Suppose he had gotten hit in the head and was wandering around someplace that wasn't safe, like Chicago, not even knowing who he was. Maybe he had better tell Officer Mac. Wasn't nobody else around here who would help Dare, if Dare was needing help. Just as Isaac was about to doze off, that car came by playing La Cockroach. Damn. As soon as Dare showed up, they were getting out of here.

Marti was surprised to see Bigfoot come downstairs when she let herself in. "Is everything okay, boy?" It wasn't like him to leave Theo alone upstairs. "Did you hear something down here?" She didn't think he was much of a watchdog, and he sure didn't have any killer instincts. When her husband, Johnny, Lord rest his soul, picked him out at the pound, he was looking for a pet for the kids.

Bigfoot wagged his tail and gave her a look that made her feel uneasy. She checked the house from the basement to the attic. The dog followed. "You sure you're okay, boy?" Bigfoot was protective enough of Theo and the rest of the family to watch out for them as best he could. He had not been trained to guard or attack. She hoped she would never feel the need for a dog like that, not at home. When she went into the kitchen and put on the teakettle, Bigfoot padded upstairs. Marti paced from the stove to the window and back to the stove, unable to shake her unease. Sharon wasn't home yet. Should she page her?

This was probably just a part of a guilt trip for leaving the children alone. They did not need an adult in constant attendance.

They weren't little kids anymore. Her ability to protect them was diminishing every day. She walked to the window again. Whatever happened within these walls was her responsibility and nobody else's. She knew what happened in nice neighborhoods: the same things that happened everywhere else. She had to keep this house safe.

For a moment, she thought of Ladiya. Mrs. Norris could have been talking about her and Joanna. The Norris house was smaller than this one but just as nice. It wasn't in a terrible neighborhood. What made the difference? How could she protect Joanna from something she couldn't identify or understand? What was Barry Knox to Ladiya Norris? What did he represent? What did he give her that had been lacking? Or did their being together have anything to do with any of that?

Marti assumed Joanna was too smart, too secure, to ever become involved with someone like Knox. But even Ben could see that Joanna was unsure of herself with boys. Would having Ben around make a difference? It seemed to be making a difference now. The only answers she could come up with—having a father, having a mother who spent less time at work—seemed so much more simplistic than the questions. She'd probably never figure out what she should know and never understand whatever else it was that she should do. "Children," Momma would say. "Walk on your back when they're young. Walk on your heart when they're grown." Marti was just beginning to understand the work it took to raise them when they were young and the worrying that came as they grew up. Lord knew that Ladiya was walking on her mother's heart now.

It was after one in the morning when Sharon came in. Marti was about to go up to bed. Sharon draped her jacket over the back of a chair, sat down, and put her face in her hands. "Damn but six-thirty is going to come early."

Marti didn't speak. She hadn't met the current Mr. Wonderful or any of the others and had no inclination to do so, but something about this one was different. Until this one, Sharon had had a strict rule against dating on weeknights, and she never stayed out all night on weekends, but she had done both several times in the past month. Maybe this was serious. Maybe he was "the one." Or maybe Sharon was feeling a little desperate because Marti was engaged to Ben. Sharon resigned herself to being alone only when she had no other choice. Her preference was to be with a man. Sharon never introduced Mr. Wonderful to anyone. Not for the first time, Marti wondered how such a pattern would affect Sharon's daughter, Lisa. Again she thought of Ladiya Norris. No, she wouldn't talk to Sharon about that tonight.

"Want something before you go to bed?" she asked.

"Shrimp," Sharon said with a short, bitter laugh.

Maybe Sharon was in love this time. She sure didn't seem happy, but she hadn't been happy very often with Frank, her ex-husband, either.

"Are you okay?" Marti asked, wishing she could bite back the words. She hated it when anyone said that to her.

"What's okay?" Sharon asked. "Because I think I should be. This Mr. Wonderful really is. I've got everything a woman could want in a man and yet I never want to see him again. In fact, he is so damned wonderful that when he calls, or when I see him, I can't seem to tell him I don't want to see him again. If I married him, I could really lord it over Frank. He's got everything— money, looks, charm. Marti, this man is the ultimate revenge. If you only knew how sweet, how perfect it would be to get even with Frank through him, especially since we've both known him since college. But I just . . . What is wrong with me?"

"Maybe nothing," Marti said.

Sharon looked at her for a minute. "You think it's okay if he's not only perfect but the perfect way to get even with Frank and I still don't want him?"

"Why do you have to get even?"

"I thought I wanted to, but . . ."

"See? You're a bigger person than that. And what's perfect?"

"You think it's okay?" Sharon said.

"Yes. Whoever he is, I think it's okay."

"Marti, my other friends all think I'm crazy."

"Well, I know you better than that."

"And you don't think I'm crazy?"

Marti had never heard Sharon sound so insecure and uncertain.

"I think whoever's telling you that might be. Trust yourself. You've done all right so far."

To Marti's amazement, Sharon jumped up, threw her arms around her, and burst into tears.

3

Five ambulances and both fire trucks from the midtown station were at the scene of the accident when Ben Walker arrived at Lincoln and Jefferson. It was two in the morning, so there wasn't much traffic, but Jefferson was a major thoroughfare, and four cars had managed to be in the same place at the same time. One had gone through the plate-glass window of the furniture store on the southwest corner. Another had plowed into a parked car. A third had run into a brick wall. The fourth was at the gas station on the northwest corner. Uniformed police officers had blocked off the intersection. Only a few bystanders were watching, several in nightclothes. Ben turned, to see Allan, a rookie riding with him for the first time tonight, standing at the open door of their unit, his back to the chaos. He was breaking in another kid again—red hair, freckles, and stunned by what he saw. At least he wasn't vomiting—yet anyway. One of the uniforms came over.

"Over there, Ben. Little girl. Inside, alive. Doors opened while it was in midair, elderly male and female were ejected. Both dead."

He pointed to the model 240 Volvo wagon that had sheared a light pole. It had proceeded to the gasoline station and now lay upside down where the gas pump had been. The front was crunched up, but the back was intact.

Ben crossed to the car at a trot, with the uniform beside him.

"We can't get at her," the cop said.

"Sure we can. How much time have we got?"

"Another forty-three minutes."

He had already lost seventeen minutes of the golden hour, that window of time when the child might survive.

He could hear noises more like whimpering than crying, but he couldn't see anyone inside, despite the lights that had been set up. Two men were trying to pry an opening to the interior with the scissorslike manual Jaws of Life. Too risky to use the gas-powered pump. The manual was not as fast. He pointed the beam of his flashlight toward the front of the car.

"Damn." If that's where she was, it would take them at least twenty to thirty minutes to hand-crank an opening.

Ben said a quick prayer as he went to the back of the Volvo. He used the flashlight to break the window. The front seat had been pushed back. He could see a bright pink-and-purple jacket where the dashboard was, and long dark hair. The crying had stopped. He couldn't hear any breathing.

He extended his arms as far as he could and gasped air. He wedged himself in a little farther and touched leather. He groped on the side of the front seat until he found the lever that released the back. Nothing. He held the lever down with one hand while he pushed on the back of the seat with the other until it gave. An extra push and something snapped. Twisting, he managed to get far enough into the vehicle to touch the little girl. He put his hand near her mouth and felt her breath on the palm of his hand.

"Allan?"

"I'm right here, man."

"Make sure they've ordered a medevac to get her to Milwaukee."

He found a pulse in her neck and counted.

"Pulse thready . . . a hundred and one." She was scrunched up on the dashboard. He could see her shoulders but not her legs. Her right arm was stiff, muscle tone good. There might not be a spinal injury, but . . . her legs—almost tucked under her. He would have to get her stabilized, immobilize her neck and back, then get her out. "Have a C-collar ready. Backboard, too."

The little girl moaned.

"Hi, honey. Can you hear me?"

"Ummm."

"Good girl. Don't move, okay?" He checked her pulse again. "Pulse weak, one oh six. Respiration ten."

Allan repeated that. They were in radio contact with the hospital.

"Here, Ben." He had remembered to bring a stuffed animal.

"What's your name, hon?"

"Stephanie."

"I've got something for you. I'm going to put him right here."

He wedged the brown bear with the big eyes where she could see it.

There was a cracking noise as the metal was pried farther apart.

"Come on, man. Come on," Allan said. "Get it open."

"Time?" Ben asked.

"Thirty-three minutes."

"How do you feel, Stephanie?"

"My legs hurt, and my back."

"Just don't move. We'll have you out of here real soon."

"I want Grandma! Where's my grandpa?"

"They've already gone to the hospital."

"My kitty."

"Your kitty?"

"We just got her and she came for the ride."

"Is she a real kitty, or pretend?"

"She's real."

"What's her name?"

"Goblin."

"Hey, Allan, see if anyone has found a cat."

"Anybody got a cat?" Allan yelled. "Hey, Ben, is it yellow and white?"

"Yes," the little girl said.

"Then we've got it. It's fine."

"Stephanie," Ben said. "Can you move your toes and your fingers?"

After a moment, she said yes.

"Good girl. Hey, Allan, pediatric kit."

"Right here."

"Good. Stephanie, I need your left arm." He felt along her shoulders. She was lying on it. "Does this hurt?"

"No."

"Does this?"

"No."

He didn't think her arm was broken.

"Can you help me get your arm from under you? Good girl. Say, Allan, can you get the light closer?" Ben glanced at the space between the jaws. "I've got to get a line going."

His partner peered in though the space that was slowly widening, then began passing in what he needed to start an IV.

"More light!" Allan called.

Two uniforms came over with high-beam flashlights.

Ben tapped her arm lightly and felt for a vein. "Keep still, Stephanie. You're just going to feel a little stick, okay?"

"Okay."

Ben swabbed the little girl's arm. "DFiveW drip. Five drops a minute," he said when the line was in and taped in place. "Give me the board." He immobilized her arm.

He checked her pulse again. "Ninety-seven. Weak."

As Ben called out Stephanie's vitals, Allan radioed them to the hospital. Her skin felt clammy, and he could smell the "sick sweat." If there were internal injuries, internal bleeding . . . They had to get her out of here.

"Let's move it," Ben said.

"It's coming," the fireman said. "We're almost there."

"Time?" Ben asked.

"Twenty-six minutes."

He took her vitals again. "How old is your kitty, Stephanie?"

"I don't know."

"Do you know where you are?"

"In Grandpa's car."

"How old are you?"

"Six and a half."

Good, she was still coherent.

With a loud crack and a crunching sound, metal gave and the door opened. Two firemen were on each side of the car. One had the backboard.

"Three count," Ben said. "We'll do a log roll at sixty degrees." He held her head. "One, two, three."

As Ben kept her head stable and the IV intact, they slid the backboard in and got it beneath her. "Now, we go out the passenger side at three." He counted again and they got Stephanie out and onto a gurney.

"My bear," she said.

Ben put it on her chest and covered her with a blanket. "Don't move, okay? We're going to put you in the ambulance now. You're a big girl and you're doing just fine."

Stephanie gave him a wobbly smile and closed her eyes.

When Marti and Vik arrived at the scene of the accident, there were three fatalities, an elderly man and woman and a teenager.

"Stupid," Marti said. "Senseless and stupid."

If one car had been just a little faster, another a little slower, would this have happened at all? If the driver at fault had used one ounce of common sense, three people might not be dead. "Damn."

The intersection was closed off and what traffic there was was being rerouted. The local radio station and two Chicago television stations had crews at the scene. Because there were fatalities, the scene had to be processed before the cars could be towed. An evidence tech was taking pictures. Lights seemed to be set up everywhere.

"Jeez," Vik said. "My driver's ed teacher always used to say, 'Man your weapon' when we got in the car. Something like this makes you understand why. How in the hell . . . ?"

Joanna would be taking driver's ed next semester. Chris, her boyfriend, was taking the course now. Marti would have to come up with a whole set of car rules, but even if she did, there would still be no way to prevent something like this. Uniforms and firemen crowded around one car, holding flashlights to augment the bright spotlights.

"They must have a live one," Vik said. "Usually it's only the drunk who causes it who walks away."

"Maybe whoever is trapped in there will get lucky, too, and come out of this a quadraplegic."

"PMS?" Vik said.

Marti didn't answer. Accidents with fatalities tended to have this effect on her, but he was right about the PMS. That annoyed her. Vik wouldn't have made that comment six months ago. He was being corrupted by his peers.

"Say, there's your fellow."

She recognized Ben and his new partner as they ran alongside a gurney, heading for an ambulance. In the short time she and Ben had been engaged, Vik's only acknowledgment was the tag "your fellow." His tone of voice wasn't much different now from what it had been when they first became partners three years ago and he'd said, "Men's work, policing." His attitude toward her hadn't changed, but she suspected he was going to have as much difficulty accepting Marti the married woman as he had accepting Marti the cop.

A uniform walked by.

"Who was in there?" Vik asked.

"Little girl," the uniform said. "No way anyone was supposed to get her out of that car. Hell, big as Walker is, no way he was supposed to get in."

"He's a damned good paramedic," Vik muttered. Marti couldn't tell from his tone whether he was pleased or disappointed.

One of the firemen handed Marti a marmalade cat. "Walker said to give it to you when you showed up, on account of the fatalities."

The cat was wrapped in a blanket, probably so it wouldn't scratch. It watched her with wary green eyes but didn't try to escape when she held it.

"A cat?" Vik said.

"It belongs to the little girl," the fireman said.

Marti stroked the cat between its ears. "Do you know how she is?"

"Alive," the fireman said. "And that, my friend, is a miracle."

As Marti watched, the ambulance headed for the hospital. The cat settled in the crook of her arm. Had they acquired another pet, or was this temporary? Last summer, it was a goldfish. This cat was a pretty good size, and it seemed friendly. Theo wouldn't want to give it back.

"Okay. You're going to be a good cat and wait in the car while I do a little detective work. Think you can handle that without destroying the upholstery?"

She had just driven the car off Rockenbach's lot a month ago. It still smelled new.

She tried not to think about fur on the upholstery as she got the cat settled on the backseat, cracked the windows, and went to find Vik.

"What's the count?"

"Two drivers okay, neither at fault. One dead passenger, one seriously injured. Grandma and Grandpa are dead. We'll see what happens to the granddaughter. The driver and female passenger in the Geo are dead, too. Both drunk, and he was the cause of the accident. He was on a suspended license for driving under the influence and he'd already been involved in an accident with a fatality, so I don't feel too bad about him not being on the road anymore. Maybe MADD will give him some kind of posthumous award for taking himself out this time."

"Too bad the grandparents didn't deserve this, or that little girl," Marti said. "I guess it's just too damned bad about that."

After she completed the paperwork, Marti drove over to the fire station. Ben was in the kitchen, slumped in a chair pulled up to the table. He was looking down at his hands.

"Coffee?" she asked.

He shrugged.

She filled two mugs and sat across from him. "How's the kid?"

"Stephanie. They airlifted her to Milwaukee. We don't think

there are any spinal injuries. No seat belt. She'll probably be okay."

Ben seemed more tired than depressed. She liked being able to figure out his moods. Her late husband, Johnny, had come home from nights much worse than this, put on some doo-wop music from the fifties, took her into his arms and danced. Ben wouldn't do that. She would always know what he was feeling. Even if he didn't tell her, she would see it in his eyes or in the angle of his shoulders or from the way he walked. How could two men go off to the same war and come back so different?

"Why are you frowning?" Ben asked.

She traced the pattern on the checkered tablecloth for a minute. "I think there was a time when I knew everything about Johnny, how he thought, how he felt. But not after he came back from Vietnam."

"I got lucky," Ben said. "I was a medic. I watched a lot of people die, but I didn't have to kill." He reached across the table and covered her hands with his.

"Hey. I came here to make sure you were okay," Marti said.

"Tonight, I'm okay. But you're upset."

For as long as Marti could remember, everyone assumed that no matter what happened, she was, or would be, okay. The Sunday after Johnny left for Vietnam, her minister said, "You're a strong woman." He said the same thing the day Johnny died. And she was strong, but with Ben, she didn't have to be, not all the time.

"Thanks," she said. Ben didn't ask her what she meant.

He walked around the block twice, checking parked cars and looking behind Dumpsters, making sure there were no strangers loitering about before he went into his apartment building. He took the stairs, unable to tolerate being shut up alone in an elevator. When he opened the door to the third-floor hallway, he checked the series of strings and toothpicks carefully placed in the door to his apartment. Satisfied that none had been disturbed, he went inside.

It was just a studio apartment, furnished only with the necessities. He always left the lights on and the cabinet and closet doors open. His cot was made up military-style so that nobody could hide underneath. Still, he checked carefully, making certain he was alone. He searched for bugging devices but had found none, so far.

This apartment had been carefully chosen. No carpet, a wooden chair and table, his cot, his footlocker, his weight-lifting equipment, and a portable radio. He ate out, and he kept only coffee and some clothes here. While he was here, it was almost as if he didn't exist. He felt certain that if he left in the morning and never returned, nobody would ever find out who he was.

WEDNESDAY, OCTOBER TWENTY-EIGHTH

He waited for half an hour before approaching the house. Wednesday morning, even though the cop left a little before daybreak and everyone else left on time. The dog sniffed at his hand as soon as he closed the back door. He reached down and rubbed between the dog's ears. When he reached into his pocket and pulled out a king-sized Hershey bar, the dog began wagging his tail.

"See what I brought you, big boy. A great big candy bar."

There was a begging expression in the dog's eyes. He unwrapped it and let him have the whole thing. Then he thought, What the hell, and gave him the other chocolate bar, too. What if he didn't kill him? Dogs couldn't ID people. Not that he would ever get caught. A sudden movement caught his eye and he turned. A cat. A damned cat. Where in the hell had that come from?

"Here kitty, kitty," he coaxed. When it came close enough, he grabbed it by the tail and flung it halfway across the room. It yowled, landed on its feet, and ran from the room. He couldn't kill it, not yet, but it would be the first thing to go. For now, he just wanted it to stay away from him.

He went down to the basement again, to the den, and sprawled in his favorite chair. He should have thought about stealing their keys sooner. It hadn't been like this with the others. He had to watch them from a distance. He had to call them while they were at work. He had to be satisfied with casual encounters while they were shopping or commuting. And at the end, when they could no longer bear the separation, he had to take them to an unfamiliar place, where they couldn't relax or feel at ease. He had to frighten them much sooner than he wanted to, kill them before he was ready. This time, having a key made all the difference. He was able to become close to them. He wanted only one of them at first, but that was when he was watching from the outside. Now that he had become so involved in their lives, he realized he could kill them all. And the more time he spent here, discovering their secrets, the more he wanted all of them dead.

He checked to see what movie was in the VCR, then read a page that had been printed out on the computer. Theo seemed to be working on a science report about Saturn. Six copies of the same report, each with changes and corrections, and the final version wasn't much better than the first. If it had been Joanna's, it would have been perfect the first time. Joanna didn't have any files saved. No need to: She did things right the first time. Sharon saved most of her correspondence. She wrote boring letters to her mother, told her sister in Philadelphia a lot of lies, and wrote love letters to Frank, her ex-husband, that began, "Even though I will never mail this . . ." She had a program for budgeting and for balancing her checkbook that hadn't been used this year, but she kept track of her students' grades. Dull, all of it. After she was dead for a few days, nobody would notice that she wasn't around.

Superficial Sharon, going from man to man, still obsessed with Frank, pretending to have a life without him. The thought of killing her pleased him. He had devised several plans for killing everyone but had found flaws with them all. He was dealing with a cop. He would have to keep focused on that and not get distracted by any of the others. She was the smart one, the cop. The detective. The homicide detective. Of course, if she was that smart, by now she should have realized someone was coming in here. It was absurd how secure, how invincible a person could think she was with nothing more than a badge and a gun. He sat in the recliner with his feet up and his hands behind his head. His initial plan was the best. Even before he ever entered the house, he could almost see this room in his mind. He liked it down here, felt safe here. This was where he would attack from. When he was a child, whenever he wet the bed, his stepfather would lock him in the cellar and make him sleep on the concrete floor with the lights out. For a long while, he had been afraid. Then, he had conquered the darkness and the cold. A place where he was once weakest had become his position of strength.

When he went back upstairs, the cat hissed at him, then ran when he stamped his foot. He had killed lots of cats. He could hardly wait to wring this one's neck. Maybe he'd half-drown it first. Cats hated water. He checked the sink. Everyone had had either oatmeal or dry cereal for breakfast. He looked in the refrigerator. Fish for supper. He helped himself to ham and fat-free cheese and made a sandwich, drank some milk, and left the glass in the sink with the rest of the dirty dishes.

It was messier upstairs than usual. They all must have been in a hurry. The cop hadn't even bothered to throw the comforter over the rumpled sheets. He sat on the edge of her bed. This had all been unexpected. Six people, not one. And he had come to know them so well without even meeting all of them. He would kill the boys first, then Lisa and Sharon, then terrify Joanna into submission, but this one—she wasn't just big; she also knew how to use her strength. Worse, he would have to shoot her as soon as she knew he had the drop on her. He might even have to shoot her in the back without even letting her know who he was or what he had done to the others. But he wanted her to know.

He went to the bureau. He opened the drawer in the middle and felt like gagging at the familiar smell of lavender sachet. It made him think of old, sick people and bedpans and nursing homes and IVs dripping into arms so thin, you could see the veins. First Gramps and then Nana. He slammed the drawer shut and opened another. This one never folded anything. Bras, panties, slips, and mismatched socks were all thrown together. Sloppy, but she was a woman, after all. Even if she was a cop, she was still just a woman. With the others dead, and the element of surprise, maybe he could risk making sure that she knew. He took some undergarments out of the clothes hamper and mixed them in with the clean ones. She was such a slob that she would never notice. He kicked a shoe out of his way and hummed as he walked from the room.

Sharon's room was a shambles. He picked up a handful of mail on the edge of the bed and leafed through it. Her charge-card payment at Carson's was a month overdue. She had charged to her limit again. And Frank would be late with his child-support payment. He had extended a vacation to the Bahamas to give his wife a break from the baby and was a little short on cash. And her mother, her blood pressure was up. Give it a week, lady, when she's dead. Maybe you'll have a stroke and miss the funeral. And what was this? He unfolded a piece of paper. A note: "Robert A., 7:00 P.M. Wed." He refolded it and put it in his pocket. On his way out, his foot caught in a sweater on the floor and he almost tripped.

"Son of a bitch." He picked it up and tried to tear it. He pulled until the yarn gave. "Soon," he panted, tearing at it. "Soon."

By 9:15 A.M., Marti and Vik had spent over an hour at the Edison plant, interviewing workers as they entered the parking lot on the off chance that someone might have seen something. They spent an hour at the site where Ladiya Norris had been found, and then attended her autopsy. The only information they had gleaned thus far was at the autopsy. The victim had been seven weeks pregnant. Now they were standing on the damp sand near the edge of the pond. A few late-season anglers had set up their gear, but the man they had interviewed yesterday was not among them.

"Maybe finding a body taught him something that frigid weather and this wind off the lake couldn't," Vik said.

"Maybe he's just found another place to fish—someplace where bodies are less likely to turn up and there might not be any half-frozen cops wandering around asking questions." Marti turned up the collar of her jacket. The sun was deceptively bright. The wind blew cold and sharp as ice off the water. Despite a sweater, scarf, and wool slacks, she had felt chilled to the bone earlier this morning. Now, after thawing out at the coroner's facility and warming up with coffee, she was shivering again. The wind tugged at her scarf. There was something about this compulsion to fish that she didn't understand. "There are at least half a dozen dead fish just tossed on the sand. Why would anyone stand around in this to catch one and not even bother to keep it?"

Vik waved his arm in a wide gesture. "They're nuts, all of them, fanatics. The beaches close on Labor Day. There's a reason for that. Some things are seasonal sports."

They approached a man who was just setting up for the day.

"Sir," Vik said, showing his shield. "Police."

"What's that?" the man said, cupping his ear. There were brown spots on the backs of his hands. Marti guessed his age at about sixty-five. "What did you say?" Either he couldn't hear above the wind or he was hard of hearing.

"Police!" Vik said, louder, holding up his shield.

"Oh," the man said, close to shouting. "Something I can help you with?"

"How often do you come here?" Vik said, also speaking loudly.

"Most every day, unless Lorna's not feeling well."

"That your wife?" Vik asked.

"No, my dog. She's got arthritis real bad. Has a hard time getting around. I can't bring her down here anymore, least not this time of year."

Marti could tell by the pause that Vik wanted to ask him why he came.

"Were you here yesterday?" he asked.

"Yes."

"What time?"

"Oh, early. Lorna had a vet's appointment this morning. I get here a lot earlier than this most mornings."

"How early?"

"Four, five o'clock maybe."

"See anything unusual?"

Vik was beginning to sound a little hoarse. Marti scrounged around the bottom of her purse and found a cough drop.

"Depends on what you consider unusual."

"Something you don't see every day."

"Oh, like a hearse?"

"Yes," Vik agreed. "Like a hearse. Is that what you saw?"

"No. I was just asking."

Vik rocked back on his heels and looked at the man for a moment. Then he said, "See those rocks?"

The man looked where he was pointing and nodded.

"We found a body there yesterday. Now, did you see anything unusual?"

"Well . . ." The man scratched his chin. "Can't say as I did. Depends on what you consider unusual. That's why I was asking about the hearse. I didn't see nothing down by the rocks yesterday, but I could have swore I saw someone over in those tall bushes maybe three, four days ago. I could have swore it. It looked like a ghost."

"A ghost, sir?" Vik said.

"Coulda been. A ship went down not seven miles out from here in '68. The *Seabird*. All aboard were lost. Now that Archaeological Society has been out there diving the wreck. Maybe there is such a thing as disturbing the dead."

"'Sixty-eight?" Vik said. "Nothing went down around here in 'sixty-eight."

"Eighteen sixty-eight," the fisherman said. "Of course, it coulda been my eyes playing tricks on me, too. It was right about daybreak. The light can be kind of tricky then. I caught a two-pound catfish, and time I looked again, it was gone."

"You haven't seen anyone dressed up like a pumpkin, have you?" Vik asked.

"Now look, I told you it most likely coulda been my eyes playing tricks on me. No need to get sarcastic."

Marti smiled.

"No, sir," Vik said. "I'm serious. You take Sherman Avenue to get here?"

"Sometimes."

"Have you seen anyone dressed like a jackass . . . jack-o'-lantern?"

"Of course not."

Vik shrugged and took down the man's name and address.

"It was worth a try," Vik said as they walked away. "What the hell, if a man's seeing ghosts, who knows what else he might see. Besides, he was lying."

"About what?" Marti said.

"About the fish. There aren't any catfish around here. Salmon, brown trout, carp, but not catfish. And he was lying deliberately. He probably thinks we were dumb enough to believe him. The only thing I think he told the truth about was his eyesight. I don't remember hearing anything about a boat going down that close to Lincoln Prairie, either."

"Oh, Vik, that doesn't make sense. Why would he bother lying about something like that?"

"Because he's a fisherman," Vik said, as if that explained everything.

All the way back to the precinct they argued about whether to have fish or burgers for lunch. Vik kept insisting on fish just to annoy her.

Marti went through the reports on Ladiya Norris again. According to Dr. Cyprian, the extent of the injuries seemed excessive for the height of the fall. The blow that killed her was a direct frontal contact with a jagged rock that pentrated her skull between her hairline and her eyebrows. There was a second blow, closer to the scalp, that appeared to indicate a rebound or bouncing action as opposed to a reflex. Cyprian was not able to explain how that had happened. There were also bruises and contusions that could not be explained by the fall but that had occurred at approximately the same time, as well as healed fractures in both arms and in the fingers on her right hand, all of which had been properly set. Several ribs had been broken. Ladiya wore a partial denture, replacing three of her upper front teeth. Except for the lack of identification when they found the body, there had been no obvious attempt to destroy or eliminate evidence. They had all kinds of fibers, hair types, soil and sand samples.

"I don't know how the coroner's jury will call it, but I don't see how they can rule suicide or accidental."

"Stranger things have happened," Vik said. "It's not like she was lying faceup, with a bloody rock beside her body."

"There are bruises on her arms and the back of her neck and a second blow that couldn't have been self-inflicted."

"That's what you say." Vik flipped through his report again. "Feast or famine. We finally get a case with enough physical evidence to convict a small army and nickel bet the coroner's jury rules against us or we never find the perp." He weighed the report. "This is like having the tooth fairy show up at a nursing home after some old geezer looses his dentures. Much too good to be true."

"Well, we're going to have to proceed as if that won't happen," Marti said. "Assuming somebody did kill her, do you think whoever it was knew the area or got lucky when he decided to head in the direction of the lake and went past the Edison plant? They work two shifts, and from midnight until about four in the morning, that area would be deserted. But with all of the lights, who but a local would know that?"

Vik rubbed his chin. He hadn't taken the time to shave this morning. "Suppose the perp did know where he was going? What if he remembered the place the way I did—with access to the beach—and didn't know everything had been fenced off. Suppose he thought he could hide her, bury her."

"That implies premeditation."

"She was pregnant."

"There's always abortion. Maybe it wasn't premeditated. Officially, it's not even homicide yet." Marti shoved the Norris files into a folder. "Everything about this seems a little off center, including the second blow to the head. Maybe somebody just had a bad day and nothing went the way they planned."

"And we wind up with a corpse and a joker who saw a ghost."

Marti had decided that the old codger was just having a laugh at their expense. "I didn't buy that."

"Me, neither. But suppose he did see something. You know

how these old coots are. They'll do anything for attention. He was probably just trying to lay out enough line to make us go for the bait and question him a few more times. So he comes up with this little game so we'll have to pry whatever it is out of him."

They might have to. The coroner's jury would convene in the morning. And if their fisherman friend was making everything up, he'd already had more than enough time to think about what he wanted to tell them next.

Vik ran his fingers through his hair. Instead of springing in all directions, it fell limp.

"Jessenovik. Don't tell me you didn't shave *or* shower."

"I took a shower."

"Next time, wash your hair."

"I did."

"With shampoo."

"We didn't turn up anything on Knox," Vik said. "Not that I believe the man is clean. Lucky maybe, but not clean. You got any contacts in the city who might know something or be able to find out?"

"I'll see what I can do."

Vik watered the spider plant with the dregs of his coffee. "Time was when killing was a much simpler thing—greed, hate, envy. Now we've progressed to boredom, and looking at women and children as disposable commodities. Either way, bang, you're dead." He held up a few dangling spider plant babies. "Look, this thing is at it again. Do they have plant doctors? Can we neuter it?"

"I don't think so." Whoever had abandoned the plant in their office might have done it as a practical joke, but Marti thought the odds were better that the person just hadn't been able to kill it off.

After lunch, Marti and Vik met with Denise Stevens, head of the Juvenile Probation Department. Denise was as tall as Marti and about ten pounds heavier. Unlike Marti, she was not pleased with her size and had a collection of hats that she wore to draw attention away from her hips. Today's hat was brown felt with a narrow brim decorated with a metallic bronze bow. Denise was what

Momma would call a handsome woman, a term that included looks and size. Denise's face was full-featured and attractive, with dark oval eyes, a generous mouth, high cheekbones, and flawless skin the color of rich chocolate.

"So," Denise said as she sat in a chair midway between Vik's desk and Marti's. "You've got another dead girl on you hands. Twenty-two is a little old for me to be of any help, especially since she's not a local."

"As far as we've been able to determine so far, she didn't know anyone here. We don't know if she was just passing through, had been here for a couple of weeks, or was visiting someone for the day. If she needed to maintain her habit or get an abortion, where might she go?" Marti asked.

"Just about anywhere she wanted to. None of that makes her unique, or differentiates one neighborhood here from another. Not anymore."

"Suppose she was keeping a low profile and didn't want to be noticed?"

"Lower end of the business, maybe," Denise said. "South Side. The drug activity there is more visible. She could get whatever she needed and not be conspicuous. Nobody would be likely to notice her at all unless there was something distinctive about her."

Marti shrugged. Ladiya had been pretty, but not outstanding. "She wasn't a local," she said. "That was about it."

"Then somebody might have looked at her twice, but who would care?"

"Can you ask around, informally?"

"Sure. You talk with Narcotics yet? Or Vice, maybe? She might have needed to turn a few tricks to support her habit."

"The narcs are next," Vik said. "Slim and Cowboy have got a flasher on their hands. I don't think hookers are high on their list of priorities right now."

Denise adjusted her hat. "I'll ask around and see if there's anything on her out on the street, but your guys might be a lot more helpful."

Lupe Torres was the liaison between the Gangs and Narcotics

divisions. They found her in the locker room. Lupe was shorter than Marti, broad-shouldered, wide-hipped, and street-smart. She worked a tough detail that tended to wear people down. Although she was only twenty-six and hadn't been on the force quite four years, she had those city-cop eyes that suggested she had seen it all. Marti hoped she wasn't getting burned out.

Vik explained what they had.

"I don't think I can help you." Lupe put on a bulletproof vest, adjusted her holster, then slipped into her flak jacket. "Since your victim was involved with drugs, why don't you keep me advised as to what's going on. We've got covert operations going on out there all the time. I wouldn't want you to blow a good bust asking routine questions. If I do hear anything, I'll let you know."

Barry Knox had come up clean except for two possession charges. He had two known addresses, the house they had gone to in Chicago and another in Elgin. His wife and three kids lived in Elgin. His gave his occupation as financial adviser, self-employed, and listed his Chicago address as his place of business.

"Everything about Knox screams drug dealer," Marti said. "It would be nice if we could connect him with someone here in Lincoln Prairie." She made a few phone calls. Maybe one of her fellow officers in Chicago could find out something about him. Next, she called a girlfriend who worked at a Chicago hospital.

"What was that all about?" Vik asked when she hung up.

"The fractures in Norris's arms were set. My friend can access computers."

"Which could mean a legitimate accident."

"Maybe." If Mrs. Norris was aware of physical abuse, would she have told them? "Mrs. Norris can't stand Knox, but you know how it is with abuse. Nobody knows anything. Everyone's so surprised."

Vik drummed his fingers on his desk. "Finding out who treated her or where she was treated could be a logistical nightmare in a city the size of Chicago."

"Not to mention confidentiality and all the red tape it could take to get at her medical records."

"Maybe she had some kind of convulsion," Vik said. "Maybe that's how she died. That could explain the second blow to the temple."

Neither of them believed that, not with Dr. Cyprian handling the autopsy.

5

After Isaac left Queenie's, he walked back to the house and sat on the front steps to watch all the comings and goings. The last time he had seen Dare, it had been about five in the morning. It was still dark then and Dare had left real quiet, going off to see if there was any work. He never made it there. Whatever he decided to do, he made up his mind before daybreak and without any cash in his pocket—maybe while he was walking down this street.

Isaac sat with his back against the railing, pulled his cap down, and closed his eyes, acting as if he was sleeping. He didn't like it here, so he tried not to be here too much, going back to the old place and sitting in the sun on a tree stump instead. Might be time he got familiar with the neighborhood. Maybe, once folks knew he belonged here, he could ask if anyone had seen Dare—if Dare wasn't back by then.

Before too much time had passed, he was shivering and ready to head back to Queenie's place. There was too much happening here for him. Just like Dare to pick someplace where something was always going on. Cars going back and forth, not a one of them a police car. Kids hanging around and strolling along who shoulda been in school, not just teenagers, mind you, young kids. And folks practically lining up a few houses down. Dare had put them right by a drug dealer and business was good. Dare always did like being where there was a little action, but that wasn't no reason to move so close to it. A man's home didn't have to be no castle, but it should at least be a safe-enough place.

Isaac didn't know too much about local gangs. The city got rid of the graffiti almost as fast as it got sprayed on, which made it hard to keep track, but that's probably what those shots he heard the other night were all about. Some of these kids must be gang members. He didn't think he had to worry too much about them coming after him. Not unless they just wanted to have a little fun. He didn't have nothing for nobody to steal. Time his check came, Dare better be here. He wouldn't want to move on without him, but he would have to find some other place to stay. Best thing would be to let Queenie know where he was. That's the first place Dare would go.

"Whatcha doing, old man? You live here or something?"

Isaac opened his eyes and adjusted the visor of his cap so he could look up and see who was talking to him. It was some skinny little kid who didn't look more than nine or ten. No sense asking why he wasn't in school. Fool might get offended and try to beat up on him. "What's it to you? You looking for a place to stay?"

"Naw, got a place. For now."

Isaac wanted to tell him to go about his business, but the kid was just making conversation. Probably trying to find out if he had anything worth coming back for and stealing when he got drunk.

"How come I ain't seen you here before?" the kid asked.

"'Cause normally I'm someplace else."

"Oh. You a friend of that other dude who lives here?"

The kid had to be talking about Dare. Isaac tried to act like he wasn't much interested. "Other dude?"

"Yeah. About your height, dark-skinned, wears sunglasses all the time?"

"I might know him. Why?"

"Nothing. He just told me he'd bring me something and he ain't."

"Might not have had time to. How long's it been since he told you?"

"He told me Thursday night. Said he'd have it by Sunday at the latest."

This kid hadn't seen Dare since the last time Issac had. "When he comes around, if I see him, I'll let him know you're looking for him."

"You do that, man. You do that." The kid looked him up and down and adjusted the direction of the visor on his cap.

"So?" Isaac said. "You got a name?"

"J.D. Tell him J.D."

Isaac stood up. Time to go. One thing he couldn't stand being around was kids. Now that he'd called attention to himself sitting out here, no telling who'd bother him next. Time his money came, he'd better be gone, 'cause sure enough this kid or one of his friends would come looking for him. Wasn't nothing friendly about no neighborhood no more and no such thing as a neighbor. He might as well be in Chicago.

Marti was just getting back from lunch when Ben called. "How's that little girl?" she asked. Toward morning, she had awakened from a jumbled dream of gunshots, fire engine sirens, and a de-molished car.

"Stephanie's doing okay. Her parents were on vacation. They flew in from Jamaica this morning. I told the mother about the cat and asked if I could drop it off, but it doesn't sound like they want it."

"Ben, at this rate . . ."

"You took home that goldfish before."

Theo did love having pets.

"Did you get a call from school?" Ben asked.

Her stomach lurched, even though a teacher hadn't called since last year. Now what?

"No. why?" Nobody ever called to give her good news.

"It's the end of their first six-week grading period and Mike has a stomachache, which probably means his grades don't look too good. I take it Theo is okay?"

"Theo is a perfectionist when it comes to schoolwork. In my opinion, he is too compulsive. That's not okay, but so far, I haven't been able to do much about it."

Sharon had told her so many good things about the fifth-grade teacher the boys were supposed to have had this year. And for that one month, before they fired her, Theo finally seemed to be enjoying school. "I think this teacher they've got now wants them all to be Rhodes scholars. With all the time Theo puts in doing homework, you'd think he was in training for some kind of academic decathlon."

Ben laughed. "I don't think I'll ever have that kind of problem with Mike. I'll have a little talk with the teacher when I pick him up."

"Find out how Theo's doing, too."

After she hung up, Marti tried to ignore the slow churning in her stomach. Theo had been putting in much too much time on his homework. He had even missed a Cub Scout meeting last week because of a paper he was working on. Maybe she should be glad that he was so focused on his studies. Maybe that was good, even if her gut didn't think so. And Mike—just a couple of years ago, he was a chubby little kid who was alternately the class clown and a bully. She wasn't sure how he and Theo had become friends. She suspected it was something that each saw in the other and couldn't emulate. Back then, Ben seemed to be floundering as the parent of a child whose mother had died in a car accident. Since then, he had become a take-charge parent instead of taking a wait-and-see approach. And he was a good parent, with good instincts about kids. Over time, Mike, like Ben, had become one of the family. Marti couldn't imagine one boy without the other, just as she could no longer imagine not having Ben around.

She looked down at the snapshot of all of them crowding the frame during a picnic last summer. Funny how things had changed since she'd come to Lincoln Prairie. She and Ben had not set a date—marriage was just "out there." She wasn't sure she wanted to wait much longer, and she knew Ben didn't. Would this snapshot of happy, smiling faces change when they were married? It still seemed like such a vague idea that she was sure the children hardly thought of it. They all had gotten used to things the way they were, casual. Marriage was a little more intense.

Vik cleared his throat. When she looked at him, he was watching her and scowling. She'd already been married to a cop when she joined the force in Chicago. She didn't know what impact cops' marriages had on the people who were their partners on the force. So far, Vik seemed much less than pleased with the idea. Sooner or later, she would probably figure out why. Maybe one of the people she should be concerned about was sitting across from her.

She picked up the toxicology reports on Ladiya that had just come in. The girl had ingested cocaine, which didn't tell her anything, even if she had gotten the drugs here. Cocaine was everywhere. The test results on the cocaine she had found at Knox's house would be in later, but these lab results indicated there was nothing unusual about the chemical makeup and potency of what Ladiya had been using.

Vik began scanning the *News-Times*. "They didn't get her picture in. Too much going on with our Halloween flasher. Look at this."

The front page had a picture of several students and instructors. One was holding up a poster. It said, "HAVE YOU SEEN THIS JACK . . . ?" Below this was a caricature of a small jackass whose head was a huge pumpkin. The jack-o'-lantern had a big grin and its very small tongue was sticking out.

"They aren't taking him the least bit seriously, Vik. The guy's a joke."

"Let's hope he has a sense of humor."

Ben arranged an after-school meeting with the boys' teacher. Marti had decided to meet him at the school. The classroom was so orderly that she looked around for a minute at the desks and tables cleared of all clutter, the blank chalkboards and the precisely thematic bulletin boards, and she wished for the busy disorganization and happy children she had walked in on not more than a month ago. Theo's new teacher, Mrs. Hinkston, was an older woman, short and heavyset, with straight gray hair cut in an old-fashioned pageboy. Marti thought of the energetic young woman she had met in September and wondered why she had been replaced with someone who looked as if she had been brought out of retirement. Tenure, probably, or something equally stupid.

Mrs. Hinkston indicated two chairs that were the perfect size for an elementary school student. Marti could see Ben struggling to suppress a smile as they sat down. Mrs. Hinkston remained standing. She leaned against her desk, her arms folded. "Mrs. MacAlister, as I explained to Mr. Walker earlier, we are quite certain that Mike and Theo should be separated—at once."

Marti could see that just as Ben had explained to her, the "we" was imperial, not the consensus of the school staff.

"Since there is only one fifth-grade class here this year, I'm recommending Dunsworth Middle School for Mike. Theo is so much more advanced. He takes full advantage of the opportunities offered here."

Both boys attended the Science Academy middle school. Gang activity and drugs had invaded the Lincoln Prairie school district, along with every other school district across the state, but here the children were required to wear uniforms, and this and other regulations seemed to make the problem manageable and allowed the students to focus on getting an education. Marti had heard Dunsworth referred to as the "dumbbell" school, something Mike certainly was not. Student fights were not uncommon there, and one student had tried to stab another at the beginning of the school year.

Marti looked at Ben and raised her eyebrows. "And just how is Theo doing?"

"Theo is an excellent student. We could not be more pleased with his progress. He's the most advanced student in class."

Marti didn't like the sound of that. Theo was not a gifted student. He had a natural aptitude for math and a lot of curiosity about nature and science. He worked hard for everything else. Good grades in all subjects meant that he wasn't having much fun. Children were supposed to have fun.

"Is there any reason other than an academic one why you feel they should be separated?" she asked.

"Mike tends to encourage Theo to . . . be less attentive in class."

"They clown around?" Ben said.

"And distract the other students. And Mike even encourages Theo to go out for recess when he'd rather stay in and work."

"Good Lord," Marti said. "Fifth grade and Theo still gets recess?"

Ben pressed his lips together, then covered his mouth for a moment.

Marti stood up. Sitting in that chair was giving her a backache. She resisted an impulse to stretch. "We'll discuss this and talk with the boys about it, then get back to you."

"Mrs. MacAlister, we do not feel that discussing a classroom and school change with two young boys is appropriate. In our opinion, this is a decision made by the teacher and communicated to the child. We would certainly not recommend your approach."

Ben stood also. *"We* don't make decisions that way at our house. *We'll* get back to you."

"We" looked much less than pleased.

As soon as they were outside, Marti said, "I have no intention of separating the boys. I don't like her attitude toward either one of them, or her expectations." Her stomach was churning again. "A year of her and I'll have an ulcer. Is Mike okay?"

"After I explained that one A, two B's and three C's don't make you a bad human being, the stomachache went away and he was ready for lunch."

"Good. He's probably in better shape than Theo, or me, for that matter. There's always a private school, but damn it, public education should be made to work!"

"They had a really good teacher earlier this year," Ben said. "Mike couldn't wait to get to school. And there was no good reason for letting her go. Does anyone in this system just stop and think only of the kids and what's good for them?" His frustration echoed her own.

Isaac sat on the stump in the clearing where their last house had been. Pretty soon he wouldn't be able to come here anymore. They had brought in the bulldozers and already there was a wide path of dirt where trees and bushes had been. A place had burned down three blocks from here that was like a halfway house for teenage ex-cons. He'd heard something about that place buying this land. Wouldn't be no place to go pretty soon.

He didn't want a room or an apartment, didn't want to be bothered with folks, except for Dare. Friends wasn't nothing but trouble, family no more than a heartache. He was better off alone. Ten, twelve years he and Dare had been hanging out together, and now even Dare just took off like it hadn't been nothing. Before Dare, it had just been freight trains and open spaces. He'd left St. Louis and rode all the way to Oregon. Saw the Pacific Ocean before he turned around and came back. Wasn't enough colored folks in Oregon for him to get comfortable being there. A man needed to be around his own, even if he didn't have nothing much to do with any of them. He wasn't gone but five, six years, but time he got back, most things had changed. Aunt Minnie was dead. She'd been about the only person in the family who'd had anything to do with him after.

So he'd just moved on again. He didn't like it here no better than he'd like living anywhere else, but he had gotten used to the place over the years. It didn't matter much where he was, long as he had a post office box and some place like Queenie's where folks weren't too particular about the people they drank around. The world was changing, though. It wasn't safe nowhere no more. The more he thought about it, the less he knew where to go, or what to do. When Dare got back from wherever he was, they was going to have to do something. There must be another place in this town like this, with lots of trees and not too many folks around. There must be just one more place like this.

Marti got another call from Ben a little after five.

"This is disaster day," he said.

"Now what?"

"Bigfoot is sick. He vomited all over the kitchen floor. It looks like chocolate. Dogs get a reaction like this when they ingest it. We're taking him to the vet."

"How's Theo?"

"Very upset."

"I'll be right there."

It took her seven minutes to get home. Traffic was light, so she didn't have to use the dome light. Bigfoot was in the van when she got there. Theo was standing at the open door. His face was streaked with tears, but he had stopped crying. She took him to one side. "I know you're worried about him, and he's never been sick before, but . . ."

"He's going to die."

Everyone was going to die, Marti thought, unless what they said about the rapture was true. She couldn't tell him that, not now. "Let's not panic until we hear what the vet says. It sounds like he just ate something he shouldn't have."

"But we don't give him anything but dog food. He doesn't go near the garbage, he can't get at the plants, and we walk him. What else could he have eaten?"

Ben stuck his head out of the van window and made "let's go" motions.

"Let's let the vet have a look at him."

Sharon and Lisa were out grocery shopping. Everyone else piled into the van. It was half an hour before the vet came to the waiting room.

"He's been eating chocolate. It's great stuff for most people but a big no-no for dogs."

"He isn't going to die?" Theo said.

The vet put his hand on Theo's shoulder. "I'm sure he'll be fine, and I wouldn't tell you that unless I was certain. I do want to keep him here, though, at least overnight. I've got him on an IV and I'm giving him some antinausea medication. Why don't you come and see him for a minute? And if you want to stop in on your way to school in the morning, just call first, okay?"

They all trooped back to the examining room. Bigfoot opened his eyes, gave them one flick of his tail, and went back to sleep. Theo rubbed the shaggy hair between Bigfoot's ears and whispered something in his ear.

The vet came in and timed the IV drip.

"He's not used to sleeping by himself," Theo said.

The vet smiled. "I know. I'll have him back home as soon as I can."

"I didn't give him any chocolate," Theo said as soon as they were back in the van.

"Me, neither," Mike agreed. "Joey came over to play yesterday. Do you think he did?"

"I don't remember him having any chocolate."

"Dante was there for a while," Mike said. "He's always eating something."

Marti exchanged looks with Ben. Dante was Lisa's boyfriend. Boyfriends weren't allowed in the house unless an adult was there.

When Ben dropped off Marti and the kids, Sharon was upstairs and there was a lot of thumping. "Damn it," Sharon yelled. It sounded like another cranky-mood day.

Marti hurried upstairs.

"First my sweater disappears and now I can't find my earrings—those yellow-and-green parrots I brought back from the Bahamas." Clothes were thrown everywhere, the contents of drawers dumped on the floor. "My keys . . ."

"Your keys? You lost your keys?"

"Yes, but I found them."

Marti wasn't so sure. "Look, I'll have the locks replaced."

"Marti, I found them. I've got two sets of keys, swear to God."

Marti joined the search. The parrot earrings were just cheap carved wood, but Sharon had repaired them numerous times. The trip to the Bahamas was the delayed honeymoon Sharon and Frank took two years after they got married. Sharon had waitressed at a second job for six months to save up for it. It might have been the only good time she and Frank ever had.

"Sharon, I don't see how you can find anything in here."

"Like you can talk."

"Well, at least I keep things in the same place." An organized mess, she like to think of it as. "And I don't keep my jewelry in the same drawer as my underwear."

"Neither do I. I thought if I dumped the jewelry box into the drawer so I could see everything . . ."

"Sharon, don't explain." Marti squatted and picked up some fibers that were clinging to the rug. "What color was your sweater?"

"Lots of colors. Stripes. You know the one."

"Looks like I found some of it."

"What!"

Sharon began picking at the fibers, too. "So, Miss Detective, what crime have we here? Has a certain houseguest with fur who goes by the name of Goblin attacked my sweater and absconded with the evidence?"

"She probably dragged it to a corner somewhere and made a bed. Was it irreplaceable?"

"I'll survive."

They had no luck finding the earrings. At five to seven, Sharon called off the search. "I've got to run. School board meeting. Back by ten. You home for the night?"

"As far as I know," Marti said. "I'll beep you if I have to go out on a call." She would have to wait until later to tell Sharon about Lisa and Dante.

He wanted to stretch but could not. The back of the station wagon was filled with boxes and other junk. It had been easy enough to move them forward a bit and lie behind them, against the back of the seat, but there wasn't enough room to move. The dust was enough to make him want to sneeze. He'd gotten used to the tickle in his nose, and he found he could relieve it by pinching his nostrils. Despite the discomfort, it was a good thing he had thought of this. She might have noticed if he followed her in his car. He was going to find out who this Robert A. was.

Where in the hell was she? She would pay for keeping him waiting. He'd have cramps in his legs for a week if he didn't move soon. Bitches, all of them, never on time. Sharon slept around like a whore. Who was she meeting? This Robert A. could be anybody: a produce boy who caught her eye while she was grocery shopping, the dentist—she had her teeth cleaned last week—or almost anybody from the school where she taught, from the janitor to the principal.

The door opened just as he was shifting his weight a little. The radio came on full blast as soon as she turned the key in the ignition. She backed out of the driveway, slammed him against the back of the seat as she braked to a stop, swung the station wagon around in what felt like a complete circle, and drove off much too fast, braking again. Must be the corner.

After a few minutes, the odor of burning tobacco wafted back. She was sneaking a cigarette again. He smiled. She thought she was alone. What would happen if he spoke? If he sat up? Would she become frightened enough to run off the road and crash into something? He could kill her right now, without laying a hand on her, just by scaring her to death. If the crash didn't kill her, he could just bash her head on the dashboard and walk away. She could be a dead woman. All he had to do was surprise her. Stupid, all of them. He could step into and out of their lives at will. What if killing them wasn't as much fun as planning their deaths? What if stepping over their bodies wasn't as exciting as walking through their lives? What would he do when they were dead?

The car stopped sooner than he expected. Where were they? Was this just a quick stop at the store? He waited until she got out, listened, but he didn't hear the locks click. He didn't hear her speak to anyone, didn't hear a car door close or drive off. Where was she going? He gave her three minutes and sat up. A school. Who in the hell was she meeting at a school? The parking lot was filled. Maybe he hadn't been able to park nearby. Had she gotten out of her car and into his?

He got out carefully, stood watching as people went into the building, wondered if he could go inside without being noticed.

He was wearing jeans, didn't look too rumpled. Not everyone was dressed up or wearing a suit. The building was well lit. He followed three women who walked as if they knew where they were going. The gymnasium. There was a meeting. Was Sharon going, or was this just an opportunity to rendezvous with someone for a couple of hours? She was probably getting laid in the janitor's closet. He sauntered over to the doorway and looked in. It took a few minutes, but finally he caught a glimpse of her bright green scarf. A man was sitting beside her! He was right! He knew she was here to meet someone.

When Sharon came out of the building an hour and a half later, she was alone, but he was not fooled. They had gone somewhere together. There had been plenty of time. That bitch! For a moment, all he could see was an orangy haze. When his vision cleared, all he could see of the station wagon were the taillights. The palms of his hands stung. He unclenched his fists and took half a dozen deep breaths. That whore. He smiled. A whore, a cop, and the beautiful and innocent Joanna. And soon, all of them would be his.

Isaac sat on the steps in the dark. He hadn't felt like being bothered with folks long enough to go to the church for something to eat, and now his stomach was grumbling. It was just the way they fixed that chicken most Wednesday nights—floating in a sauce with carrots and green peas, and that crust on top. No matter, though. He wasn't hungry at all. Queenie had let him fill a pint jar with house whiskey and that would get him through the night. Just six more days now and he'd have some money. Time enough to worry about what he'd do then.

At least it quieted down a little around here at night. The cops drove past a couple of times, slowed but didn't stop. The kids had someplace to go, the third house from the corner. As long as he'd been sitting here, they'd been going in and out in ones and twos. A dope house maybe, or a gang hangout. No place that he or Dare would go. They was just alcoholics. Now dope, that shit would kill you. A car circled the block a couple of times. Not the kind of car that belonged here. It came back again and stopped, probably because he was the only one sitting out here.

"Can you tell us how to get to Christ Church?" the woman in the passenger side asked. Another woman was driving. Nice-looking women, both of them. Churchgoing women, like Aunt Minnie had been. No place for them here.

He got up, brushed off his pants, and walked down the steps, getting just close enough for them to hear him without him having to yell and let other folks know they was here. "Y'all want to get away from here. This ain't no place for nice ladies like yourself. They be selling drugs around here. There's a gang hangout." He gave them directions to the church. "And you keep them windows up and lock them doors," he warned.

They were real ladies, both of them. Recognized that he wasn't looking for no handout and didn't offer him one.

A three-quarter moon was sitting high in the sky and the jar of whiskey was half gone when he decided to call Officer Mac. Dare wasn't coming back tonight. Maybe he couldn't. Maybe he was like those two church ladies and needed a little help. Isaac didn't have a wallet, but he did carry a little change purse, just in case he had something to keep in it. Big Mac's card was there—a little ragged around the edges, but he could still read it. He didn't have any change, so he when he got to the pay phone, he dialed 911.

Marti was stretched out on the recliner in the family room, trying to summon the energy to get ready for bed, when her beeper went off.

"Sorry to bother you, Mac. Someone who calls himself Isaac wants to see you. He said you'd know who he was. Said you'd find him on Fourth, near the corner of Eureka."

She put on her shoes, went upstairs to the kitchen, and grabbed her jacket from the back of a chair. After making sure Sharon was home and knew that she was leaving, she went out. She was going to have to have a talk with Sharon. What if Sharon hadn't come home after her meeting? The agreement was that Sharon would be there with the kids during the week. Until the current Mr. Wonderful appeared on the scene, Marti had been able to come and go as necessary. All of the kids would be offended if she so much as suggested a backup sitter. Maybe it was time to install an alarm system, but an alarm would only keep out the unwelcome guests. Lisa wasn't ready to be responsible for saying no when a boy wanted to come over, and maybe Joanna wasn't, either. Maybe she was out of step with the times.

Marti stopped for coffee at a drive-up along the way, picked up sugar and cream, since she didn't know how Isaac liked his, and gave serious thought to whether she would let him get in the car. It was almost the end of the month, almost time for Isaac's monthly trip to a motel for a bath and change of clothes. Her best bet was to get out of the car, stay upwind of him, and shiver if she got cold.

She found him sitting out on the steps of an abandoned building on Fourth.

He didn't seem pleased to be offered coffee. That didn't surprise her, but it didn't bother her, either. She'd help him find a warm place to sleep, give him a cigarette, even, but he'd have to find his own liquor.

She tested the railing before leaning against it. "How're things?"

"Could be better."

After about five minutes of watching her breath, she decided that Isaac wasn't going to say anything without a little prodding.

"So, is this your new place?"

"For the time being."

"Neighborhood's a little rough."

"You're telling me. Got a dope house or gang hangout right over there." He pointed. "Kids out here messing around all times of the night and day. Someone ought to make their butts go to school."

She made a note of the location. "Too bad about the other place."

"Yeah. You know of anywheres where there's something like it?"

"Not that I can think of. Dare can probably find something."

Isaac was silent again. She watched a cluster of clouds drift across the night sky and partially obscure the moon. Two cars pulled up at the house Isaac had pointed out as the drug house. Marti watched as teenagers jumped out, ran in, and emerged quickly. Maybe Narcotics already knew about the activity and for some reason hadn't closed the place down. She would call Lupe first thing in the morning.

"This street is a real hotbed of activity," she said. "More to Dare's liking than yours."

"He couldn't find us no place else on such short notice."

"Well, he'll spot something, riding the garbage truck and all."

Isaac was silent again. Marti shivered. Isaac was going to speak up real soon or she was leaving. "Is there something you want to talk to me about? Other than that house over there."

He asked for a cigarette. She dug a pack out of her purse, certain that they were stale, certain that Isaac was stalling for time. She decided to let him, and she sat on the stairs, hunkering down from the wind.

Isaac inhaled deeply. "Can't find Dare," he said, blowing smoke.

"Since when?" she asked.

"Last Friday, early."

"Is that a long time?"

"For Dare it is."

"Got any idea where he might be?"

"Ran out of 'em."

"Okay. I'll see what I can do."

Isaac flicked the lit butt in the direction of the sidewalk. "Called the hospitals, and the jail."

"I'll see if I can find out anything. Is there anything else I should know?"

From the way Isaac sucked in his breath, she was sure that there was.

"Whatever it is, you need to tell me. I might not be much help if you don't."

"Wasn't nothing . . . or maybe something, but . . ."

"Or something?"

He rubbed his hands together. The man needed gloves, and a

warm coat. Too bad the alcohol was more important. She'd have to see what she could do.

"Ghost," he said.

"A ghost?" Terrific. Jessenovik would love that. First a jack-o'-lantern, now not just one but *two* people who had seen ghosts. Maybe Vik was right and it was the time of year.

"Something white, sheet maybe, something in the rosebushes. Can't say for sure. Wasn't no hallucination, though."

He shivered. Marti didn't think it was from the cold.

"What's wrong?"

He shivered again. His whole body shook.

"What's the matter, Isaac? Are you all right?"

It wasn't a convulsion, but his whole body seemed to be shaking.

"Need a drink?"

He shook his head.

"Doctor?"

He shook his head again; then he buried his face in his arms. "Jesus. Lord. Jesus, Lord."

Marti sat down as far away as possible from the odors of liquor, bad breath, sweat, and dirt. What it was about ghosts that caused this? "Did you see anything else, besides the ghost or whatever?"

"No. Nothing. Isaac don't never see nothing. Isaac don't never see nothing, never."

"Are you okay?" she asked again. "Do you need anything?"

"Isaac don't never see nothing" was all he would say.

When the trembling stopped and he seemed calmer, she said, "I'll do everything I can to find Dare. You need me for anything else, you just call."

She sat in the car for a minute, reluctant to leave him. Another car turned the corner and stopped in front of the house. She had seen several other cars while she was talking to Isaac. This time, an older man went into the house for a few minutes and came back out. Dare loved a little action. There was almost enough of it here to keep him happy, but it was a little too much for poor Isaac.

Isaac drank the rest of the whiskey and went into the house. He pulled out the blankets and huddled under them, waiting for the liquor to make him feel warm and sleepy. Instead, he shook until his teeth chattered.

What had he seen? God as his witness, he didn't never want to see nothing, not ever again. Lord Jesus, whatever it was, this time it wasn't his fault. He hadn't meant to see nothing. It wasn't his fault. What kind of trouble had he gotten himself into now, telling Officer Mac? Now something bad *would* happen to Dare. It was his fault Dare had gone out that morning. His fault. Dare went looking for work because of him. Jesus, God, Jesus, God, what had he caused to happen now? He needed a drink. God but he needed a drink. Where was Dare?

6

Marti had Dare's name and description run through the computer. Nothing turned up. She called every place she could think of, from the jails in Lake County and the surrounding counties to the mental hospital in Elgin. She called every coroner's office that had a John Doe. Wherever Dare was, he wasn't sick or in jail, and he hadn't turned up dead anywhere in the state. Isaac was so upset. Ghosts. It had to be the time of year.

When Marti got home, neither Sharon nor Theo was asleep. She went to Theo first. "Did you call the vet before you went to bed?"

"Uh-huh."

"What did he say?"

"He said Bigfoot was sleepy but feeling a lot better. And he put the phone to Bigfoot's ear and let me talk to him. He said Bigfoot can come home tomorrow."

"Meanwhile, you don't have your sleeping buddy hogging space at the foot of your bed."

"No."

"But he is getting better." She stretched out beside him, and he snuggled close.

"I got pretty worried when Ben called," she said.

"I know. You came right home."

"Well, Bigfoot's a member of the family. He's not just a dog."

Theo giggled. "I bet he's sleeping real good now that I talked to him."

"And you need to get some rest, too. Want me to stay here until you fall asleep?"

"Ummm." Theo pulled the comforter up to his chin and closed his eyes. After a few minutes, he said, "Ma, is Ben family, too? And Mike?"

"They will be soon. How do you feel about that?"

Theo was quiet for so long, Marti thought he was falling asleep, until he said in a quiet voice, "Mike is my best friend."

"And Ben?"

"He's not my dad."

There was so much sadness in his voice that tears came to her eyes.

"Do you think Dad can see us from heaven, Ma?"

"I think he knows how we are."

"That we're okay?"

"Yes."

"That we miss him and want him back?"

"Yes."

He didn't say anything else, and soon the evenness of his breathing told her that he had fallen asleep. She relaxed beside him, certain that he had told her exactly how he felt about Ben and Mike being part of the family, but there was something else. Was he concerned that Johnny might not be pleased?

When Marti woke up a couple of hours later. Sharon's bedroom door was open, but she was not in her room. Marti hesitated. It was almost three in the morning and it had been one hell of a day. The lights were still on downstairs. Sharon was in the kitchen, sitting by the window.

"I'll sit with you for a while if you promise that you will not cry about anything," Marti said.

"It's been that bad today, huh?"

"Damned near it." In spite of herself, she asked, "What's wrong?"

"Mr. Wonderful called. He thinks maybe we should discuss getting married. Actually, he wanted me to drop everything and go out with him tonight. But I was too worried about Bigfoot and the kids. So then he dropped that on me."

73

"Nice guy," Marti said. "Great timing." She remembered something Sharon had said. "Is this that guy you were dating on the q.t. while you were in college?"

"He's the one."

"As I recall, things didn't work out that time, either." Sharon had married Frank. It sounded like both men were losers.

Sharon rested her forehead on the palms of her hands. "He's so . . . everything. He really is Mr. Wonderful. But it's, like, he knows it, and everything revolves around him." She laughed. It sounded brittle. "Back in college, it seemed like there would be other men. Now, one part of me wants to be with him, and the other says, No, you'll get swallowed up in this black hole where nothing exists but him. Another part of me says, 'Vanity, thy name is woman.' He's been talking marriage for over a month now. How do I get out of this? I know how I got into it—I should have just said no."

Marti felt too tired to come up with an answer. She wasn't sure Sharon expected one. "I think we could all use a night's sleep. Trouble is, it's almost morning. It's obvious that you don't want to marry this guy, so you can't. How you tell him, I don't know. Since you don't, either, tell him you need a little time to yourself to think things through. There's not much he can say to that."

"Oh, there's plenty he can say to just about everything," Sharon said. "Whatever will get him what he wants."

"Look, I hate to bring this up now, but the night before last, while you were out, Dante was here with Lisa."

"But they're not . . . are you sure?"

"I'm sure. And nobody tattled. The boys were upset about Bigfoot and were trying to figure out who might have given him the chocolate."

Sharon slumped in her chair. "I'll talk to her. What I really need to do is stay home. I don't need to go out on weeknights, and it isn't just because of our kids. I've got another thirty at school to deal with every day. But when I don't go out sometimes, I feel so cooped up, so . . . trapped."

"It sounds like there are some things about this arrangement that we need to change."

"Oh, Marti. I love the kids. I want to be there for you. And I do have one of my own. If Dante is showing up when I'm not around, it's pretty obvious I need to be home, like it or not. At least for a few more years." She massaged her temples. "No, I don't think home is the problem. I've just been so—this guy has always had this effect on me."

"Do you want me to say something to him the next time he calls?" She had relayed a few messages when Sharon didn't want him to know she was here.

"Like what? Back off? That's something I have to tell him myself. The trouble is, I have to mean it, and sometimes I don't. God, but I hate inconsistency."

As he walked down the street, he got a glimpse of the back of the house. The lights in the kitchen were still on. Timing was everything, but the cop just wouldn't cooperate. She never came home at the same time. At least she always came home late. She was the only variable in the equation. He had no way of knowing what time she would show up. She hadn't made it home before eleven during the week that he had been watching, but he didn't know what kept her away. Her shift began in the morning.

He couldn't risk following her. She was trained to tail people without being observed. She'd spot him right away. He had walked past the precinct for several days, watching for her car to determine if she was there. Then he had seen her get out of an unmarked police car.

She didn't have a schedule clipped to the refrigerator like Joanna, or a "To Do" list like Sharon. He had listened to phone messages on the answering machine, but there were none for her. He needed to know where she was, have some idea of when she'd be coming home. Once he began killing them . . . If she walked in before they were all dead . . . He would have to come up with a contingency plan for that.

The dog didn't greet him when he let himself into the house Thursday morning. He searched upstairs and down but couldn't find it. The damned cat was there, but it kept well away from him. He tried to entice it closer but could not. He had worked out a new plan last night for killing them, and it didn't include chasing the cat. He shouldn't have thrown it. He fixed a cup of coffee in the kitchen, went to the basement, and leaned back in the recliner.

The most important thing was timing. He'd have to do it on a weeknight, when their activities were most predictable. Tomorrow night? Joanna didn't have a date penciled in on the calendar. Or Monday? Tuesday maybe. He'd have to check Joanna's volleyball schedule first. Theo had Cub Scouts on Wednesday. He finished his coffee and did a walk-through. The boys first. If either of them woke up, he would do exactly as told when he saw the gun. Aside from that possibility, it would be easy to hold them down for the five or six minutes that it would take for them to die. Then Sharon. One hand over her mouth, the other holding the knife. A knee on her chest would immobilize her. Then the other girl, Lisa. How? He couldn't decide. Lisa was short like her mother, but fat. He hated the fat ones. They were worse than ugly. His sister was fat. He knew all about them. They were self-centered, self-indulgent, greedy pigs. He would choke her to death. He flexed his fingers. Brute strength, flesh pressing into flesh, squeezing tighter and tighter. He liked the sound of it.

He stood at the doorway to Joanna's room. With everyone

dead, it would just be him and her. Joanna was a big girl. She would struggle. He would have to subdue her. He rubbed his hands together. That could be a lot of fun, subduing Joanna. He thought of the way silk panties felt. He would keep the knife after he used it on Sharon, and when the struggle stopped being fun, he would put it to Joanna's throat and . . . He smiled.

Then he would wait in the basement for the cop to come home. She would go to the kitchen, warm up something to eat perhaps. The gun was for her. Could he make her go upstairs and see what he had done before he shot her? If not, he would just put it in her mouth and pull the trigger. Either way, it would be just him and the cop. And, he would have the drop on her. He would tell her what to do and she would obey. The cop. Soon. Very soon.

Marti checked in with Lupe Torres right after roll call. The Narcotics and Gang units were aware of the activity at the house Isaac had pointed out to Marti the night before. If Marti did anything to jeopardize three months of undercover work, they would be more than a little upset. She agreed to be careful. By eleven o'-clock, Marti had exhausted every avenue she could think of trying to locate Dare. His given name was George Washington Jones. There were no other arrests, just the misdemeanors. His mother and brother refused to talk with her, beyond saying that they hadn't had any contact with him at all in at least five or six years. They refused to file a missing persons' report, and Isaac couldn't file one because he wasn't a relative.

"Awful lot of work for one drunk who's AWOL," Vik said. "George Washington Jones. He's probably wrapped in newspaper in a doorway somewhere, in the middle of a blackout."

Marti told him about the "ghost" Isaac had seen.

"It's got to be the time of year," Vik said. "They need to stop putting up those Halloween decorations. Everywhere you go, you see witches and ghosts and carved-up pumpkins. The power of suggestion. Drunks and old folks haven't got too much sense left anyway."

"The guy at the beach seemed okay to me."

"That joker," Vik said. "A real wise guy. I'd love to harass him."

He pulled a few new danglers from the spider plant. "Birth control," he said. "Maybe we should question him again. With this other 'ghost' sighting, why not. They might tie in."

Marti did want to talk with him, if only to watch the expression on Vik's face if the man mentioned a ghost.

The fisherman lived in a bungalow on the far northeast side of town. Red maples and silver birches lined the street and every yard had yews or other evergreens. There was a tall blue spruce in the center of the old man's front yard. He opened the door without removing the chain and squinted at them. When Vik reminded him of where they had last met, he said he couldn't remember and demanded to see some ID. He looked at their shields for what seemed like several minutes before letting them in.

"You can't be too careful."

A Irish setter rushed up to greet them, wagging its tail.

"This must be Lorna," Marti said, thinking of Bigfoot. "Mine's at the vet."

"What breed have you got?" he asked.

"Oh, Bigfoot's at least six or seven."

He gave her crooked smile. "Lorna's got a little collie in her."

"We need to know more about this ghost you saw while you were fishing," Marti said.

"Oh." He led the way into the living room and pulled an afghan covered with dog hair off the couch so they could sit down. He sat in a chair with a hassock and put his feet up. The dog hesitated, sat on her haunches on a threadbare Oriental rug, and nudged Marti's hand. The dog's hair was long and silky, not coarse like Bigfoot's, and shiny, as if recently brushed.

"There wasn't no ghost," the man said. "Least not as as far as I know."

Vik smirked but said nothing.

Marti tried not to stare at a fish mounted on a board with its mouth open. People really did stuff them and hang them on walls. Maybe there was some reason for doing this that she didn't understand.

"Are you saying that you didn't see anything?" she asked.

"Oh, I saw something. A deer, maybe. Hard to tell. My sight's none to good when I'm looking off in the distance. The noise is what got my attention. I can still hear pretty good. Branches breaking, dirt being pawed at. I got a glimpse of something moving that was dark, didn't pay much attention after that. Whatever it was wasn't coming over that fence, and it's not like there're any bears around here." He pulled out a pouch of chewing tobacco and stuffed some in his jaw. "The way they been taking the land around here, cutting down the trees and building something every place they can, deer and skunks and raccoons and such ain't got no place to go. I'm so far north that deer come right in my yard, and I can't keep a garden no more for the rabbits."

"Damned shame," Vik agreed. It was one of his favorite complaints.

"Well," Vik said when they got back in the car, "so much for that. I don't think he was telling the truth this time, either."

Marti wanted to ask him if there was something symbolic or traditional about hanging dead fish in the living room, but if she did, he'd probably tell her. She had heard enough fish stories for a while.

"I told you he was a liar, MacAlister."

Maybe that was why he had the fish stuffed, so when someone asked, he could tell them about the one that got away.

"Ghosts," Vik said. "It's either something that nuke plant is emitting or the full moon. Maybe it's a combination of both."

This talk of ghosts was bothering her. Someone was seeing something. In the old man's case, it probably was just an animal, but what had Isaac seen? Was it just an alcoholic delusion? Isaac "never saw nothing" and, for whatever reason, it had cost him dearly when he decided to tell her that he had seen whatever it was. His reaction was still puzzling.

"Maybe we'll just go over to Isaac's neighborhood and talk to whoever lives in the house where he thinks he saw the ghost."

"Look, Marti, Dare's just off drinking somewhere. If anything had happened to him, you sure would have found out by now.

You know how unpredictable drunks are. We need to be working on the Norris case."

He was right, but the Norris case was cold and she needed to occupy her mind with something trivial. Something useful might come to her if she let go of Ladiya for a while.

Isaac lived in what city planners called a "transitional neighborhood." This one was transitioning in a downward spiral, with pockets of blight, like the street where Isaac lived, and pockets of modest but well-kept old homes, like this street, a block over.

"Doesn't look like a haunted house to me," Vik said as Marti pulled up in front of a tidy white-framed two-flat building with lace curtains at the front windows. Nobody answered the first-floor bell. An older woman came down from the second floor to let them in. Vik took one look at her short, curly gray hair, sensible shoes, and the bib apron that covered a blue pleated skirt and long-sleeved white blouse and gave Marti a look that said, There won't be any ghost nonsense now. After checking their shields, the woman introduced herself as Elizabeth Stiles.

Upstairs, they sat in a tiny living room with Queen Anne chairs and pineapple doilies on mahogany tables. Vik straightened his tie and inspected his fingernails while Ms. Stiles made tea.

"Ghosts?" the woman said, pouring from a silver-plated tea service. "Oh, that poor girl won't harm anyone." Vik looked as if he'd just swallowed vinegar. "She just can't find rest, for some reason. She died such a violent death that she may never rest easy. It happened twenty-three years ago and her spirit is wandering still."

"Not the old Milford case?" Vik said.

"That's the one. She lived in this flat with her mother. Not that they could ever prove exactly where she was killed, or, for that matter, who did it, but the way she lingers in this place, it must have happened here."

"You've seen her, Ms. Stiles?" Vik said.

"Just glimpses."

"And that doesn't bother you?"

"Oh, no. I'm a witch, you see. I understand such things."

Vik almost choked on the tea he was sipping.

"Are there many witches around here?" Marti asked. She was beginning to enjoy this.

"There are just the three of us, as far as I know."

Vik coughed again.

"Are you all right, young man?" Ms. Stiles said.

"Just fine," Vik gasped. He put the teacup on the tray and pushed his chair farther away from her.

"Is there anything else you can tell us about this ghost?" Marti asked.

"Just that I'm surprised that someone who doesn't live here has seen her. I have such a terrible time keeping the downstairs apartment rented. I tell them she's harmless, but people are so skittish about spirits. And you say she was seen outside? I've never know her to go into the yard." She paused for a moment. "Perhaps you should dig there." Her voice was just above a whisper. "Maybe there's a clue, a weapon or something. They did find her body, right here in this room, but there wasn't enough evidence to find out who did it." She leaned forward and spoke to Marti. "They always did think it was her nephew, but they couldn't break his alibi. Since she didn't find rest when he died, maybe he wasn't the one. I would dig, if I were you," she concluded. "Right away. Wherever this person saw her. Did they say?"

"Is that a rose trellis out there?" Marti asked.

"Why, yes. Those rosebushes have been there for years. Would you like to take a look at them?"

Vik's expression suggested that he would rather do just about anything else.

"Sure," Marti said. "I think we'd better."

Ms. Stiles put on a gray cape with a hood that framed her face.

Marti couldn't help smiling as they went out the back door.

"I can't imagine her leaving the house," Elizabeth Stiles said. "I've lived here seventeen years and I've never known her to do anything like that."

As they followed her across a concrete path and onto damp

grass, Vik said, "All of this because of something a wino told you. Not only does that man *not* have any grip on reality; he probably hallucinates *and* imagines he's had hallucinations when he hasn't."

The rosebushes were a thick, tangled mass of bare branches.

"Oh, my goodness," Ms. Stiles said. Marti bumped into her as she stopped. "I don't think we should go any closer. There is such a terrible aura here. I can't imagine . . ." She paused and cocked her head to one side, then shook and said, "If she did come here, she was quite disturbed by something. I would truly appreciate it if you would tell me if you find out anything of significance about this place."

"If I can," Marti said.

Vik shifted from one foot to the other, eager to get back to the precinct. In another hour, Marti would be as much of a joke as the Halloween flasher.

"These roses have been here for years," Ms. Stiles said. "Much longer than I have. I used to come back here and prune them, but she didn't seem to approve, so I've just let them grow wild."

The rosebushes were thick at the base. A tangle of low branches had spread across the entire corner of the yard and now threaded their way between the links of the fence.

"The roses are completely wild now. Hundreds of yellow flowers not any bigger than a joint on your thumb."

Marti squatted, trying to look among the branches without getting pricked by the thorns. She picked up a stick and poked among the branches, moving paper and other debris that had caught there. The stick broke as she jabbed at a thick wad of newspaper. Vik handed her another that was sturdier. There was a purple cloth bag beneath the newspaper. It was lodged at the base of one of the bushes, wedged between two thick stumps. Marti recognized it as something liquor was packaged in. She couldn't think of the type or the brand.

"Well," Vik said, "what do you know. Someone threw away an empty booze bottle right here in Ms. Stiles's garden. It sure couldn't be something that belonged to Isaac. Too expensive for his taste, not to mention his wallet, if he has one."

Marti whacked the bag with the stick. There was a bottle or something else inside. She maneuvered the stick between the yellow drawstring at the top of the bag. It was wedged too tightly to move. "If you went around to the other side of the fence, Vik . . ."

"Marti, give it up. All you've got there is an empty booze bottle."

"There is something out here that she doesn't like," Ms. Stiles said. "I would certainly appreciate it if you got it out of there. I've never felt such a sense of foreboding in this place, and there's nothing else here."

Vik went out to the alley that abutted the fence and found a tree branch that fit between the links of the fence. It was just the right size to dislodge the bag. Marti maneuvered her stick until the drawstring was looped over it. "Heavy," she said as she pulled the bag from under the bushes. When she opened it, there was a gun inside.

"No wonder!" Ms. Stiles exclaimed. "After all the violence that poor dear experienced, having something like this in her rosebushes must have really upset her."

"Great," Vik said. "Now we've got a weapon and no victim to match it up with. We don't have anything open involving a bullet wound."

Marti snagged the wad of newspaper with the stick so that it wouldn't blow away. "Let's just get an evidence tech over here, okay?"

"Maybe we'd better dig up the rosebushes, too," Vik suggested.

Ms. Stiles gasped. "Oh my goodness, no. Why, she is already so upset."

"She's been gone for over twenty years now, ma'am," Vik said.

"But her spirit. And that gun so distressed her that she left the house. She's never done that before, not as long as I've been here."

"Yes, ma'am. I think you mentioned that." Vik muttered something that Marti couldn't quite make out except for "nutcases."

The evidence tech was not impressed with the gun. "It's just a Sig Sauer thirty-eight," he said. "A friend of mine in Cook County confiscated an Uzi last week. It had a thirty-two-round magazine. This Sig is just a two twenty-five, nine rounds."

Regardless of the firepower, Marti knew it wouldn't have been thrown away without good reason.

"A witch," Vik said to Marti when they were in the car. "First ghosts and now a witch. What if she put something in the tea?"

Marti stopped for a red light and turned to look at him. "I don't see any warts growing on your chin yet."

"Be serious. There's no such thing as a witch or a ghost. But people like her learn a lot about herbs and poisons. She could have put something in the tea. I will never accept another cup of anything from anyone I don't know."

"It was good tea. I've never tasted any quite like it. I should have asked what it was so Joanna could buy some."

"If I get so much as an upset stomach, I'm having that woman brought in."

"What about the victim? Did she die right in the house? Was the weapon a gun?"

"No. She had dozens of stab wounds, but there wasn't much blood. The killer cleaned the place up afterward, so there was always talk that she died someplace else. Wishful thinking. People just don't like that kind of thing happening in their neighborhood."

"Are there any other stories about a ghost?"

"There are always stories, Marti. People thrive on them. Don't tell me you believed her."

"I don't know," Marti mused. "People do such weird things that when you think about it, hanging around and haunting people doesn't seem that strange."

She didn't think there was any point in talking with Isaac again to determine what he had really seen. The old fisherman had admitted he hadn't seen a ghost, but Isaac had probably been too drunk to know what he was looking at, assuming that he actually saw anything at all.

"The coroner's office has released Ladiya's body," she said. "Maybe we should talk with the mother again. There has to be some connection to Lincoln Prairie."

"Unless this was just some random act of violence."

"Come on, Vik. What are the odds on that?"

"At least as good as seeing a ghost. We're two for one on that, so far."

Mrs. Norris led Marti and Vik to a bedroom at the rear of the house, next to the kitchen. Posters of athletes and rock stars Marti didn't recognize were hung on the doors and the walls. A wall unit held a stereo, speakers, and dozens of tapes and CDs. Clothes were folded and sorted near the foot of the bed. The closet door and several dresser drawers were open. Boxes were stacked against the wall.

"I always thought she'd come back," Mrs. Norris said. "I left her room just as it was." She went to the window. "Even the bird feeders. She was always convinced that she'd lure some finches here one day, but it was always just the sparrows that came."

Marti could see the small plastic seed containers attached to the outside of the window with suction cups. They were empty. She looked at the clothes: jeans, T-shirts, skirts on the bed, prom dresses and party clothes in the closet. In a collage of school pictures that hung on the wall, Ladiya went from a pretty little girl with pigtails and two front teeth missing to an attractive young woman in an off-the-shoulder formal with sprigs of baby's breath in her hair.

"I can't imagine what she was doing in Lincoln Prairie, or why she would have been near the lake. Ladiya couldn't swim very well. She wouldn't have learned at all if it hadn't been required. She very seldom went to the beach."

"You don't know of any friends who moved to that area? Because of jobs or marriage, maybe?"

"I can't remember anyone in the family or any of her friends ever mentioning that place. I didn't even know how to get there until yesterday." She frowned for a moment, then busied herself refolding a neat stack of blouses.

"Did Ladiya keep any papers or letters—a diary, maybe?" Marti asked.

"She kept journals in high school. I've never read them." Mrs. Norris went to the closet and took down a shoe box from the shelf. Marti opened it. There were four notebooks inside. The covers were flowery and Marti suspected the writing was trivial but detailed, with all the minutiae adolescents considered important.

Mrs. Norris sat on the bed. "It's funny, the things you remember. Instead of thinking of the shopping trips and the time we went to Atlanta, all I can think about is rushing out the door to get to work, or rushing to some event at school and getting there late or when everything was just about over. There was this one piano recital, and I made it before it was her turn to play. When she saw me, she gave me this big smile. There were other recitals when she must not have smiled at all." She plucked at the lacy pattern in the lavender bedspread. "If I could just do it again. Those other things that had to get done, a clean room, a clean house, even a second job—a lot of that might have waited."

Marti thought of her own kids and took a deep breath. "We do what we can," she said. "There's always so much. Especially when there's no father."

Mrs. Norris reached out and gripped Marti's hand. "Do you think they understand?"

"No," Marti admitted. "Not until they get there themselves. I think they accept it, though."

"You don't think . . . they . . . get . . . angry enough to get even?"

"I hope not."

"If I could just understand why she did this."

Marti swallowed hard and stared at the bird feeders. "Can you remember what you talked about the last time she was here?"

"We were very . . . careful with each other. I didn't mention . . . him. She didn't mention . . . whatever she was doing. Mostly we just sat for about an hour not saying much of anything. Small talk. She needed to go to the dentist. She'd been having a constant toothache. She'd seen some shoes she thought I might like at Marshall Field. She had been in Milwaukee the week before.

When she didn't say why or with whom, I didn't ask. Just small talk, nothing important." She smoothed the bedspread.

"Did she seem any different from the last time you'd seen her?"

"Not really. She had lost too much weight. Her clothes hung on her. And looking back, she seemed more tired each time she came. Just tired. That last time, she came to her room. She never did that. But that time she did. She was standing by the window when I came in. 'They never came,' she said. 'Not one. Maybe if I tried different seed . . .' Then she said she was running late, and she left. Do you think maybe she was ready to come home?"

"It sounds that way," Marti said, not quite believing it, but curious. "Do you suppose that since she did come in here, we could take a look around?"

"Of course. I don't suppose you'll want me here while you do." She hurried out of the room.

They removed drawers, checking behind and underneath them, and went through the pockets of everything in the closet. They stripped the bed, checked the mattress and box springs, and then remade it. They looked everywhere Ladiya might have hidden something, even in the tiny china teapot, but they found nothing.

When they got back to the precinct, Marti put the box of diaries on her desk and avoided opening it as long as she could. When there was nothing left to catch up on and her in and out baskets were empty, she reached for it. She wanted to toss one to Vik, but they each had to read them sequentially, just in case. Patterns— they were always looking for patterns. What would she find out, reading something that would have been none of her business if it weren't for the way Ladiya died?

The first two journals were depressing—a child's mind, a woman's body, a simplistic concept of good and bad, right and wrong, and confusion. Bad things happened to people who didn't deserve their misfortune; teachers, parents, and life in general weren't always fair. There were changes in Ladiya's junior year: more maturity, adult decisions. Smoking made her cough and cigarettes tasted like "dried leaves and old newspaper, which is all that they are, so why garbage up my lungs? The look is not worth it. Shenea says the boys just think it means you'll put out." A well-thought-out decision, at least as good as her decision not to have sex until she was married. "Shenea says they get inside and push and grunt and sweat while you get all wet and sticky and slimy and she wouldn't have starting doing it if she'd known that's all it was." Shenea, the girlfriend who lived next door.

By the end of her junior year, Ladiya was experimenting with drugs. "It was like being someplace wonderful and no place at all. A kind of between space, like having a porch and hiding under it, only you haven't gone anywhere at all and everyone is still there, but it's like they're not, like finding your own hiding place while everyone thinks you're still there." What did Ladiya want to hide from? Or whom? Why did she need that isolation?

Ladiya used drugs recreationally throughout her senior year. Marti marveled that her mother never knew. She probably did, and just denied it. Drugs brought change. Ladiya began to enjoy the dances and parties with boys, which in prior years were "nonproductive activities, not like Junior Achievement, where you learn something useful, or student tutoring, things that make the teachers like you and give you good grades." She was concerned about her grades going down in her senior year, but she wrote, "Momma likes it when I go out. I think she worries about sex and drugs (ha ha), but she likes telling everyone that I'm going to a dance or a party."

The final entry was made the night before she graduated: "Who will I be the day after tomorrow? Will I still be me? Who is me? Do I want to know?"

As she passed the journals to Vik, Marti wondered if Mrs. Norris would read them.

They gave their boss, Lieutenant Dirkowitz, an update on the Norris case before they went home.

"She's not a local," Marti said. "Two arrests for possession of narcotics with intent to sell. We've talked with Narcotics. No suspects, no motive. Not yet. It looks like it might end up being a matter of someone dropping something or giving us something to try to buy their way out of a drug-related bust."

The lieutenant had earned the nickname "Dirty Dirk" as a football player, locally and then at Southern Illinois University. At thirty-five, he worked out and watched what he ate; he still had the build and thick neck of a linebacker. He ran his fingers through blond hair that was beginning to thin. "What about this Halloween flasher?"

"He's making his annual appearance," Vik said.

"But he's not getting his annual reaction," Dirkowitz said. He picked up the apple-shaped defused hand grenade he kept on his desk as a memento of a brother who had died in Vietnam. "Should we be concerned?"

Marti hesitated. "It seems passive, sir, showing yourself. And this guy, he really does act like a clown."

"But—"

"It is an act of aggression, sir, not buffoonery."

"Do you think he might be dangerous?"

"The department psych can't call it one way or the other."

The lieutenant looked at the grenade. "And you, MacAlister? Jessenovik? What do you think?"

"Better to be safe than sorry," Vik said. "We've got a body count of one right now. It's a manageable number."

"I can't disagree with that. I want him out of the limelight and out of the news. Lake County will be having a special guest next weekend. All I need is to have punkin' puss and his little pecker all over the front page of the local newspaper. I might have to assign a few extra men to Vice temporarily. Since you and Slim and Cowboy are roommates, you might know them better than anyone else. See if you can provide any input." The lieutenant dropped the hand grenade on his desk, a signal that the meeting was over.

"Just what we need," Vik said as soon as the door to the lieutenant's office closed and they were out of earshot. "I have never worked Vice. Have you?"

"Once, but just for a couple of days." It had been an experience that she had tried to forget.

8

He stepped into the alcove just outside the boys' bathroom and waited until loud voices told him that volleyball practice was over. When he stepped into the hall, the girls were just ahead of him. He paused, caught a glimpse of Joanna, almost a head taller than most of the others, then took long strides to catch up. He passed among them, close enough to Joanna to touch her long, thick braid. He wanted to jostle her, bump into her, whatever it took to touch her breast. Before he could think of a way, she turned down a corridor with her team-mates and was gone.

Isaac wanted to be drunk. He wanted to be so drunk that tomorrow he would not be able to remember wanting to be drunk today. Instead, he had to nurse this sorry high, careful not to get sober enough to go into the d.t.'s. Without money, that wasn't easy to do. He'd gotten lucky today and run across a couple of Dare's friends and shared a few pints with them. They cooked up a pot of mountain oysters smothered in gravy and made some biscuits that tasted so good, it made him think of his grandmother. He couldn't remember the last time he'd eaten hog nuts. Lord but they was good. He couldn't leave without having some, couldn't eat as much as he wanted to, and was still feeling hungry for more.

Where in the hell was Dare? If that fool walked in right now, he'd slap the something out of him for being gone for so long. The folks he had been with today hadn't seen him, neither. Hadn't nobody he talked with seen hide nor hair of Dare. A man didn't just disappear, didn't just up and walk away. Dare had to be somewhere. If anyone could find him, Big Mac could. Why did he have to talk so much? All she needed to know was that Dare wasn't around. He didn't know what he had seen in the middle of the night, just that he had seen something. Why did he just have to go and tell? He wasn't used to telling folks nothing. Didn't want to tell them nothing. Didn't want to know nothing that he should tell them. He reached in his pocket. A full bottle. Thank you, Jesus, for another day and another bottle. If only he could just drink the whole thing, instead of sipping and praying for tomorrow.

Marti thought about Isaac as she drove home from the precinct. His jacket wasn't warm enough for the weather and those thin jeans he was wearing had holes at the knees. He did not look well. Every time she saw him, he seemed frailer than the last time, and older. It wouldn't take much more than a gust of wind to knock him over. She wished she could talk him into staying at the new rehab center for men, but she knew Isaac had no plans to be rehabilitated, that he intended to remain just as he was. There was no point in her worrying about him. There was nothing she could think of that would make him change. Like Vik said, it was a free country, and Isaac wasn't doing anything to hurt anyone.

Bigfoot was home when she got there. Theo and Mike were on the computer. The dog was stretched out close to Theo's feet. He wagged his tail a few times when she came in but didn't get up. "Hi, boy, how you doing?" She rubbed the fur between his ears. "I bet you're glad to be home. Where's your new friend Goblin? Are you getting along okay?"

The cat, friendly at first, had become skittish and stayed away from the family, preferring a hiding place upstairs to their company. It probably missed the little girl, but she was going to be in the hospital for another week. Her parents were spending as much time with her as possible, and nobody had time for a cat.

"Schoolwork?" Marti asked, sitting in the recliner.

"Ummm," Theo said.

"How's Bigfoot doing?"

"Okay."

"What did the vet say? Do we have to do anything special? Did he have any prescriptions? Do they give dogs prescriptions?"

"Uh-uh."

"Uh-uh what?"

Theo frowned and kept typing.

"Can you type without looking at the keys?"

"Umm."

They were back where they'd started. She decided to leave him alone.

"How's it going, Mike?"

"Okay."

"Have you met the cat?"

"No." Mike was a friendly child who smiled a lot, but tonight, he was reticent and frowning.

"Get the encyclopedia," Theo said. "And look up the comet entry again. We've got to make sure everything is right. This has got to be perfect."

Good, Marti wanted to protest. Very good, but not perfect. They were only ten. What would they be like in another five years if they thought everything had to be perfect now?

She woke up to the sound of Theo shushing Mike. "Shhh. Joanna thinks we're in bed. She never checks if the door is closed. If she hears us down here, we'll never get this done tonight."

Marti remained still.

"What if Mrs. Hinkston doesn't like it?" Mike said. "Are you sure she can't tell that you helped me? She'll throw it away and give me an *F* if she doesn't think I did the whole thing myself."

"You did do the whole thing yourself. I just asked the questions and helped with the typing."

"I know, Theo, but we're not working on this in teams. I should have done everything myself. She'll find out and I'll get in big trouble."

"Mike, if you don't get everything exactly right from now on,

Mrs. Hinkston is going to get you transferred to a different school. You did this report. You looked everything up in the encyclopedia. You found the answers."

"But I probably won't remember any of it. Ask me a bunch of questions again."

Marti knew it was after ten o'clock. They should both be in bed. While Theo quizzed Mike on comets, Marti wondered what she and Ben were going to do.

Isaac wasn't sure what had awakened him. He hated being woken up. Worse, he had drunk all of the muscatel and had nothing to help him get back to sleep. He heard the noise again: a creaking sound. The floorboards in the other room. They were coming to rob him, but he didn't have anything for them to steal. They'd kill him if they didn't find nothing. He listened but didn't hear anything else. Maybe it was just the wind. He'd gotten so used to being safe at the other place that he hadn't even bothered to start sleeping with a knife when they came here. Now someone could come in here and kill him, and here he was, couldn't even defend himself. There wasn't no noise now. Musta been the wind. The night wasn't half gone and here he was wide-awake, and all because of the wind. No way was he going to look out the window. That was what'd happened the night that Dare didn't come home, and nothing good came from that. Man worked most of his life at making sure he didn't see nothing and one accidental trip to the window and he blew it.

Now what? It was too cold in here to get up. There wasn't no place warm to go to this time of night and he didn't have nothing to help him get to sleep again. Another squeak. What the hell? He eased from under the covers and slipped to the floor. Better to just get out of here, then figure out whether or not something was in here with him. It might be that ghost. He had seen something the other night that was not alcohol-induced. He had had the d.t.'s often enough to know that much.

He tucked one tennis shoe under each arm and began backing away in a crouch from the direction he thought the noise was coming from. There was an open door behind him. As soon as he was in the other room, he stood and tiptoed away. The front door was half open. He had closed it when he came in, but there wasn't a lock or anything. The wind blew it open sometimes, but when it did, it always slammed against the wall, and he knew what that was.

He waited and listened again, until he heard another sound that was too far away for him to figure out what it was. Might be nothing. He'd just go around to the side and peek in through the windows. He found a spot where he couldn't be seen from the street and put on his tennis shoes. He was going to have to get himself a pair of socks soon, start looking for some boots at Sally's before it snowed. That's what Dare called the Salvation Army, Sally's. And he'd go see the old priest about a coat. Get one for Dare while he was at it—if Dare wasn't back by then—so Dare wouldn't miss out.

The windows were high. He had to stand on tiptoe to peek inside. And the moon was full. No hiding out here. He went to the back to a spot where a tree kept out most of the light, then peeked into the room where he'd heard the noise. Nothing. He went to the room where he slept.

Someone was standing over his bed with a knife, sticking it into the mound of blankets again and again. Isaac watched the arm swing up and come down. Then he backed away, careful not to make any noise. When he was far enough away from the house, he ran.

Marti was wide-awake. Overtired, probably. After the boys were in bed, she went to the computer and picked up the stack of printouts. There were six versions of Theo's project on Saturn, nine copies of Mike's paper on comets. Theo had a lot of curiosity when it came to science. She hoped this phase of technical perfection with Mrs. Hinkston wouldn't stifle it. The content of Theo's first paper was as good as the final draft, but he had gone over it anyway, making small changes. She couldn't remember being that conscientious as a student, but maybe this was good.

Having met his teacher, she knew Mrs. Hinkston would be pleased with his efforts. Maybe Marti just missed the little boy who had sticky fingers and dirt smudges on his face and this was part of growing up.

She put down the papers. That wasn't what was bothering her. Theo had a tendency toward perfectionism and she didn't want anyone to encourage it. The effects of Johnny's death on her children were more subtle than obvious. Not only did they have to deal with one parent who had died in the line of duty; they also had to deal with another parent who was also a cop, another parent who could die much the same way. They didn't misbehave, didn't act out their grief or their anger. In their own way, they sought to please her. She didn't know if they thought good behavior was some kind of mantle of protection that would shelter them from more hurt if it couldn't shelter her from harm, or if it was more like the compromise she had made with God when her father died. It had been simple and direct: Dear God, I promise I will always do whatever you want me to do, if you just don't let Momma die, too. She had not always lived up to her commitment, but Momma was still here.

She felt that over time, Theo and Joanna were becoming a little more willing to risk her displeasure, or maybe God's. But it seemed like just when she began to relax, something like this happened. Once, not long after Johnny died, Theo had reached the point where everything had to be in its proper place. Now, although he would never reach Joanna's level of indifference, he could manage the occasional pair of socks left on the floor and didn't always hang up his jacket or sweater. He hadn't even gotten too upset last month when he left his baseball glove outside in the rain. Of course now, thanks to Mrs. Hinkston, Marti was sure all that was about to change. Once again, Theo couldn't even leave a misspelled word and a few misplaced commas alone.

Thank God for Mike. Before Marti got to know him, she hadn't liked him. Not for any particular reason, except that she didn't want to like him, or Ben. She didn't want anyone to get that close, not then. But like Ben, Mike had become very special. His behavior had been awful in the years following his mother's death, when he was five, but now, although he was still overweight, he had calmed down. She couldn't remember the last time Ben had mentioned a temper tantrum, and, unless Mike was overtired, he seldom talked back. There was an eagerness about Mike. He was always ready for whatever was going to happen next, and with the expectation that it might be fun. While Theo anticipated how things could go wrong, Mike saw the humor in things. When Theo aligned a slide in his microscope and saw things right side up, Mike would flip the slide over and look at it upside down. They balanced each other so well. There was no way anyone was going to separate them. She was going to have a talk with Mrs. Hinkston about both boys, but she didn't expect the woman to pay any attention to one word she said.

She went upstairs. Mike was in the top bunk, on his back, arms flung open, a half smile on his face. Theo had kicked off the blankets and was all curled up. She adjusted the covers, then sat beside him. There were two encyclopedias and a dictionary on his desk. His wastebasket was half filled with crumpled pieces of paper. The model airplane he had started a month ago was still unfinished. And the telescope he'd been so excited about when she gave it to him two weeks ago hadn't even been taken out of the box. Theo was ten years old, and he didn't have a dad. Ben could not replace Johnny, and she neither wanted nor expected him to. She did want Ben to be important and influential in Theo's life. No matter what, Theo was going to have a childhood. She was going to have a talk with Mrs. Hinkston. She was a cop. She did know how to make people listen.

When she looked in on Joanna, she had to step over a volley-ball uniform and two sets of sweats to get to the bed. At least nothing seemed to have changed here. Joanna, who looked so much like Momma, and like Marti, was just as untidy. Did Joanna keep a journal? She doubted it. Joanna hated to write anything, including homework. Joanna wasn't anything like Ladiya. She was going to parties. She was less shy with boys. She had one hell of a volleyball serve. She was only compulsive about everyone's eating habits. Nobody that concerned about what went into her body could even consider doing drugs. Reaching down, Marti smoothed the soft strands of auburn hair that had come loose from Joanna's braid. Not everyone did drugs. Her children were too smart for that. She was going to have to spend more time with them.

Sharon came to the door. "What's the matter?"

Marti shook her head.

"Want some tea?"

Marti thought of the tea the nice witch had served her and Vik. Maybe the woman had a potion that would make her a better parent, or just make her kids think she was. "Sure."

They sat in the light from a small lamp, hunched over steaming mugs of strawberry tea. Marti wished Ben were there. He thought she was the intuitive parent, and she thought he was the most practical. She needed some commonsense idea of what to do. She could use some clear idea of what the problems were, too. She explained the situation with Theo and Mike to Sharon.

"Good luck" was all Sharon said.

"But Sharon, you're a teacher."

"Yes. I think so. At least for the most part. I was today."

"What does that mean?"

"I don't know. Teaching is changing. The system is changing. Last year, a principal was fired. She might have played just a little loose with the rules, but she was a gifted motivator, encouraged innovation, and her students' test scores were among the highest in the district. She maintained the highest attendance and best parent participation and got kicked out of the district within two years. So this year, everyone's in a save-your-own-ass mood, and everything is done by the book."

"Is that why the teacher Theo began the year with is gone?"

"Yes. She was much too enthusiastic and creative."

"What about Theo and Mike?"

"Hinkston has been around long enough to do whatever she wants to, and she only wants to teach children who are fast learners. She's very hard on anyone who is not, tries to get them out of her classroom, into special ed or behavior-disorder classes."

"And the parents let her?"

Sharon laughed. "We are always right. Weren't you impressed by her authoritativeness?"

Marti cussed, then caught herself. "I wonder how impressed she'd be with mine."

Sharon laughed again. "Good luck, Detective MacAlister, good luck."

"Have you talked with Lisa yet?" Marti asked.

Sharon fidgeted with her hair. "He doesn't have any kids. He insists that ours aren't babies anymore, that I need a life of my own, and in a way, he's right: They are growing up and I am . . . confined. But there is so much out there, Marti. There is so much out there, just waiting for them. It's like the reverend says: If you don't keep watch at the gate, the wolves come in."

Sharon pushed her chair away from the table and stood up. "So, I will talk with Lisa. And I will keep my butt at home. What's a few more years of child rearing? She'll be off to college soon. And I'll only be forty-three when she leaves."

Marti detected an unfamiliar tone of resentment in Sharon's voice.

"Sharon, I'm the one who never dated anyone but Johnny. I had the curfew and the church, no dating until sixteen and then double-dating through high school. You got to do pretty much what you wanted. You dated a lot of boys before Frank and you've dated a lot of men since."

"Then why in the hell do I feel cheated? Why do I feel like I got the short end of the stick? Why do I feel so damned trapped?"

Sharon rushed out of the room before Marti could answer.

Isaac had nowhere to go. He considered going to the emergency room, complaining of chest pains, but he didn't like dealing with strangers and he didn't like anyone touching him. There were parks not too far from here that were okay, and this time of year he could sleep there without worrying about cops or robbers, but it was too cold to be sleeping outdoors. He walked fast—

wandering, really, but looking like he had someplace to go. They didn't keep the churches open anymore. Time was when he could have slept there. They kept the train station locked up. Even with boarded-up places that looked empty, it was tricky. Rats, for one thing, two-legged and four-legged. There weren't many apartment buildings that were unlocked, and no public buildings that were open. This just wasn't Chicago. Not that he liked the city, but at least if nothing else, there was the Lower Drive, and nobody much cared if you slept on a grate where some heat was coming out.

Damn shame the way they just came in and tore down the old place. That place had been home for going on four years. They had even brought in a few pieces of furniture, a couple of chairs and some mattresses, a table, too. No matter that it wasn't like anything that most folks would call home. It had what he wanted: peace and quiet. No La Cockroach song playing in the middle of the night. Nobody nearby. Crickets and fireflies in the summer and that family of skunks he had to watch out for. And when it got cold like this, he could build a little fire under the trees and roll up in a sleeping bag right under the stars and go to sleep. There might not be any more places like that around here. There might not be any place left to go.

Eventually, he found a garage. The door was open and there was no car inside. It looked like it was about to fall down. He found a corner out of the wind and wished for some cardboard or newspaper to wrap up in to keep warm. His knees had got to aching and sometimes he didn't think anything was circulating in his fingers and toes. Wasn't no need to complain none, though, he thought. At least nobody would come looking for him here and he could give his legs some rest. In the morning, he'd go get the trash out for old Queenie and she'd give him some coffee and doughnuts and a couple drinks. Then he'd head over to see the old priest.

He kept trying not to think about that man, just standing there and stabbing them blankets, but there wasn't much else on his mind but Dare, that and finding a place to stay. Just remembering made him tremble all over. Man musta been a fool coming in there like that. Probably one of them fools let loose from the mental hospital what didn't have nare bit of sense. That's what it was—some fool out there took notice of him when he was dumb enough to ask a few folks questions about Dare. Well, he wouldn't be going back around there no more. He sure wouldn't be going around there. And he wouldn't be saying or seeing nothing else.

He stretched out on the army cot and stared up at the ceiling. He was too keyed up to sleep. He had touched her, hadn't he? Yes, he had finally touched Joanna. She had looked at him with such eagerness. Her breast had looked firm, her nipple erect. He had been close enough to feel her breath on his face, close enough to smell her sweat mingled with perfume . . . close enough to see that little black mole on the side of her neck. A minor blemish, but it marred the smoothness of her skin. The more he thought about it, the more that imperfection bothered him. If he bit it off . . .

9

When he let himself in Friday morning, there still was no dog waiting to greet him. He had brought another candy bar, assuming that there was some logical reason for the dog's absence the day before. Instead, it was gone, and just when he had almost decided to allow it to live. He liked the dog. Who did they think they were, getting rid of it?

The kitchen was clean, except for two coffee cups in the sink. He checked the coffeepot—still warm—rinsed a cup without disturbing the lipstick smear, and filled it. Bright red lipstick. It was Sharon's. He sat away from the window, but close enough to see outside. The wind chime didn't clank anymore. Damn but that had been an annoying sound. He had removed one of the pieces and nobody had noticed. From where he stood, he could see two blue garbage containers. Theo had left them by the garage again. They were supposed to go into the shed. There was not enough discipline in this house. When he was a boy, he couldn't imagine ever doing anything other than exactly what he was told. For some reason, the hardest thing was to mop the kitchen floor every night. No matter how carefully he inspected it when it was dry, he always missed something. "I expected more from you" was all his stepfather ever said. "I expected much better than this." Then he had to wash the entire floor again, on hands and knees. He drank the coffee and returned the cup to the sink, with the lipstick smudge intact.

Then he went to Joanna's room. He hadn't gotten to sleep until almost daybreak, thinking of her, remembering how close they had been and the smell of her perfume and the way her breast looked. He didn't imagine that, did he? He really had touched her. He knew by the way she had looked at him that she was excited by him. If only they had been alone and her teammates hadn't been there.

He stepped across her uniform, a pair of sweats, socks and pajamas. What a mess. As neat as she was, as much as she hated disorder, it must have been difficult for her to come home to this last night. She must have been exhausted, stepping out of her clothes like this. Too bad that mother of hers never had any time for her. With all that Joanna had to do every day—schoolwork, athletic practices, games, baby-sitting, cooking, housework, studying—how often did she find it impossible to take care of herself, too?

He picked up her underpants and a sports bra. She had been wearing these yesterday when he saw her. They smelled of her. He wanted to keep them. Would she notice? Everything was such a mess. He dropped them on the floor and went to the hamper, took undergarments from there instead, and stuffed them in his pocket. Then he stretched out on her bed, right where he knew she must have lain, and looked up at the ceiling. Soon they would lie here together. He knew from the expression on her face yesterday that she could hardly wait for him to come to her.

When he got up, he went to the dresser. Just as he was about to open a drawer, a box of tampons stopped him. Tampons. Open. He couldn't. Not while . . . He would have to wait—four days, maybe five. He counted on his fingers. Tuesday or Wednesday. Could he wait that long? He patted the bulge of underwear in his jacket pocket. He would have to. He couldn't come to her while she was dirty. Too bad there wouldn't be time for a ritual bath, like in the Bible.

When he glanced in Theo's room, the dog was there, at the foot of the bed.

"Hey, boy, where were you yesterday?"

The dog wagged its tail once but didn't come to greet him. He took the chocolate out of his pocket.

"I thought maybe they had replaced you with that cat. Don't

worry, I'll take care of it, right along with everyone else." Maybe he would just take the dog with him afterward. There wouldn't be anyone else to take care of it.

The dog sniffed at the candy, then put his head down and closed his eyes.

"Hey, what's the matter? I brought you something. Here! Eat it!"

He stuck it under the dog's nose, but the dog didn't even open his eyes.

"Hey! What is this? I thought we were friends. I bring you something every time I stop by and now all of a sudden you're too good to accept it?" He got up and shoved the candy bar back into his pocket.

"The hell with you." He had intended to spare the dog's life, and this was the thanks that he got. "When they find the rest of them, big boy, you'll be right there with them."

He wanted to hit it with something, but he remembered how the cat had skittered away from him. What if the dog growled or barked? He needed to pretend they were friends for a while longer, but now the dog would get it, too.

Isaac sat with his back against the cinder-block wall. He was either shivering or going into the d.t.'s, he wasn't sure which. The dreams had come back and he didn't know how he was going to get enough to drink in the next couple of days to keep them away. He had already run up a tab at Queenie's, unless Dare came back and paid her. Dare would be back anytime now, hopefully before his check came and the tab came due. Isaac didn't like owing nobody, liked it even less when the cash he had coming in was already spent before he got it. He was always real careful about not getting nothing on credit, but this was an emergency.

If Dare didn't come back, he was going to have to find some way to supplement his income. Township office, maybe. They were good for letting you shovel snow or sweep or do something to earn what little they gave you. He'd have to go early in the morning, when they first opened up and he at least looked like he might be sober. He was damned near sober now. Sober, and dreaming, and hiding. Who was that sneaking into his house, standing over his bed and trying to kill him? Wasn't nobody he could remember ever seeing before. Sure enough wasn't nobody he had ever done nothing to. He hadn't done nothing to nobody or even said much to nobody for years.

Maybe it was just some fool who got disoriented. Or one of them psychotics. You couldn't be too careful these days, there were so many crazy folks running loose on the streets. No. It couldn't have been nobody looking for him. Wasn't no reason for nobody to do that. It was all a mistake, and now here he was with no place to stay. Didn't have nare blanket, neither. All the time he had spent collecting them blankets and all the trouble it took to haul them to the new place, and now here he was with nothing. No way he'd go back there to get them. Nobody any-where near that house would ever see his face again. Sitting on them steps was what did it. Till then didn't nobody even know he was there. Sure was a lot to be said for keeping yourself to your-self and minding your business.

His stomach grumbled, but he didn't feel hungry. He needed a drink, not food. Bad enough he was cold. And almost sober and broke. Tired, too, probably. He'd made himself stay awake when the dreams came. All he needed was to wake up hollering and have some fool call the cops. Cops. Damn. Was Officer Mac out there looking for him? He sure didn't need her to call attention to the fact that he knew a cop, or that he had been hanging around there and wasn't hanging out there no more. Be best if those few folks who had seen him forgot he'd ever been there at all, and real quick, at least those one or two who might have cause to re-member him. Best not to be seen or heard. Best if you just wasn't nowhere at all besides by yourself. He didn't never have no trou-ble being alone. And if Dare didn't come back, he wouldn't have no trouble being alone now. He sure would like to know where Dare was, though. At least he wasn't sick, or in jail, or dead, for that matter. Between the old priest and Officer Mac, one of them would have found that out by now.

The priest. Isaac was supposed to stop by and pick up some

coats. He'd best get on over there, take the long away so he wouldn't have to go nowhere near that house. He hadn't had nothing but bad luck since they'd tore the old place down, but he'd had bad luck before and outlasted it.

The old priest was in the church basement. None of the church ladies were there yet, but there was a big pot of coffee and the smell got his stomach rumbling again.

"What do you say to a doughnut with that?" the priest asked.

Isaac's hand shook as he tried to fill the cup.

"Oh, I've got something upstairs for that. Be right back."

He returned with a bottle of altar wine a little over half empty. Isaac unscrewed the cap and gulped some down, grateful for the burning sensation in the pit of his stomach and the warmth that began to spread across his belly.

He wiped his mouth on his sleeve. "They'll be thinking this was you."

"There was a time when it would have been."

"And you're giving me wine and not preaching at me to quit drinking?"

The old man smiled. "Some would call it wrong. In fact, many would, I suspect. I've always had trouble doing the right thing, and not because it was too difficult. A lot of the time, it's just too easy."

Isaac wasn't sure what the old man meant.

"It would be much easier, Isaac, to tell you to get help. The hard part is forgetting that craving I always felt, those feelings I always had to push down with another drink."

Isaac wondered what the priest's dreams had been about and how he was able to keep them away now without drinking.

"If I didn't give that to you, Isaac, I'd spend the whole day feeling pious. As it is, I'll be back on my knees. I've never been a very good priest, you see. But I rather like trying, so I keep at it."

What the hell was pious? Sometimes what the priest said didn't make a bit of sense, but he had given him the wine, and in a few minutes he'd have a winter coat. For now, that was more than enough.

Marti trailed Vik, Slim, and Cowboy to the elevator. It would have been healthier to take the stairs, but for some reason she didn't feel that energetic today. If she could just remember more of the dream that kept waking her. Bullets, fire engine, cars.

"I think we're real close to nailing that flasher," Cowboy said as he measured coffee into a filter. "We've got him running for cover."

Marti disagreed. "Those college students and faculty members have forced him to step up his level of aggression."

"This guy has been around fifteen years now and hasn't hurt a fly."

"How do we know that?" Marti asked. "We don't even know who he is." She wanted to feel relieved because the flasher had surprised someone in a dorm hallway last night and got the desired reaction, but it was difficult to feel relieved that a woman had been scared out of her wits, even if she hadn't been hurt.

"The man is happy again, Mac. He's got them running for cover. He's back in control."

"You don't even sound convinced, Cowboy," Marti said. "He's got them organizing a campus patrol. They've got a community group coming in to conduct a seminar on date rape, the Lake County Council Against Sexual Assault. The instructor who gave self-defense lessons to Joanna's gym class last year is organizing a class for them. What's he going to do when he can't get into that dorm tonight? Go home and sulk? Or hurt somebody?"

"First cup, Marti." Slim filled her mug. "We hear what you're saying, but there isn't much more we can do. The woman couldn't give us much of a description. She did insist that this wasn't some little old man with some shriveled thing that didn't work anymore. She didn't even think he was middle-aged. And according to her, what he lacks—" Slim glanced at Vik—"where his tattoo is, she said he more than makes up for with arm muscles. Not exactly good news."

"Sugar?" For once, Slim didn't flash his Cupid's bow smile or give Marti's hair a tug that was much too familiar. As she accepted a packet of sugar, the odor of Obsession for Men seemed less irritating.

"She was frightened, Slim. She could have been exaggerating. Nobody else has given us a description like that."

"Maybe," Vik said. "With all of this publicity, we've probably got a copycat out there."

Cowboy pulled his five-gallon hat forward and hunched over his cup. "Oh, give me a break, Jessenovik. There can't be two fools out there like that." He ran his fingers through the wave of white-blond hair that had fallen across his forehead. "The lieutenant wants the guy off the street pronto, so we've got a few extra patrol units out there. That's about as much of a police presence in the area as we can muster, given the circumstances. The man's hardly a challenge, let alone a threat. We can only guess at what might be going on inside his head, how frustrated he feels, what he might do about it. Most flashers are just exhibitionists. Some of them are downright timid."

"And some of them are psychopaths," Slim said. "I think Big Mac's right: By going into the dorm to confront them, he's stepped up his level of aggression. And that, my friends, is not a good sign."

"Might not bode well at all," Cowboy agreed. He yawned again and stretched. "I don't understand why we haven't caught him. We're damned near spending the night patrolling that area. He has to bring that pumpkin costume with him and put it on somewhere, but we haven't even seen someone carrying a bag. How does he put it on? When? Maybe it's inflatable."

"Nobody ever says much about it," Slim said. "Except for the 'tongue,' there must not be much about it that's distinctive."

"Maybe his mother made him one like it when he was a little boy," Vik said, "and all of the kids made fun of him and now he's getting even with her."

Cowboy frowned. "Maybe he's got a pumpkin fetish. Lord knows what will happen tonight. I sure as hell hope this one is Marvin Milquetoast."

Marti read her phone messages. There was one from Ben. He

had made a late-afternoon appointment with Theo's and Mike's teacher. If he didn't hear from her, he said, he would go to talk with the woman anyway. Marti returned the call and got Ben's machine. "I'll do my best to be there," she said. "If I'm not, make sure she knows that the boys stay together." Ben could handle this as well as she could, and probably with more tact.

She reached for Ladiya Norris's file. More forensic reports had come in. "I've had cases where I would have killed for this much evidence," she said. Ladiya's picture had run in yesterday's late-afternoon edition of the *News-Times*. There hadn't even been a prank call.

"If it wasn't for the second head wound," Vik said, "the coroner's jury might have ruled it accidental."

"There was no identification. I wonder if whoever did it knew her fingerprints were on file. If they didn't, it might not have seemed that important if the body was found. Does the water get much deeper than five or six inches where that channel is between the pond and the lake?"

"Not much."

"Then they could have carried her across, climbed those rocks that jut into the lake, and thrown her into the water instead of leaving her where they did. The current is so strong along the shore that warning signs are posted there. She might never have turned up, or even *have* been reported missing until who knows when."

"Either the perp didn't know the area that well or it had changed a lot since the last time he saw it, since as far as we can tell, the victim wasn't familiar with Lincoln Prairie."

"If the boyfriend bailed her out, then he'd know about the fingerprints." She made a few phone calls. "Well, I located the bail bondsman. He doesn't know who put up the money."

"You believe that?"

"Could be, unless he had a reason to know the person, or remember him."

Vik scowled. "Or not know the person and forget him?"

Marti tossed the Norris folder into her in basket and scanned what she had on Knox. "Nothing on the boyfriend. We've come up empty so far. I can't even get a line on what he does as a financial adviser. No known connections here. Nothing."

"Maybe they were taking a ride up the coast, she ticks him off, they argue . . ."

"And Knox just happens to pull off Sherman Avenue where the coker plant is and just happens to find that fishermen's cove. There are a lot of missing pieces out there, Vik. We need a break with this one."

"Right," Vik agreed. "And you know what that means."

"Legwork."

"And more legwork," Slim agreed. Marti had almost forgotten that he and Cowboy were still there. "Time we were all out of here, partner. Conversation ain't getting us too far this morning."

Slim stifled a yawn and rubbed his eyes. "So far, legwork hasn't helped us much, either. I guess we need to go back and talk with folks again. Maybe we should focus on the costume. I wonder if it's the original?"

Cowboy swung his feet off the desk. "Maybe he makes a new one each year and comes up with some variation."

"Geez," Vik said. "Maybe it's a real pumpkin and he grows it himself. It's a good thing you two don't have any important cases to work on."

"Thanks," Slim said. "We appreciate the input. The lieutenant suggested a little brainstorming session with you two. He thought you might come at it from a different perspective. If this is the best you can do, forget it. Let's go, Cowboy."

"You got it, Slim. Damned shame when you work your butt off protecting the streets of this city and some homicide dick makes it seem like Trivial Pursuit. Of course, they have important things to do, like drinking coffee and reading coroner's reports all day."

When the door closed, Marti said, "I think we're back to where we started on this one."

"Hah! We never left the starting gate."

Marti tapped one of the journals. Ladiya's friend Shenea was mentioned throughout. "We didn't say much to her best friend the other night."

"Nobody saw much of her once she went to live with Knox."

"Maybe not, Vik, but Ladiya did go to see her mother occasionally, and Shenea lives just next door."

"I got the impression they had been out of touch."

"Maybe we were supposed to think that." She checked her watch. It was a little past ten. Her meeting with Mrs. Hinkston wasn't until 4:30. "It might be worth a quick trip to the city. We'll need something before we can talk with Knox again."

Marti found Shenea's phone number, but she hung up when a young woman answered. "Well, if she works or goes to college, it looks like she's got the day off. Let's go. Either we'll surprise her or she'll surprise us by not being there."

Traffic on the Eden's Expressway was light until they reached the merge with the Kennedy and incoming traffic from O'Hare. Once they got past that, it was a quick trip on the Dan Ryan Expressway to the South Side. Shenea was at home. She was a tall girl, and angular. Not as pretty as Ladiya. There was an outbreak of tiny pimples on her forehead.

"You're those cops," she said. She was wearing slippers and a robe that just covered her thighs. Momma would have said her knees were knobby, Marti thought. "If Ladiya's mother didn't answer the door, she's at work."

"We wanted to talk to you," Marti said. Shenea just stood there. She didn't appear to be anxious, nervous, or even interested.

"Is it okay if we come in?"

"No, it's not. I don't feel good and I don't think I want to talk with any cops today."

"I'm sorry to hear that. I guess I got the wrong impression when I was reading Ladiya's journals. I thought you were best friends."

After a moment's consideration, Shenea stepped back and let them in. The front door opened onto the living room. The furnishings were ultramodern, black leather upholstery and shiny black tabletops, ceramic lamps with odd-shaped white bases, bright multicolored abstracts on the wall.

Shenea waved them to the sofa and sat with her legs over the arm of a chair. "There's nothing I can tell you."

"When's the last time you saw her?" Marti asked.

"Last summer."

"When?"

"The date? I don't know."

"Where did you see her?"

"It was this Italian restaurant on the North Side, near Halsted. I was there with some friends."

"What did you talk about?"

"Nothing. She was with him."

"Him?" Marti said.

"Yes, him—Knox."

"The two of you used to talk about a lot of things," Marti said. "When you were in high school. You even persuaded her not to start having sex."

Shenea frowned.

"When you were juniors," Marti added. Shenea looked as if she had no idea what Marti was talking about. Maybe she didn't remember.

"Sticky and slimy?" Marti said, referring to the comment from the journal.

Shenea's eyes got wide.

"What else did you read in there?"

"At the moment, nothing else comes to mind. Have you thought about anything that happened that night at the restaurant?"

Shenea smirked. "Ladiya acted like she didn't even know me. And I did the same. I sure didn't want no introductions to him."

Marti was certain they must have managed at least a few minutes in the ladies' room.

"Did you spend any time with Ladiya when she came to see her mother on Labor Day?"

Shenea looked away. "Maybe a couple of minutes."

"What did you talk about?"

"Things." Shenea got up and stood by the door to the dining room, her back to them.

"You went to high school together. Did you go to the same elementary school, too? There wasn't any mention of that, but it sounded as if you might have been in junior high the first time you sneaked some of your mother's wine."

"We've been friends since before kindergarten." She leaned her head on the doorjamb. "We were friends, damn it. We were friends."

"Did you go to college together?"

"No. That wasn't what I wanted to do. I'm a secretary at City Hall. I wanted a job, my own money, a car, maybe even an apartment. Everything is so expensive. I was planning to move out of here by next spring."

"And now?"

"Maybe I'll just stay home awhile longer. I don't know. Maybe it's safer."

"Did you ever visit Ladiya?"

Shenea turned. "Where she was staying? With him? Are you kidding?"

She sucked in her breath, then hesitated. Marti waited.

"Once," she said. "Once. She called me. He wasn't there. Ladiya had a black eye and one side of her face was all bruised and swollen. I promised her I wouldn't ever tell her mother, and don't you dare tell, either. If you do, I'll swear every word is a lie." She came a few steps closer. "Why don't you just arrest him? Who else would have killed her but him?"

"We don't know what happened, Shenea. And unless people talk to us, there's not much chance we'll find out." The entries in the journals made Marti think Ladiya was someone who liked to take risks. She didn't think that was something Ladiya's mother would have encouraged.

"If we had just stayed friends. If it had just stayed the way it was when we were kids. If only . . . I should have just hung in with her, no matter what she did. I—"

Shenea's voice began rising and Marti cut in. "What was going on with Ladiya when she met Knox? Did she think she was in love? Or was it drugs? It seems like she got into them pretty heavily her senior year."

"Ladiya wasn't a junkie, if that's what you're trying to say!" Shenea retreated to the chair. She sat with her legs tucked under her, hugging herself. "Ladiya liked . . . she liked getting high. Not all the time, and just for fun. She started taking uppers when we were juniors. We stayed friends, but I didn't want to do that. Maybe if I had just hung out with her more, even though she was popping pills. It was just hard to keep being close friends. We weren't doing the same things anymore. But she never snorted or shot up or anything like that. She never did. She just liked the high, I swear to God."

"Did she buy from Knox?"

"I don't know much of anything about him. One day, he wasn't there. One day, he was. I know it was all his fault, though. After she met him, she started doing cocaine. The next thing I knew, she had dropped out of school and moved out of her house and was living with him. It happened so fast, it was scary. Ladiya wouldn't have given someone like him the time of day if it hadn't been for the drugs."

"How long had he been beating her before she died?"

"I don't know. She called me last May. I told her that if he'd hit her, he'd kill her. She laughed and said he brought her flowers and presents afterward."

"What did she say to you that night in the Italian restaurant?"

Shenea blinked back tears. She sniffed, then wiped at her eyes with the back of her hand. "Nothing," she said. "Nothing."

"Not even in the rest room?"

She shook her head. "No. I was— She was so scared . . . so afraid, I didn't dare."

"Why was she frightened? Because she was with him?"

"Her arm. It was in a cast. He must have broken it. When we walked in and Ladiya looked up and saw me, she looked like she was scared to death." Shenea took a handful of Kleenex. "I didn't know what to do. If I had known he was going to kill her, I would have walked right up to them and made her leave with me right then."

"Why didn't you? You knew what must have happened to her arm."

Shenea stared at the abstract painting with the green and yellow cubes and sniffed a few times. "Because she said she loved him. I didn't think she would come. Besides, she knew a couple of the girls I was with. I didn't want to embarrass her any more than she already was."

"Shenea, Ladiya's mother thought she was unhappy the last time she came home. Was she?"

Shenea nodded. "He knocked out three teeth. She had to get a bridge. She said he would be so good to her afterward that she knew he hadn't meant to hurt her, but she just didn't know how she could take it anymore. I wanted to tell her mother. I wanted to help her. I just didn't know what to do." She began sobbing.

"Was she going to leave him?"

"I don't know if she would have. But she wanted to."

"Did she think she could come home if she did?"

"Ladiya knew she could always come home."

Marti drove around the block a few times and when a car pulled out, she squeezed into a parking space three doors down from Knox's house and across the street.

"We might need a crane to get out of here, MacAlister," Vik said.

"I've parked in much tighter spaces many times."

"You couldn't have, Marti. You're touching that guy's hood and this guy's bumper."

"Trust me, Jessenovik, we've got plenty of room. Just keep your shield handy in case whoever is parked behind us shows up. I think I nicked his fender."

They didn't see Knox's car, but parking was always a problem in this part of the city. He could have parked anywhere within walking distance. It was a quiet street, an upscale area where solid, well-crafted older homes had been rehabbed.

"Looks like a real safe neighborhood," Vik said. Tall fences with padlocks bridged the distance between each house and burglar bars secured windows and doors.

"No place is safe," Marti said. "Not if someone wants to get in."

When nobody answered the bell, they returned to the car. Vik flipped open a can of pop. "Looks like this guy might not be coming home. The curtains are drawn. Think he's left town?"

"When we get back to the precinct, I'll check out what's happening in the suburbs. See if his wife is at home and the kids are in school. It'll just take a couple of phone calls and a few lies. No need to tip him off that we know about that any sooner than we have to."

They waited until three before leaving. There was no sign of Knox, and neither of them wanted to get caught in rush-hour traffic. As it was, if they hadn't been north of the Loop, it would have taken two and a half hours to get back to Lincoln Prairie, instead of an hour and a half. Marti dropped Vik off at the precinct and rushed to meet Ben at Theo's school.

10

The teachers' lounge was a homey place. The couches were lumpy but comfortable, the upholstery worn. Two teachers sat on vinyl kitchen chairs at a Formica kitchen table that could have come from Marti's mother's kitchen. Someone had filled a vase with white mums.

Mrs. Hinkston looked as formidable as she had on Wednesday. Marti's stomach began to churn, and she wondered what ogre of a teacher the woman reminded her of to cause such a quick gut reaction. Second grade, she decided, unable to remember her teacher's name. Did the similarities end with physical appearance, or had that teacher been an implacable autocrat, too?

"We are pleased that you've responded to this situation so quickly. The sooner these adjustments are made, the better it will be for both boys," Mrs. Hinkston said.

Ben gave her his most engaging smile. "If we can agree on the arrangements."

"Oh." Mrs. Hinkston arched her eyebrows and pursed her lips. Already she was not pleased, and they hadn't discussed anything yet.

"We, Ms. MacAlister and I, do not want the boys separated."

Mrs. Hinkston straightened in her chair.

"Mr. Walker and I are going to be married," Marti said. "The boys are inseparable now. They'll be stepbrothers soon. Separate schools don't seem appropriate."

"We feel that separating them now, given these circumstances, is the most appropriate thing to do."

"Mrs. Hinkston," Ben said. "We're hoping that we can agree on what is best for the boys. Since Marti and I have known them since birth, we think we're the ones who are best able to decide that."

"Quite to the contrary, Mr. Walker. We have been working with young boys for forty-two years. We know the best thing to do."

"Mrs. Hinkston," Marti said. "I don't have the patience for this."

Mrs. Hinkston's eyebrows arched a notch higher.

Marti supposed the woman considered her disrespectful. "If we can reach an agreement on what we want for the boys, fine," she said. "If we can't, then we will discuss this with the principal and look at other options."

Ben smiled at her and winked.

"We . . ." Mrs. Hinkston began.

"No, *we,*" Marti said. "The parents. Now, I want Theo to go to recess every day. I want him to complete his assignments and do everything else that is appropriate in that classroom. However, he's already a perfectionist. If you can't accept a report that he didn't spend forty hours perfecting, please do not communicate that to him. I'm putting some limits on the time he spends on homework and insisting that he have a social life, too."

Mrs. Hinkston looked alarmed. "But Theo has a fine mind. He must be challenged."

"Theo is ten years old. He must learn, he must play, he must have time to spend with his friends, and he must exercise—his body, not just his mind. I expect you to take all of that into consideration before you make excessive demands."

"But he is gifted."

"Perhaps, but I think not. Theo is curious. He is interested in almost everything, but there are those things that he works for; they don't come easily. He has to find some kind of balance. I want him to have time to think and imagine and dream and even dawdle over those things that grab his attention."

It was obvious that Mrs. Hinkston did not agree.

"Now think about it over the weekend, and if you can't adapt to what I think Theo's needs are, just give me a call and we'll find someone who can."

Before the teacher could react, Ben said, "And as for Mike, feel free to push him a little more, make a few more demands. If you let him know what you expect, he'll most likely comply. He isn't lazy, and he isn't stupid or slow, either. He just has other priorities, like having fun. I can't imagine you having any difficulty motivating a child to work harder."

Mrs. Hinkston appeared somewhat appeased by that. The arch of her eyebrows smoothed just a bit. "We do not agree with you at all. But I am going to call Michael to task, and I am going to demand less from Theo."

"No," Marti said. "Don't expect less than his best; just be realistic about what his best is and allow for some variations. Let them be children. They have such a long time to be adults."

"When his grades go down, and Michael's grades don't go up . . ."

"I don't think that has to happen," Ben said. "Not unless you expect it to. I'm sure you are much too good a teacher for that."

When they got outside, Ben said, "How was that for a good cop–bad cop routine?"

"You're getting the hang of it."

Ben grinned. "I love it when you come on like a cop."

"Oh, you do? Well, I suppose that's okay, while I'm on duty."

"And when you're not?"

It was Marti's turn to grin. "I think this is going to have to be a short courtship."

"And the lady never lets on that this is how she feels."

Ben walked her to her car. Then he was whistling as he walked to his van.

J.D. walked past the empty house at least seven times before he decided to go in. He had told them about talking to the other man who stayed here, the same as he had told them about Dare. He figured they must have run him off, too, same as Dare. But he didn't know why. He wasn't sure he really wanted to know exactly what had happened, but it seemed weird, two guys just disappearing. He knew the difference between real and TV. This was real. People didn't just disappear, not for real.

The place looked pretty clean when he went inside, at least cleaner than other abandoned houses around here that he had been in. There was no junk lying around. There was even a broom. Place must have been swept up. When he came to the room with the blankets piled up in the corner, he knew this was where the man slept. When he went close to the blankets, he couldn't see nothing that made him think anyone was under them, but then, the man was so skinny. Did he want to know if the man was under there? He hadn't been outside today looking for someone to keep him company. J.D. had told them about him yesterday afternoon. He had never smelled a dead body. Those who had said the smell was real bad. He didn't smell anything now, but the dust made him sneeze.

He lifted the edge of one blanket, then pulled up a couple more, real slow. There were cuts in the blankets, lots of cuts, like from a knife. Is that what they did? He yanked at the blankets. Wasn't no dead body here. He was right. There wasn't even any blood.

J.D. went to the window. The night was clear and there was almost a full moon. The man wasn't here. Was the man in trouble? Was J.D. in trouble? He had told them. If they hadn't found the man, either, would they think he had lied? As nosy as Dare was, it wasn't no surprise that he was gone. J.D. was kind of glad that he was. People always asking a lot of questions made him nervous. But this man, what had happened to him? He probably should have just kept his mouth shut. Be best to just wait, act like he never came in here, act like he had never said a word about the man sitting on the steps. Most of the time that was best, just doing like you were told and not saying too much and not knowing anything.

By the time it was dark, Isaac's feet hurt from walking most of the day. He was much too close to being sober, and his stomach felt like someone was jabbing him with a little bitty pocketknife. As soon as he had left the church this morning, he had set about finding a place to stay. He'd been looking all day, carrying the shopping bag with two jackets and a coat. The bag was heavy. He needed a drink, some food, and some place to lie down. He went to Queenie's.

"Isaac, you ain't seen Dare yet?"

He sat on the bar stool with the bag touching his leg and accepted a drink. He didn't ask if it was free or on his tab, didn't want to worry any more today about being beholden to anybody. The old priest had let him sweep the leaves from the walk in return for the coats, but that was hardly anything to do for warm clothes. He wished Queenie would let him work, but this tight-fisted old lady didn't want anything from nobody but cash.

"Seems like we ought to do something, Isaac. It's been what, a week now? I can't even remember it being this long and Dare ain't come in."

She looked as worried as he was.

"Whatcha got in that bag?"

"Jackets and a coat for winter." He didn't want to tell her because he knew what was coming next.

"Let me have a look."

Queenie took everything out, admiring the sheepskin jacket with the fleece lining. "My man sure would like to have this. It's worth me forgetting all about your bill."

Isaac talked her out of a half-pint of rum, which he hated, but it was all she would part with. He left feeling like he had stolen something from God by giving her the coat.

Sharon thought about turning off the ringer on the phone. She thought about getting another line put in. She thought about hiding somewhere, in the basement maybe, so that the kids would think she wasn't home. Phillip would call tonight. She had put him off last night and the night before, but he would be insistent tonight. She would become trapped somewhere between saying yes and saying no. Just her luck. After years of finding fault with every man she dated, someone had finally come back into her life who seemed almost perfect. What she considered a flaw, his self-centeredness, everyone else seemed to insist was just typically male.

She had first met Phillip while she was going to school in Atlanta. She was just dating Frank then, and it was flattering to have two men courting her. She had teased both of them, flirted with both of them, and married Frank. Frank thought he was the only man she had slept with. Phillip was more experienced. He knew better.

She had felt so . . . noble . . . at the time, choosing Frank, a poor, struggling prelaw student, over Phillip, who was wealthy, charming, suave. Part of the truth was that she could not abide Phillip's mother, Lord rest that woman's soul. No matter what she ever did, she would never be good enough for that woman's son. Nothing was worth having to put up with the look the woman gave her every time Phillip took her to his house.

Not that she told Phillip that. As far as he was concerned, true love had conquered all. She did love Frank. She had followed her heart. Why was it that Mr. Right and Mr. Wonderful never came in the same package? Why couldn't Frank have loved her the way Phillip did?

When Frank was accepted at Yale and they moved there so that he could complete his law degree, Phillip found reasons to visit the campus and, until she became pregnant with Lisa, excuses to call her with desperate pleas until she agreed to see him. There were periods of time when he left her alone. Years, in fact, but eventually Phillip came back. After all these years, nothing had changed. Phillip wasn't Frank. He never would be. She needed to tell him that, so that he would leave her alone.

Alone, that was the problem. Alone. In a couple of years, she would be forty. She plucked the occasional gray hair, stuck her finger down her throat when she lacked the willpower to stop eating, but the women in her family began aging early. Her mother went through menopause before she was forty-five, and Sharon's periods were already irregular. Why couldn't she say yes to Phillip and marry him? Soon nobody would want her.

The one teacher whose opinion she trusted almost as much as Marti's had said, "Once burned, twice shy," as if the failure of Sharon's first marriage explained it all. "But," she added, "if you let him get away without at least giving it a try, you know you're always going to ask yourself what might have been."

The phone rang. She picked it up on the fifth ring.

"Well, hello, hello. And what have you been doing this evening?"

"I, um. Marti's not here."

"Look, I've got a great idea. It's only a little after seven; let's just go out for a drink."

A drink would stretch out to two or three, dinner, a few dances, a motel room. It would be midnight and the kids would be alone and Marti would be upset.

"Phillip, you know I can't leave the kids." She had never been to his condo in Bolingbrook. It was an hour and a half drive when traffic wasn't backed up, and just too far from home if she was needed.

"Two days is a long time, baby, too long to be without my sweet thing."

"I know." She could feel herself giving in. No, the kids might be all right, but if anything happened . . . Theo had become almost hysterical when Bigfoot got sick.

"Look, as soon as Marti comes in, I'll call you. I promise."

Why couldn't she just say no? That had never been a problem before.

"Well . . ."

She steeled herself against the hurt in his voice.

"I will, Phillip, I promise."

"I'm going to call back in an hour. It'll be a little late for dinner, but I'll wait. I'll wait for you, baby, just for you. You know, you are one fine woman."

What if everyone else was right? What if, after all the bad times with Frank, she was magnifying Phillip's one little flaw—this tendency toward self-absorption—making more of it than it was, using it like a shield to protect herself?

"I'll make it special tonight, baby," Phillip promised. "Real special."

"I know you will, Phillip. I know you will."

She couldn't deny the relief she felt as she hung up the phone. He had probably thought of something special she could do for him. No, that was unfair. Phillip always wanted to please her in bed. He'd doze for half an hour afterward and then want rave reviews. Damn. She was doing it again. Maybe Marti was right. Maybe she was too concerned about how she thought she should feel. Maybe she just wasn't ready for the right man yet. Maybe that was why she couldn't keep herself from being critical of Phillip. It was as if she had to find fault. Was it just so she could keep him at a distance? What would happen if she just let go and got lost in the moment? She'd make a fool of herself again, just as she had with Frank.

Frank. That's what it was. No matter where he was, who he was with, how miserable he still tried to make her life, that bastard would always be there to remind her of how foolish she had been. Sharon in love: That was the joke. Sharon, who loved Frank so much that she would just make Frank love her, too. Even when he told her that he came first, that his feelings for her were not as strong as hers were for him, she told herself that he didn't mean what he said. She convinced herself that he felt too vulnerable to admit how much he cared for her, how important she was to him.

Now she was confronted with smooth talk and finesse in bed again. Unlike Frank, Phillip said she was number one, that he loved her, wanted to marry her. This time, she was the one who was pursued, the one backing away from commitment. And for all that she thought Phillip was rich, spoiled, and selfish, she also believed that he did love her, just as she had believed that about Frank. Suppose Phillip was for real? Could she afford to send him out of her life? At her age, what were the odds on someone else like him coming along?

Damn. Maybe she should go upstairs and look for her earrings, and the cat's hiding place, and her spare set of keys. If she didn't find the keys soon, they would have to have the locks changed.

When Isaac thought it was late enough, he left the woods near the ravine where he'd spent most of the evening nursing the half-pint of rum. There was no way what was left was going to get him through the night, but he had just paid off his debt with Queenie. He wasn't going to start another tab the same day. When a man got himself out of debt, it seemed like he ought to stay that way, least for a while, even if it was only for a day.

The garage wasn't as far from where he was staying as he thought it was last night. No matter. There still was no car in it, and it didn't smell like anyone ever used it. It was well behind a house that someone was living in, but all the lights were out except one in the little window that was most likely in the bathroom. And the way one side of this roof was caving in, it didn't seem likely that anybody would use this place for anything. It was clean except for dust and cobwebs and dead leaves that had blown in. If he was careful, he might be able to stay here until Dare came back and they found someplace else. He took off the winter coat he was wearing, folded it so it wouldn't get wrinkled, and put it in the bag. Then he put on the jacket that Queenie didn't want and used his old jacket as a mat. It was cold as hell, but there wasn't any wind like there was when he was sitting under that tree in the woods. It was damp there, too. This place was dry. It might be nothing compared to the place they lost, but he could make do. He could easily make do. Dare should be coming back anytime now. He'd best just go around to Queenie's every day and see if Dare had been looking for him, rather than tell her where he was. Wasn't like this was abandoned property. Folks were living in the house dead ahead.

As soon as Marti got home, Sharon went out. Sharon had called her at the precinct to find out what time she'd be home. She seemed more anxious than she did eager to leave. Marti was becoming curious about this Mr. Wonderful. One thing was for sure so far: Nobody could say that the second time around was the charm.

Joanna came into the kitchen with a towel wrapped around her hair.

"Let me comb it for you," Marti offered. They hadn't had much time together lately. Marti wasn't sure they ever spent enough time together. She remembered how her mother worked long hours cleaning houses or cleaning trains, and nights falling asleep on the sofa waiting for Momma to come home. The only time they had together was on Saturday, when Marti helped with the cooking, and Sunday, when they were together most of the day in church. Joanna didn't even have those times with her.

While Joanna made tea, Marti laid out the combs and brushes. When Joanna was settled on a pillow on the floor, Marti began at the nape of Joanna's neck. She relaxed as she worked her way though the damp, thick, tangled mass of hair.

"Ben called while you were out."

"Did he say what he wanted?"

"He talked to Sharon, but I think he was checking up on us."

Marti smiled. "Sharon's been out a lot lately." She thought about Lisa's boyfriend, Dante. "And I take it that Dante and Chris know that you two are here unsupervised."

"How did you find out they were over here? Mike and Theo?"

They? She didn't know "they" were over here. "Chris was here, too?"

"Gee, Ma, just once. I'm fifteen now. I'll be going to college in a couple of years, living in a coed dorm. Guys will probably be in my room all the time then."

"They were in your room?"

"No, Ma. They were right here in the kitchen while I was fixing supper. At least Chris was."

"Oh." Marti thought about last week's meals. She couldn't remember one that included meat, and there was that vegetable lasagna last Thursday with the broccoli, squash, and string beans. "If you were cooking, I guess he didn't stick around too long."

"Ma!"

"Look, I don't want him over here when there's no adult at home. That's the rule."

"I knew you were going to be impossible about this. Sharon is lightening up, Ma. Of course, Sharon knows a lot more about men than you do."

"You think so?"

"Oh Ma. You don't even . . . you know, with Ben."

Was this the same person who only a year ago had had no interest in dating?

"Sharon says there was never anyone but Dad."

"By choice," Marti said.

"Look at Sharon, Ma. She's had lots of guys. She doesn't pull this courtship stuff or have celibate relationships."

"Oh? And I do, and you have a problem with that?"

"No, not me, but you do."

"Joanna, have you . . ." She stopped brushing her daughter's hair.

"No, Ma, not yet. I'm not sure Chris is worth it. He's a nice guy and all, but who knows, maybe he's got a big mouth."

"Joanna!"

"Look, Ma, let's just say I'm beginning to appreciate Sharon's approach to . . . life. Am I going to do anything about it? At fifteen, no. I don't need the reputation. But when I go to college, why not? If the time is right, the person is right. I mean, why this big deal about courtship and marriage and all that? Maybe I'll never get married. Who knows?"

Marti touched a damp strand of Joanna's hair. She was glad Joanna was being honest with her, but she didn't want to be having this conversation. All this time, she thought she was setting a positive example for her children, waiting to sleep with Ben until they were married, and her daughter thought it was just lack of experience. As if there was something wrong with that. Joanna didn't have any respect for what she was doing. Joanna thought she was being stupid and that Sharon was the one who was smart. She blinked back tears and began brushing Joanna's hair again.

"What do you think of this guy Sharon's dating, Ma?"

"I haven't met him, have you?"

"Of course not. She never brings them home."

"He doesn't seem to be making her happy," Marti said. "I don't think Sharon's ready to be happy with a man yet."

"She still hasn't stopped feeling miserable about Frank."

Marti tugged at a kink in Joanna's hair, then separated it into smaller sections. Were all fifteen-year-old girls this smug in their knowledge about adult women's foibles?

After a few ouches, Joanna said, "I don't know about that cat."

"She doesn't seem to be sure about us, either. She doesn't even come out to eat until we're asleep."

"I wish I could find her hiding place."

Marti remembered Sharon's sweater. "Has she taken something of yours, too?"

"I'm not sure, but she has some real bad habits. I don't know if she sleeps on my underwear or what, but she's always messing with it."

"Maybe if you didn't leave your clothes on the floor, that wouldn't happen."

"I'm going to start closing my door. I thought I did this morning, but I guess the latch didn't catch."

Too bad Joanna's incisive analysis of everyone else didn't extend to her own small flaws.

"Ouch, Ma, don't pull so hard."

"Sorry." Marti brushed the sections of hair that she had combed, then ran a comb through again. "How do you want it?"

"Will you oil my scalp and cornrow it in one braid that hangs down my back? That way, I don't have to comb it for a while."

"How long is a while?"

"Just a couple of days. With practice and three games in a week, I'm going to be busy."

Marti hoped she'd be too busy to have Chris over when Sharon wasn't home. Sharon. Damn. Going wishy-washy with some man just when she was needed here.

"Is everything at school going okay?"

"Oh, I've got this really cool French teacher. I can't believe I had so much trouble with it last year. It's so easy now."

"I missed your game."

"You've missed a few games, but that's okay. I play volleyball mostly to stay in shape. Now when basketball starts . . ."

"I'll try," Marti said. There had to be a way to spend more time with her kids, but if they were going to have conversations like this, maybe it was just as well that she didn't.

After Joanna went to bed, Marti sat in the rocker by the window and read the *News-Times*. There was nothing about the Halloween flasher today. Nothing about Ladiya Norris, either. No witches, no ghosts. How dull. She heard a scratching sound and looked up, to see the cat.

"Well, hi there." She spoke in a quiet tone of voice and didn't make any movements toward it. It didn't arch its back or snap its tail back and forth. It seemed more wary than unfriendly. "I bet you miss Stephanie, don't you, Goblin? She's going to have to stay in the hospital for a little while longer, but she is getting better. It's too bad they can't let her see pets. I bet she misses you, too."

The cat took a few timid steps closer, stopped, and appraised her with wide blue-gray eyes.

"I hear you've been getting into mischief while everyone's out. From the looks of it, you just about destroyed Sharon's sweater. Joanna isn't too happy about her underwear, either." Then there were Sharon's earrings. Not that the cat would be interested in them. Maybe they had a ghost around here, too. "I bet you've made yourself a nice soft bed in the attic somewhere. Just remember, you're going to be in trouble if you shred anything else or something else goes missing around here."

The cat skirted the room as she spoke, turned around a couple of times when she reached the corner nearest Marti, then settled down in a ball. Her fur was white, with yellow patches. Marti wanted to pet her. Although she wasn't a cat expert, she did suspect that any advances on her part would send Goblin back into hiding, so she talked to her instead.

Sharon came home earlier than Marti expected. She was humming as she came into the kitchen—off-key, but at least she wasn't close to tears.

"I take it everything was okay tonight. Or is this a new Mr. Wonderful?"

"Same guy," Sharon said. She rummaged around in the drawers in the refrigerator and came out with a package of bologna and cheese. "Beef bologna and real cheese," she said as she undid the twistie on a loaf of bread.

Marti's sandwich tasted better than steak. "I can't remember the last time we had bologna in the house. Where did you hide it?"

"Under the drawer with the fruit. Nobody bothers to go in it as long as I keep fruit in the bowl on the counter."

"Make sure you don't forget."

"Know what I think, Marti? I think maybe I'm not ready for a good man. I just can't trust myself to pick 'em, know what I mean? So, I told Phil . . . Mr. Wonderful, that we could continue seeing each other on a casual basis until I was sure I knew what I wanted. It's this intense 'I want to marry you' talk that puts me off."

"And he saw it your way?"

"He wants to keep seeing me. He didn't even insist that I stay the night with him, and I had told him I would. Sometimes you just have to be firm."

"That sounds like a step in the right direction."

"God help me, I think you and Ben are beginning to rub off on me. Do you two ever do anything on impulse?"

"I think Ben does have a devil-may-care streak there somewhere that he's careful to keep in check. He's more of a risk-taker than I am."

"He sure could have fooled me," Sharon said. "And as for risk-taking, as safe and downright boring as your job is . . ."

They both laughed. Marti was glad Sharon was beginning to sound like her usual feisty self again. There was a lot they needed to talk about, but if Sharon's mood held, it might not be necessary.

Isaac thought he woke up hollering, but he wasn't sure. It could have been part of his dream. He peered through the space where the garage roof had caved in. He couldn't see any lights on. If he had hollered, he must not have awakened anyone. He was shaking so hard, his teeth were chattering, but not from the cold. He reached for the bottle. One more swallow, not enough to do any good. He'd dreamed he was back at the creek again—around the bend, where he couldn't be seen. The trees were old and always hung low to the water, but not touching it like they were that day. He'd never seen the river run so fast before, never seen it so close to the bank. Never seen the tree branches dipping so deep into the water or so many broken branches rushing past. He could hear the rocks and pebbles being dragged along, sounding like a new kind of music. The storms had been scary. They seemed to last for days, but they had finally passed. Now the sun was shining between the leaves and flashed on the water. Birds were flapping and calling overhead. There was a low hum as the mosquitoes attacked. And then there was a terrible scream.

It was dark when Marti and Vik pulled up in front of Barry Knox's house in Chicago. The place was dark. Nobody answered the bell. The gentrified tree-lined streets lacked adequate parking spaces, so Marti circled in a six-block radius, looking for his car. When they didn't see it, they took Interstate 90 and headed west. The neighborhood where Knox lived in Elgin looked as tired and run-down as anything Marti had seen in Chicago. The bungalows were small, some well kept, most in need of paint and repairs. Bicycles had been left out to rust over the winter. Beer and pop cans and other debris littered the sidewalk and paper bags and newspapers blew about the street.

Vik spotted the car and then confirmed the address. By Marti's estimation, Knox's car was the only one on the block that wasn't at least four years old. He had parked behind an older-model Ford Escort. Marti parked in front of his house.

"Damn," Vik said, avoiding dog droppings as they went up the walk. Marti reached through the frame of a storm door that was missing both screen and window to knock on a hollow wooden door.

Knox answered. He seemed surprised to see them.

"Yeah?"

"We'd like to talk to you," Vik said.

"So talk."

"You want the neighbors to watch?"

He cursed, then hit the latch on the storm door with the palm of his hand.

Marti and Vik walked into the living room. Shabby was an adequate description: red shag carpeting, a sofa and chairs upholstered in a red-and-black pattern that had been popular fifteen years ago, an end table with a drawer missing—and a television with a thirty-two-inch screen. The box it came in had been shoved in a corner.

"So?" Knox stood with his arms folded. He dressed differently here. The *GQ* look was gone. He was just a middle-aged hustler in jeans and a T-shirt that revealed a small paunch. A bright overhead light made his scattering of gray hair more noticeable. He didn't offer them a seat, and neither Marti nor Vik insisted that he sit down. There was just enough space in the room for all of them to stand without touching. Marti signaled Vik that she wanted to do the talking.

"We wanted to talk with you about Ladiya Norris again." She hoped Knox's wife was home and her voice would carry.

"I ain't got nothing else to say."

"We heard you two did quite a bit of socializing."

"You heard wrong."

"According to the autopsy, you were going to be a daddy."

"Wrong again." He didn't seem surprised.

"Oh?" Marti said. "Ladiya was pregnant. Are you telling me she slept around on you?"

"I'm not telling you nothing."

"It might be time that you did."

"If you had something on me, you'd be taking me in." He was talking louder than necessary, given their proximity. Either they were alone or he was playing to an audience. Maybe some member of his family was home. The house was sure quiet.

"What're you doing slumming out here?" Marti asked. "Hiding from me? With that place you've got in the city, I can't see why you'd want to stay in a dump like this if you weren't going out of your way to avoid me."

"I ain't got no reason to hide from no cops. I'm just visiting my kids."

"You let them live in a place like this while you and Ladiya live like royalty in Chicago?"

His eyes narrowed and Marti could see the muscles in his jaws tighten. "My kids don't want for nothing. Can't one of them say they ever been hungry or cold or wanted anything that I didn't give them."

Marti shrugged. "It's a good thing they don't want a decent place to live."

When they returned to the car, Vik said, "You didn't mention the broken bones and missing teeth."

"There's a car parked in front of his. I'm hoping his wife was home, or if he's got a kid old enough to drive the car, that the kid's got a big mouth."

"Maybe she doesn't mind living like this while he fronts a nice place in the city."

"Assuming she's seen the place in the city and knows how nice it is."

Marti swung past the riverboat casino as she drove out of the city.

"Nice," Vik said, as she slowed near the big red-and-white paddleboat.

"Do you gamble?" she asked.

Vik patted his shoulder holster. "Every day."

*   *   *

He walked for blocks, along the street behind their house and over to the break in the fences and shrubbery where he could see the light still on in the kitchen. Why were they up so late? What were they talking about? The cop had to get up before daybreak. You'd think she would be in bed. The cop. God with a badge. Thou shalt not. Thou better not. Halt. Spread 'em. God Almighty with a gun. Or so she thought. As if she could tell him what to do. As if she could order him around. As if she could take his life and say it was good. How he hated her. How he wanted her to beg for her life. If only he could catch her alone, but she was never alone. Soon he would watch her face as she began to understand that she was going to die, that she was the one who was powerless, that she was no longer God. That he was.

11

He couldn't go into the house. It was Saturday. Everyone except the cop was at home. He went to a small store that sold army and navy surplus. The lighting inside was dim. Tables against the walls and in the center of the room were stacked with clothing and camping gear. As he browsed, he listened to the conversation between the proprietor, an older woman, and a customer, another woman, but closer to middle age.

". . . took him down with a Galil sniping rifle. Great weapon. Manufactured in Israel."

"Semiautomatic, isn't it?"

"Yup. Weighs about eighteen pounds, got a folding butt stock and bipod. It'll score a head shot at three hundred meters, a half-body hit at six hundred, and a full-figure hit at nine hundred. One hell of a weapon."

"I think I like Italy's Beretta sniper better," the customer said. "Bolt action, weighs a little less, fifteen, sixteen pounds maybe. You get less vibration when you fire."

"You fired one of 'em?"

"Sure." The customer smiled. "On a number of occasions. You really should come out to the campground with me one of these weekends. You'd have a whole lot of fun."

He stayed away from them as they talked, sorting through a stack of olive drab thermal shirts. He knew exactly what kind of guns they were talking about. He had even fired the Beretta. From the tone of their voices, he knew that they recognized the power in the ability and opportunity to use guns, just as he did. He wondered what it would be like to take that kind of firepower, walk into a house or a store or an auditorium, and make everyone do exactly as he told them to.

The conversation turned to cold-weather camping gear, and he went over to the display case where the knives were kept. He had come in once before, made a small purchase, all the while hoping that no one would remember him, but also hoping that when he came in again and made this purchase, he wouldn't stand out as a stranger. He had selected the knife he wanted then. Now, while the woman was somewhat distracted, he pointed to it.

The woman continued talking with the other customer as she took the knife from the case and rang up the purchase. She didn't even make eye contact. Once again, he had the feeling of being in plain sight and at the same time invisible. She wouldn't remember him at all.

J.D. got up early Saturday morning. His parents had gone to the riverboat casino again. They'd be home sometime tomorrow, in time to get ready for work Monday morning. His little brother hadn't been home in three or four days now, staying with his aunt, most likely. J.D. liked staying there, too, but she wouldn't let him anymore, not since he stole her watch and sold it. Not that he cared.

He went into the kitchen and fixed a bowl of cereal. The sink was filled with dishes from when he and his boys had cleaned out all of the buffalo wings, pizza, and burritos his mother had left for him in the freezer. She would be totally angry if he didn't load the dishwasher, but J.D. didn't care about that, either. He wasn't a damned maid and he wasn't cleaning up anything anymore.

He lived eight blocks south of Queenie's place and his parents didn't approve of his traveling that short distance to the ghetto. It was cold walking over there, and it took longer, but he didn't want to take his bike and have to be bothered keeping up with where it was. Queenie had opened up by the time he got there. There weren't too many ways to find out if Dare's friend was a regular customer. When he pushed open the door, Queenie was mopping the floor. It smelled like she'd dipped the mop in disinfectant and then cleaned up something nasty.

"I got to use the bathroom," he said as he brushed past her. Three women sat at the bar. Nobody was in the men's john. Dare's friend, the old dude, wasn't here yet. J.D. went outside, looked around until he spotted what he hoped was a comfortable doorway, out of the wind and someplace where he wouldn't be in plain sight. He crossed the street and stood with his back against the doorjamb and waited.

He didn't know what they wanted with Dare's friend and he didn't much care. He had sneaked out and met up with them late last night and they weren't mad at him about anything, and they said he might get to do something important, like carry a gun or deal some drugs if he could find out where Dare's friend was staying. That man hadn't even gone back to that abandoned place to get his blankets. Wherever he was staying now, unless it was one of the shelters, he sure must be cold. J.D. wondered where Dare was. Not that he cared much, but he had wanted to ask. He had decided it was best just to do exactly as he was told. That way, when he did everything right, he'd get more important things to do. He didn't ask any questions about anything. Sooner or later, someone would get to talking about whatever it was and he'd find out what he wanted to know. He had no intentions of being like Dare. Dare had to know everything, and right away. When he asked the wrong question, J.D. had to tell them. Then he had to tell Dare what they told him to. He didn't want to know any more about that than he already did. It wasn't smart, knowing too much. And it sure wasn't smart asking questions. If people wanted you to know something, they told you. If they didn't, it wasn't any of your business.

J.D.'s feet were getting cold by the time Dare's friend showed up and went into Queenie's. He could tell by the way the man walked that there was one thing on his mind—something to drink. J.D. put his hands over his ears for a minute to warm them. He was not going to wear anything on his head besides his cap and it didn't keep anything warm. He was going to have to do a little shopping real soon, though. Boost something at the flea market, maybe. Department stores were getting to be too much of a hassle. Security people weren't even dressing up in uniforms at the malls. Some old hag who looked like somebody's great-grandmother might be watching you steal and relaying the information to someone waiting at the door.

J.D. guessed it was close to twenty or thirty minutes before Dare's friend came out. It seemed twice as long, but it probably wasn't. J.D. didn't know any more about following people than he had seen in the movies and on TV, and trying something like that didn't seem to make much sense this morning. It wasn't as if there was a bunch of kids hanging around and nobody would notice him. Instead, he doubled around the block so that he was walking toward the man, and when he came alongside of him, he said, "Hi, remember me? J.D."

The man looked at him as if he wanted to tell him to keep walking. Instead, he just grunted and said nothing, but he slowed down.

"I saw your friend last night," J.D. lied.

"Where?"

"He was with some female. I saw them going into this liquor store over on Clark."

J.D. wasn't sure the man would believe him, but he had seen Dare coming on to the females who hung out at Queenie's.

The man kind of sucked his teeth and didn't say anything right away. When they reached the corner, he said, "It wasn't that one who wears a wig with rollers in it and puts a scarf on?"

"Could have been," J.D. said. "I didn't get a good look at her." He knew the woman they were talking about—at least he had seen her around—but he didn't have a clue where she lived or if the man would run into her.

"He speak to you?"

"Sure. Like I told you, he was supposed to get something for me, but he didn't. Not yet. I told him about you not living at that house anymore. He said he'd catch up with you at Queenie's.

When I saw you just now, I thought maybe you'd like to know. He been around yet?"

"Not yet."

The man started to turn the corner, then stopped. "Uh-oh, forgot something." He headed back to Queenie's.

J.D. cut between two buildings, ran to the rear of Queenie's building, and walked past just as she was about to throw out the water she had used for mopping into the alley.

"Let me help you with that," J.D. offered.

Queenie knew he was a member of the gang she paid off every week to be left alone. She knew that as long as she came up with the money, they wouldn't steal from her or damage her property. She gave him the bucket and went inside. J.D. tossed the water onto the gravel, then slipped inside.

". . . believe that fool ain't gone no further than some woman's skirt," Queenie was saying to Dare's friend. "I wonder if it is her. Wait 'til the next time she comes in here. Come to think of it, I ain't seen her for two, three days now. If he comes in here, where do you want me to tell him you're at?"

J.D. listened hard. He knew the place where they had torn down the house and he knew where the garage was, too. Wait until he told the boys how easy it was to find out where the old dude lived. He had a real talent for stuff like this. They were sure to give him something important to do now.

Isaac pocketed the half-pint of whiskey Queenie gave him after he told her about Dare. He'd already talked her out of a half-pint of vodka. If he could make it through the day without drinking all of it, there might not be no dreaming tonight. Not only that— now that Mr. Dare had been been sighted, it was a sure thing that he'd be showing up pretty soon. He knew Dare wasn't going to take off no further than some woman's skirt. He'd known that all along. That Dare, crazy, nothing but crazy. Dare must not like this neighborhood no more than he did, staying away like this. As soon as Isaac caught up with him, they was going to start looking for someplace else. And wait until Dare saw his new coat.

Isaac was whistling as he headed for the old place and a little peace and quiet. Too bad he didn't have no sleeping bag.

Marti had a message when she arrived at the precinct Saturday morning: 1156 Lee Street. It came in by telephone. She went to the dispatcher's office and had them replay the tape. It was a woman's voice, one she could not recall hearing before. The call originated from a phone booth in Elgin.

Vik scowled as he read. "Big deal. They could have told us why this address is important. You don't suppose it was a ghost calling, do you? Or maybe a witch." He crumpled up the piece of paper. "Trick or treat, what do you want to bet."

Marti took the paper from him and went to the street map on the wall.

"Don't bother," Vik said. "It's maybe three blocks west and six blocks north of the old coker. Like I said, trick or treat. Our local lying fisherman probably got his girlfriend to call."

"From Elgin?" With any luck, their caller was Knox's wife.

Vik went to his desk without answering and grabbed a sheaf of papers from his in basket.

Someone named Andrea DeMarco lived at the address. Marti ran a make on her. Two traffic tickets, moving violations.

"Let me look at that," Vik said. "There was a Milo DeMarco, owned a local car dealership. . . ." He picked up the phone.

Within an hour, Marti knew that DeMarco was a thirty-two-year-old widow; her husband had been gunned down in Chicago two years ago, an apparent robbery victim. She did not have any children. She was a real estate agent, part-time. Milo had been shot in the parking lot of an eatery in Lincoln Park, not close to where Knox lived, but within walking distance or five minutes by cab.

"We're going over there," Marti said.

"On what pretext?" Vik asked. "Trick or treat?"

"Watch it, Jessenovik. Someone from Elgin called with this address."

"Knox probably put someone up to it to make us feel stupid."

"Well, if it was Knox, he knows enough about Lincoln Prairie to give us an address damned close to the coker plant."

"Right, it's just a short hike if you slide down the bluff, slosh through a strip of wetland, and get your face slapped by bramble," Vik said, but he reached for his coat.

Marti wasn't familiar with Lee Street, which was in a subdivision that abutted the bluffs and was just beyond Bowman's Park. She drove around, trying to determine how someone could access the coker plant, but she didn't even see a way on foot unless she went to Sherman Avenue.

"You're the one who grew up here, Jessenovik. Are there any shortcuts or secret paths that you can take to get to the lake?"

"Nothing." He said. "At least nothing that I've ever seen from the beach. It wouldn't be a long walk, but you'd have to negotiate the bluff, then a lot of dense underbrush. If the tides weren't so treacherous there, or if we'd had a few drowning incidents, I'd guess that the kids had found a way to get there. Anyone going there, though, would get some scratches, maybe get their clothes caught. There would be something to indicate that was where they had been."

With all the evidence they had in the Norris case, nothing suggested an evening walk like that.

"So let's just go ring the bell."

"And say what?"

"Hell, Vik, we'll just tell whoever answers the truth, or some of the truth anyway," Marti said. "We've either got to fish here or cut bait." She was pleased to see that her comment went over about as well as trick or treat.

The house at 1156 Lee Street turned out to be a small Tudor with a tiny yard almost entirely taken up by a belowground swimming pool. The property abutted the bluff. The pool area was fenced. Marti skirted the fence as she she went to the edge of the property. The bluff was steep and covered with thick scrub and tall bushes. She estimated it was about fifty feet to the bottom, where trees and underbrush obscured a view of the sand dunes near the lake, some distance away.

A woman came out of the house. She was of average height, with brown hair that hung to her waist. There was something athletic in her stride.

"I think you're trespassing," the woman said.

"Are you Andrea DeMarco?"

The woman hesitated.

Marti pulled out her shield.

"Police?"

"Yes, ma'am. Are you—"

"Yes, and this is my property. Why are you here?"

"We're investigating a homicide, ma'am, and your address came up. I'm afraid I can't be more explicit than that."

"What? My address? I don't believe this. I'm going to go in and call the mayor's office now. This is a total invasion of my privacy. And you can just leave, right now!"

"Mind if we ask a few questions?"

"Yes, I do. I don't know why you're here and I have no interest in finding out. Nor do I intend to answer anything. I had a enough of you people when my husband died."

"This isn't about your husband, ma'am."

"Oh?"

"No. It's about a young woman named Ladiya Norris. Maybe you've read about her death in the newspaper."

The woman's hesitation was just detectable, a catch of breath. "What would I know about that?"

"That's the question, ma'am. That is the question."

Marti and Vik met with Lieutenant Dirkowitz when they got back to the precinct.

"It's Halloween," he said.

"Yes, sir," Vik agreed.

Dirkowitz had a limited view of the lake from his window. Today the sky was overcast and the lake was gray.

"Maybe we'll get some rain tonight," Marti said. "Weatherman said there was a sixty percent chance of precipitation."

"Which probably means the sun will be shining in half an hour," Vik said.

The lieutenant picked up the defused hand grenade on his desk.

"Nothing new on our Halloween flasher?"

"Not yet," Marti said. "Nobody's called in anything at least."

"Maybe he caught cold," Vik said.

"I'd like to keep him off the front page of the *News-Times*. Day before yesterday, one of the columnists made a big deal about our inability to apprehend him."

Marti wondered who next weekend's special visitor would be—the one the lieutenant had mentioned on Thursday. It had to be a politician, but other than the congressman who scheduled periodic town meetings, she couldn't think of anyone else who would come here. Maybe it was a film crew from Hollywood. They had made a film in Woodstock awhile ago. And *Ordinary People* was filmed in Lake Forest. Maybe it was Lincoln Prairie's turn.

"So," the lieutenant said. "What have you got on the Norris case?"

Marti told him about the phone call fingering the Lee Street address.

"That's it?"

"I'm afraid so, sir. The DeMarco woman did say she was going to call the mayor."

"Big deal." He dropped the hand grenade on the desk. Meeting over.

When Marti sat down at her desk, her in basket was empty. She tidied the stack of folders she didn't feel like filing, scanned the report she had written in longhand last night, then straightened a paper clip and used the strip of wire to prod crumbs from a seam along the edge of the desk.

"It's too soon to have anything on that gun," she said.

"Odd, isn't it?" Vik said. "I can't remember the last time I've had a weapon without a crime."

"There are just too many distractions. I can't remember a Halloween like this."

"Well, tonight's the night, MacAlister. Maybe tomorrow things will be back to normal."

Marti wanted to talk with Isaac, find out if Dare had showed up yet, but when she'd gone looking for him earlier, she hadn't found him. Then there was this whole business of ghosts. "We need to get a handle on these ghosts, Vik."

"Oh come on, Marti."

"No, the fisherman said he saw something. So did Isaac. It was dark, so they couldn't figure out just what it was. But they did see something, and in Isaac's case, we got results."

"That was just a coincidence," Vik said. "That woman is no different from the fisherman. We gave her an audience; she went into her act. Pumpkins, witches, ghosts. If we didn't have a body on our hands, I'd go up to my place in Wisconsin until all of this foolishness went away. And at this rate, it would be a nice long vacation." He picked up his cup, said, "Empty," and banged it down on his desk. "God knows what that woman meant when she said she was a witch. Since the drug dealers and gang bangers are taking over her neighborhood, I'm assuming she can't turn anyone into toads. Then there's this damned silly joker wearing a pumpkin. What grown man with an ounce of brains . . . I could never work Vice. As for the ghosts, forget it. There's nothing to that. No substance at all. It's easy to see things that go bump in the night when you're half drunk, or a habitual liar, or hold séances."

"Maybe," Marti said. "I've got a hunch, though."

Vik's eyebrows almost met across the bridge of his nose. She had said the magic word: *hunch*. He was as likely to have hunches as she was, but he refused to acknowledge it.

He got on the phone. Half an hour later, he was snapping pencils in half. "Well, Narcotics still can't connect Norris or Knox with anyone here. The DeMarcos are so squeaky-clean, I don't think we could connect them with anyone. There's nothing from Ballistics on the gun. According to the beat cop, there were no gunshots reported in that part of town for the past two and a half weeks. One anonymous caller reported hearing firecrackers last Thursday, but that's it."

"That doesn't mean there weren't any shots fired, Vik It just means they weren't called in. Somebody's always shooting in that part of town."

Marti decided to try to find Isaac. It might be too cold to hang around outside, but Isaac was antisocial. As busy as the new neighborhood was, he might go back to the site where the old place had been torn down just to be alone for a while. She thought of him in that thin jacket. St. James the Less Church was having a rummage sale today. Father Corrigan usually gave him a winter coat, if Isaac hadn't been too distracted by Dare going missing to remember.

She guessed right. Isaac was sitting on the tree stump. Gravel crunched underfoot as she walked toward him. She skirted the hole where the old house had been and the mounds of chopped-up tree trunks and branches that hadn't been fed into the mulcher yet. The lake was a few blocks away, but close enough to make the air colder than it was near the precinct. Marti silently blessed Father Corrigan. Isaac was wearing a heavy three-quarter-length winter jacket

"Isaac, I haven't got anything on Dare yet."

"Nice of you to try," Isaac said. "I appreciate it." His breath made little puffs of steam.

Marti just hoped he would remember her efforts later. Isaac was one of her more reluctant snitches.

"Dare's been right here all the time, though," Isaac said.

"Where?"

"Shackin' up somewhere on Clark with some woman. He got a message to me this morning. He'll probably show up sometime tonight."

The relief Marti felt surprised her. Isaac needed someone to look after him. She didn't like seeing him so alone.

"That's good," she said. "And I'm glad you called me when you couldn't find him. Glad to help. Anytime. I see you've got a new jacket."

"Yup. And I got Dare a new coat."

"Keep you warm," she said. He'd buy his monthly pair of pants when his check came, take his monthly bath, and have his monthly sleep-in with his favorite hooker in his favorite cheap motel. Then it would be back to the street again. Not for the first time, she wondered why.

"Can you tell me one more time what you saw through the window last week? What night was it?"

"Friday."

"What did you see?"

"Something white-looking that didn't touch the ground. At least I couldn't see where it touched the ground. Looked like it was floating. I took one look at it and had me another drink and went right back to sleep. If it was some ghost and it did decide to come haunt me, there wouldn't be no getting away from it no way, so's I decided to act like I didn't see it."

Marti didn't know why he was suddenly so talkative. Maybe he was just wound up because he knew where Dare was. He told her about something he had seen and there were no shakes. Talking to her this time didn't affect him the way it had the first time he'd told her.

"And that's it?"

"Yes, ma'am."

"Is that the only time you say anything like that since you'd been living in the house?"

"That's the only time I ever saw anything like that in my life. At least as far as I can remember."

Marti knew whoever dropped that gun in the rosebushes was mortal. What need would a ghost have for a gun?

Since she wasn't that far from the lake, or Con Ed's coker plant, she drove there next. Three men stood at the edge of the large pond, fishing. She could see another man holding two fishing poles just beyond the footbridge that spanned the shallows. From where he was standing on the concrete breakwater, he would have been able to see Ladiya's body. Marti had assumed that everyone fished in the pond. This man had two lines in the lake. She crossed the sand to the six-foot-high fence that led across the bridge and looked between the chain links as she walked across the metal grating to where the man stood.

"Catch anything?" she asked.

The man smiled without looking away from his fishing lines. "Not yet."

"Are you trying to get them when they come in or when they go out?"

"It doesn't matter. I'm just hoping for trout."

"Do you come here often?"

He glanced at her. "Why are you asking?"

She showed him her shield.

"Did they find that girl's body around here somewhere? The News-Times wasn't specific."

Marti didn't answer.

"I'm stationed at the navy base, had duty Monday and Tuesday."

"We found her right there," Marti said, pointing to the circle of boulders. "Do you always fish over here?"

"There's something about casting off into the deep. It loses its effect over there." He nodded in the direction of the pond.

"Did you see the News-Times edition with the girl's photograph?"

"Yes. It didn't mean anything, though. I'd never seen her before."

"You ever get here before daybreak?"

He smiled. "Lady—Detective, I don't come out here at all unless it's a fairly nice day. A little cool, a little wind, that's bracing, invigorating, whatever, and maybe some sun. It's no fun unless the water's got some turbulence and I've got something to fight when I get a bite. It's a sport, a hobby, relaxation, not a vocation. If it's cold, dark, raining, or otherwise unpleasant, I stay away."

"Were you here the Sunday before or the Wednesday after you had duty?"

"Wednesday."

"Did you see anything out of the ordinary? Not necessarily something obvious, just something a little bit different."

He thought for a minute. "No. They'd changed the Porta Potties, or cleaned them, whatever they do. That's about all."

"Do you see the same people here most of the time?"

"I come here to get away from people for a few hours. And with the way I catch duty, I don't come on a regular basis. Most of the time, I recognize a car or truck or just kind of know there's someone over there that I've seen before. The best I can tell you is that I haven't seen anything around here that seemed out of place."

Marti wanted to ask him why he had two poles instead of one. She didn't, and by the time she walked back to the car, she was curious and wishing she had. Instead of starting the engine, she leaned back and looked in the general direction where the old fisherman said he had seen his ghost, later amended to just an animal. The chain-link fence separated the area and extended across the footbridge. There was barbed wire at the top, but that stopped before the footbridge. While the fence was high, it was not impossible to scale. On the other side of the fence, sand led to the shallows. Once across the shallows, bushes and a cluster of trees led to the sand dunes. The rocks that led to the lake were beyond the dunes and out of Marti's line of vision, but she knew they were there. The old fisherman said he had seen something in the area of the bushes. Unless he'd been lying. She would have been more convinced that it was a fabrication if the area was inaccessible, but there was that stretch of fence without barbed wire.

Marti watched as the seagulls wheeled and called overhead. If it had been a clear day, she could have looked across the water to the south and seen the Chicago skyline. Today it was overcast. She watched someone with a watch cap pulled over long blond hair go into a blue Porta Potti and wondered if it was a man or a woman. She hadn't asked if women came here often. For some reason, fishing seemed more like something a man would do, although now that she thought about it, she could remember a number of Momma's girlfriends talking about fishing. Ben fished when he went to his cabin in Wisconsin, but the boys went along when he did. Fishing wasn't anything she would ever want to do. Come to think of it, gutting and scaling them didn't sound like much fun, either.

She considered the break in the barbed wire. Why would someone climb that fence and go into that wooded area? She supposed the old man could have seen something, and perhaps, like Isaac, decided it was best if he didn't keep looking. Isaac wasn't the heroic type, and people who hung fish on their wall didn't strike her as brave, either. If she went back over the bridge to the breakwater, she could climb over the railing to get to the dry sand circle of boulders where Ladiya's body had been found, but she would have to ford the shallows to get through the thicket of bushes. The water ran swiftly through that channel to the lake, and it was at least five feet at its deepest point. That left the break in the fence where there was no barbed wire.

Isaac sat on the tree stump and wished it would hurry up and get dark. He couldn't go to the garage until then. He didn't think he was welcome at the church where they were serving supper tonight. He had gotten kicked out of there for the second time last week for smelling and being half drunk. He could do without food when he had to—that wasn't a problem—but it would have been a place to keep warm and kill time for a while.

Wait till he caught up with Dare. That fool was going to get cussed out like he had never been cussed out before. Staying away this long, and with some fool woman at that. He mighta known. That was just like something Dare would do. It wasn't like him to stay away so long, though. It must mean Dare didn't like where they had been staying no more than he did. It might be a good thing that fool came in there with that knife when he did. Now Dare would have to find them another place to stay. No way Dare would like sleeping in the garage. He was going to get cussed out good first, though. Then he could go find them a place to stay. Isaac shivered as the wind picked up. He wiped his nose on the sleeve of his new jacket. Lord but he missed them blankets. Maybe Dare would go back and get them. No way he was going anywhere near that place. He was going to have to get up and get moving, though. It was that or sit here and freeze.

12

The uniform looked at Marti as if he suspected temporary insanity. The only thing he said was, "Yes, ma'am." Then he went to the end of the footbridge and climbed the fence. He walked from the sand to the grass, then turned to look at her. Marti pointed in the same direction that the old fisherman had and the uniform trudged in that direction. The sailor with two fishing rods stopped looking out at the lake long enough to turn and watch for a few minutes. Marti wasn't standing close enough to hear anything if he spoke.

The uniform skirted the edge of the bushes and came back without plunging into the brush.

"Ma'am, most of it looks undisturbed, but there is this one area near where you were pointing with a lot of broken branches. Do you want me to go in?"

"No."

By the time Vik and the evidence tech arrived, Marti felt bone-cold. The wind off the lake had penetrated her jacket, slacks, even her shoes. She had a lightweight scarf on her head and her ears felt close to frostbite.

"You watch," she said to Vik. "I'm going to wait in the car."

"What am I watching for?"

"I have no idea," Marti admitted. "Maybe nothing at all."

Vik looked as if he wanted to say something, but for once he kept his mouth shut.

Marti moved the car to a place where she could watch the technician. His progress was slow. After about half an hour, he called out to the uniform, who came to the car.

"He says there's an odor, ma'am. We might have something for the coroner."

By the time they located the body, it was getting dark. Lights were set up at the site.

"Who would have thought?" Vik said. "Two bodies within fifty feet of each other."

The body was wrapped in a bedspread and then a blanket, both light blue. Marti couldn't recognize the face. It had been blow away by a bullet.

"You don't suppose they made him get on the bedspread face-down and then shot him?" the technician asked.

"It does look that way," the medical examiner said. "The bedspread is blood-soaked, the blanket comparatively free of blood." He refused to estimate time of death. "Forensics will get you much closer than I can."

This victim was wearing faded jeans, a black turtleneck, and a denim vest—no coat or jacket, no socks or shoes. Marti went over to where Vik stood looking at the horizon. "Two victims found in almost the same place within a relatively short period."

Vik frowned. "I hope this makes some kind of sense, and that we find out what it is, real soon. Unless the victims have something in common or are connected somehow . . . I sure as hell don't want to have this whole area dug up to see if there are more bodies."

"If there is a connection, I don't know why one was buried and one wasn't," Marti said. "Maybe we'll know more when we get a make on him."

Vik shoved his hands in his pockets. "And then again, maybe we won't. We know a lot about Ladiya, for all the good it's done us so far." He got that puzzled expression on his face. Whoever had done this was trampling on his memories again. "This used to be a great place for fishing. The old man would pack a lunch and fill a thermos with coffee and let me drink some. I can't remember anyone fighting here, let alone killing someone."

His voice sounded so pained that Marti reached out and patted his arm.

When he went into the fast-food joint, the cop and her partner had already ordered. There were several people behind them and he stood at the end of the line. Would she recognize him? He wore his hair longer then, and now it was dyed a darker brown. He had dressed a lot differently then, too. These were his working clothes now, jeans. He thought she might know his voice. What did it matter if she did? She couldn't arrest him for buying a burger. And when she was dead, what would it matter? She wouldn't be able to finger him then.

When she got her order, the cop looked more through him than at him, no hint of recognition in her eyes, but even with that cursory glance, his nerve endings tingled. She would remember his face at the end. She would remember standing within three feet of him here. She would know exactly who he was. And she would be afraid. Everyone was when they realized that it was time for them to die.

He ordered a large meal and two desserts, not sure how long the two cops would sit here talking. He sat away from them, making certain that she had her back to him. If she looked at him long enough, even in passing, he was sure she would be able to place him. Her partner saw him only in the context of the other customers as he routinely panned the room.

When she stood up and went to the rest room, he hesitated for a moment, then followed. Instead of going through the door marked MEN, he pushed open the door marked WOMEN and slipped into the empty stall. He dropped his jeans and sat, the way a woman would, then listened as she relieved herself and flushed the toilet. He wasn't carrying the knife he had bought that morning or the gun with the silencer. If he had been, he could kill her right now. Who would suspect a man of going into the ladies' room, even if they saw him walking out? She thought she was safe in here. She assumed there was another woman in the next stall. Women—stupid, all of them, even cops. Dumb as hell.

When Marti returned to the booth where Vik was munching his way through his second double cheeseburger, she took a sip of her coffee.

"Don't make a point of looking up, but who's walking from the area of the rest rooms?"

She watched as Vik made another routine sweep of the room, then looked down at his food.

"Male."

"You sure?"

"Looks like it, wearing men's clothes."

"Well, he came into the ladies' room while I was there. Went into the next stall. Sat on the john, but he had big feet and was wearing men's shoes. Make a note of his face in case we see him again."

"I won't forget what he looks like," Vik said.

When they got up to leave, the man was gone.

There was a message from Ladiya's mother when they got back to the precinct. Marti returned the call. The woman was sobbing as she spoke. "I . . . I . . . I . . . there was a letter from her in the mail. When I got home today. A letter. From Ladiya. She's been . . . gone almost a week. You are sure that it was her, aren't you? How could I get a letter now? What's wrong with the post office, anyway?"

"What does it say?"

"I can't open it. I can't. She's . . . gone . . . I just . . . I can't."

"No," Marti said. "If you haven't opened it yet, just leave it right where it is. We'll be there as quickly as possible. We're leaving right now."

"A letter," she told Vik. "Still unopened. From Ladiya."

Ladiya's handwriting was both cramped and precise. Marti put the letter into a plastic bag and placed it in her purse. Mrs. Norris's eyes were red and swollen, but she had stopped crying.

"We need to have our crime lab techs handle this," Marti explained.

"You still can't prove Knox did it, can you?"

"No. And until we can, there is always the possibility that he didn't," Marti said.

"Who else could it be?"

"Almost anyone."

"Almost anyone didn't mistreat her; *he* did. He's the one who should be in jail for this. Instead she's . . . not here anymore . . . while he's still walking the street, free as a bird."

"No matter how badly we might like it to be him, Mrs. Norris, or how good seeing him locked up might make us feel, I have to arrest the right person. Otherwise, a killer is still on the loose. If it happens to be Knox, so much the better. If not . . ." She shrugged.

Mrs. Norris nodded. "I just hate him so much. If he had never come into her life, she would still be here. I have nobody else. No other children, no grandchildren. There was just Ladiya. Now there's nobody at all. How can someone just take all that you have, walk away, and sleep at night, and not even care?"

"I don't know," Marti said. And she didn't. She saw it often enough, and she heard the explanations—lack of empathy, an inability to recognize or internalize someone else's pain—but she didn't understand it at all.

She was on the phone to the crime lab as soon as she got back to the precinct. "I want someone working on that letter tonight, not Monday. And I know we did not recover a bullet with today's John Doe. . . ." She listened for a minute. "I know it's highly unlikely that we recovered the weapon before we found the victim and that it will take time to determine if the weapon was used in the commission of a crime. Send me what you've got so far and keep working on it."

Slim and Cowboy came in while she was talking. They were both dressed in black. Slim was rather stylish in a suit, shirt, and tie. Cowboy was dressed more like a young blond Johnny Cash. Marti had never seen the black five-gallon hat. The one he always wore to work was tan.

Vik leaned back and rested his chin on the tips of his fingers.

"Does this have something to do with Halloween?" he asked. "Is there a party we haven't been invited to?"

"This has something to do with our little wienie-wagging jackass jack-o'-lantern," Cowboy said.

"We've got to try to find his sorry ass tonight," Slim said. "Before he really gets himself into trouble."

Marti had never heard either of them sound so irritable. It must have something to do with going through all of those reports they had to read. "And you two call us 'the Dyspeptic Duo.' "

"Try getting as much sleep as we have in the past week," Cowboy said.

"Five, six hours maybe?" Vik said.

"Something like that."

"Try three to five, and not for a week, for three or four weeks, if that's what it takes. Then tell us how tired you are."

"And how cranky you are, too," Marti added.

Slim folded his arms on his desk and put his head down. "Don't wake me up if you hear snoring."

"What did he do last night with that dorm patrol?" Marti asked.

"Nothing," Cowboy said. "At least nothing that we know of. We've got three students unaccounted for, but only one lives in the dorm. There's nothing to indicate anything happened to them. It's the weekend. They could be anywhere. We'll track them down."

"Only three," Vik said.

"Yes. We could have that many or more unaccounted for at any given point in time. There's nothing to be concerned about. You can't always account for everybody. They'll be calling in before the night's out to let us know where they are."

"I hope so," Marti said. They didn't need any more bodies.

Marti asked Vik to describe the man in the fast-food place.

"He followed me into the bathroom," she explained. "I thought you might recognize him."

"Nope," Cowboy said. "Doesn't sound like one of the locals. Maybe the guy took a wrong turn and was too embarrassed just to walk out."

Slim began snoring.

"Hey, partner." Cowboy shook him awake. "Hell of a time for a nap. We got a loose wienie out there just waiting to wag at someone."

"Big deal."

"Small deal, based on the descriptions, but it's a matter of taste. We also got us a pervert out there who follows female cops into the bathroom."

"What?" That woke Slim up. "What's he look like?"

Vik repeated the description. "White male, short, early to mid-thirties, longish hair, dark brown, glasses."

"There was that guy about a year ago. Mole on his left cheek. Face, I mean. He liked women's underwear, too."

"No," Slim said. "MO's not the same. This guy wasn't cross-dressing. That one wouldn't have been caught dead in a ladies' room in anything but women's clothes. Undies and makeup, too."

"Thanks," Vik said. "That's enough. If you come up with anything else, keep it to yourself unless you're sure he's the one."

"Damn, partner," Cowboy said. "Some cops got no appreciation for the gritty side of life on the mean streets of Lincoln Prairie. They want their bodies wrapped nice and neat in blankets, or curled up cold and dry on the sand."

"You think whoever offed them was neat?" Vik asked when Slim and Cowboy were gone. "The medical examiner says that guy did lie down on the bedspread. He was wrapped in the blanket after the bleeding stopped. And there was no mess at all with Ladiya."

Marti doodled on her notepad. Were they dealing with the same perp? There was something about the compulsive types that she found distasteful. Maybe it was just that compulsion required premeditation. Once they figured out the compulsions, though, the perps were much easier to catch. "Let's see if these two cases have anything in common, and, if so, get a psych profile."

Vik grunted. "Hell of a lot that will do. We've got nobody to compare it with."

"That had better change soon."

"At least Dare's turned up. Isaac must have been lost without him."

That comment surprised her. Vik always made fun of her snitches. "I can't imagine why he chose that neighborhood. He knows Isaac can't stand being around that many people."

"Maybe he decided Isaac was too dependent on him."

"Could be," Marti agreed. "Maybe Dare is serious about this lady friend."

Isaac wished he had someplace to go besides the garage. He wished he had gone to the church tonight and tried to get something to eat before they turned him away. He wished Dare would hurry and show up. He really wished it wasn't Halloween. Not that he was superstitious, but he would like some explanation of that ghost or whatever it was that he saw. Maybe this time he really hadn't seen anything. Maybe it was all in his head. He thought he'd had the d.t.'s often enough to know, though. He could have sworn it was real. He got so busy thinking that he walked past the alley where he should have turned in to get to the garage, so he cut across someone's yard, picked up the alley there, and headed back.

Coming at it from another angle made the place look different. From here, he could see where the roof had collapsed. He hadn't noticed how close it was to that streetlight, either. He'd have to be careful to keep low while he was in there; otherwise, someone might see him. The lights in the house weren't on. It was a little house. He didn't think more than one or two people lived there. He wouldn't want to scare them if they were old.

Isaac patted his pockets. He'd run across another couple of Dare's friends, drank some of their liquor without offering any of his own. Not polite, but they had plenty. Two whole gallons of wine and another gallon bottle that was about half full. He patted his pockets. He still had some of the half-pint of vodka and all of the half-pint of whiskey. It was going to be a good night tonight. Maybe by tomorrow . . . Something moving in the garage caught his eye. Dare! He wouldn't have to wait until tomorrow.

He stopped. What if someone in the house had seen him in there and was waiting to catch him? Instead of rushing to the garage like he wanted to, he began backing away. If he thought about it for a minute, it might not be to hard to find out who it was. He found a low shed big enough to hold a couple of garbage cans and ducked behind it. Then he began to whistle "Georgia." If it was Dare . . .

"Isaac!"

The voice was kind of muffled. It didn't sound like Dare. No harm in letting him call a few more times, as long as he'd been away.

"Isaac! Where are you?"

The voice sounded like that on purpose. Didn't sound like Dare. Didn't sound like nobody else he recognized, either. This wasn't some game that Dare was likely to play. Isaac didn't move. He heard his name again, then footsteps in the gravel that paved the alley. He didn't move when the footsteps sounded like they were going away. He didn't move when they sounded like they were coming closer. He held his breath when they seemed like they were right in front of the shed. When the footsteps went past, he could see shoes that weren't run down at the heels and pants that weren't baggy, with the bottoms rolled up. Them was nice shoes, almost new. The pants was fitting just like they was supposed to. No way that was Dare. Whoever it was went up and down the alley until a porch light came on and a woman said, "Who's that? I'm calling the cops." Then the footsteps went away, moving fast.

It was a little before nine at night when a copy of Ladiya's letter was faxed in. Whatever the technician had found would be in a report in the morning. For now, Marti knew what the letter said.

Mom, I am such a mess. I really do need to get myself together. A friend offered me a place to stay. I need to be by myself for a few days. Then I'll be home, promise.

Love you,
Ladiya

It was dated the Tuesday before she died.

Marti passed the copy to Vik. "What do you think?"

"Depends," Vik said after he read it. "If she didn't write it under duress, it would be nice if the friend lived in Lincoln Prairie and we could figure out how to track him or her down. However, since she neglected to mention anyone by name, I don't think it's worth much of anything."

"It's postmarked from the North Side of Chicago."

"If there were anything approaching a preponderance of evidence, Marti, it might add a little weight. Given the circumstances, we could toss it."

"Did you come up with anything in the beat cop's reports?"

"No. The only oddity is the nine-one-one call about the firecrackers. Of course, with everything else, I don't know why firecrackers at the end of October should strike me as odd."

Marti checked the address. It was called in from a pay phone. "I'm going to run this by Lupe Torres first thing in the morning. It seems a little strange that someone would bother to report firecrackers. Seems a little strange that someone would bother to go out in the cold and set them off. And since this telephone is only a block and half from that drug house, we'll have to run it by the narcs, as well."

Marti called the coroner's office. They hadn't identified today's victim.

Instead of going home, Marti and Vik joined the unmarked units patrolling the area where the flasher had been seen. Despite the relatively low priority of the case, the publicity and the student and faculty reaction to the incidents had everyone a little uneasy. There was also the lieutenant's concern that it stay out of the news. They weren't the only off-duty unit on the street.

They got a call just after 10:00 P.M. from a hospital in Elgin. Mrs. Knox wanted to see them. She was in the Critical Care Unit. In addition to losing her spleen, she had broken ribs and a punctured lung.

When Marti and Vik walked into Mrs. Knox's room, a round-faced, dark-skinned woman was holding the hand that was not connected to the IV. She leaned toward the woman in the bed and spoke with a West Indian accent. Marti couldn't make out what she was saying, but she felt soothed and calmed just listening.

The woman at the bedside looked up and saw them. "Ah, so you are the officers, yes?"

"Yes, ma'am," Marti said.

"Azalea asked that I call you. She is worried now about her children."

"Are you a relative?" Marti asked.

"I am her mother."

Mrs. Knox's face was so swollen that Marti couldn't tell whether her eyes were open. Her skin was so dark, it was hard to distinguish the bruises. White bandages above her eyes and one on her chin indicated cuts that had probably required stitches.

Marti went to the other side of the bed. "Mrs. Knox. How can I help you?"

Her eyes were open, but just slits. A crooked row of stitches stretched from her left eye to the bridge of her nose. Her mouth had been wired shut.

"There is a warrant out for him," the mother said. "Coward that he is, beating a woman, he has run. Azalea is afraid that they will take her children from her. She wants me to take them to the islands, where they will be safe from him. She says he does not beat her often, but now that the twins are fourteen, he has taken to hitting them. Just slaps, but she is afraid."

"Where are the twins now?"

The woman hesitated. Mrs. Knox moved her head up and down. "I am staying at a motel. They are there."

"How many children and what are their ages?"

"The girls are fourteen. Junior is twelve."

Marti called Denise Stevens from the hospital room.

"Glad I caught you at home." She explained the situation, then listened.

"DCFS has contacted you?" Marti said to the women.

The mother seemed puzzled.

"The authorities have inquired about the children?"

"No. There have been no questions about that."

Marti relayed that to Denise, who said, "Then if she can leave her daughter and take them right away, there shouldn't be any problem."

"Are you sure about that, Denise?" It didn't seem legal somehow. Maybe it wasn't.

"The mother obviously can't care for her children. The grandmother can and she wants to entrust them to her."

"Well . . ." Marti had reservations about the children leaving the country.

"It's okay. It's what the mother wants and the state is not involved yet." Denise knew a lot more about the child-welfare system than Marti did.

Mrs. Knox's mother made flight reservations right away, then took a piece of paper from her pocket and handed it to Marti. "Azalea wants you to have this."

The writing was almost illegible. Marti repeated what she thought it said.

"DeMarco?"

Mrs. Knox gave a small nod.

"Friend? Your husband's friend?"

Another nod.

"Girl there? Do you mean Ladiya Norris?"

Tears welled at the corners of Mrs. Knox's eyes and slipped down her face.

She nodded.

There was nothing else. Since Mrs. Knox didn't give her an address, she must already know that Marti had it. Knox had made her pay for making that phone call.

"Well," Vik said as they left the hospital, "cast your nets. Looks like we reeled in a live one. Given the extent of her injuries, this note should be enough for a search warrant."

"It'll be about one-thirty by the time we get back."

"So, we wake up a state's attorney. Who knows. We might even find Knox hiding out there."

"I wonder if anything's gone down with our Halloween flasher. Tonight's his big night."

Isaac crouched behind the small shed. He didn't know who had been in the garage waiting for him. He didn't know if they would come back. He thought he'd best be getting away from here, but he didn't know where to go. He should have learned these streets better, instead of depending on Dare. His hands and feet were beginning to twitch. He felt like he couldn't keep still, but he had to. The half-pints were still in his pockets. He knew better than to take a drink unless he was going into the d.t.'s. Somebody was after him. He didn't know who and he didn't know why, but he couldn't risk getting drunk. The man in the house that night hadn't been some weirdo. That man had been after him. It could have been the same man waiting in the garage tonight. And didn't but one person know where he was staying. Queenie. Another place he couldn't go no more. It looked like he'd have to leave town.

Ben's van was in the driveway and the porch light was on. As Marti went up the walk, he came to the door and walked with her to the kitchen.

"Umm," she said as he held her. "I'm not home for the night, just waiting for a search warrant. Is everything all right here?"

"Everything is fine. Sharon is out with Mr. Wonderful. The girls are home from their dates. The boys are in the basement with sleeping bags and a couple of friends having a *Goosebumps* sleepover."

"A sleepover? Was I supposed to know that? Is that why they were so anxious to have the VCR repaired?"

"Yes, you were supposed to know, so don't let on that you didn't. I brought a VCR over. You had pizza sent in as a surprise. The pizza place delivered it."

"Thank you." She kissed him. "That isn't exactly honest, you know, ordering the pizza for me."

"Why not? You're getting the bill."

She kissed him again.

"It's such a relief, not having to worry. They always have something going on. I just can't keep up."

"You would if you had to."

"I have problems sometimes with missing so much of their lives. Is this good, relying on you?"

"I'd like to think so. Our schedules are different. I'm forty-eight on, forty-eight off. I get to sleep on the job. You're twenty-four on and twenty-four on, and you have to grab a few hours of sleep when you can. Speaking of which . . ."

"I know."

"Sit down and I'll fix you some coffee," Ben said. "With caffeine."

"Are the boys still awake?"

"Of course, that's the whole idea."

"I'm going to go downstairs first."

Marti switched off the overhead light in the kitchen and opened the door to the basement slowly so it wouldn't squeak. She slipped in as soon as it opened wide enough and closed it behind her. The boys were watching a movie with the lights out. She could hear Theo giggling. She made her way down the stairs, keeping to the side near the wall, and stood just outside the den. When the movie soundtrack quieted for a moment, she said in her deepest voice, "I am the ghost of the gingerbread village. I have come to eat up all of the children."

The boys screamed. When they saw that it was Marti, they rolled all over the floor, laughing.

She gave Theo and Mike a hug.

Back upstairs, she sat in the rocking chair with her feet on the hassock and looked out the kitchen window. Ben was adjusting the flame under the teakettle. The accident scene flashed in her mind—Ben going through the rear window of that car to reach that little girl. He could have been going into a burning building just as easily. A back draft, a roof collapse, and he would never come out. Nothing was forever. She realized she was gripping the arms of the rocker. She took a deep breath and leaned back.

"What is it?" Ben asked.

She hesitated. "My first husband was a cop, and now I'm going to marry a fireman."

"Scary, huh?"

"Yes."

Ben looked at her for a minute. "Carol died on her way to the grocery store."

"Does marrying a cop bother you?"

"I don't think of it that way. I'm marrying you."

Suddenly hungry, Marti got up and rummaged around in the refrigerator. "Chili made with ground turkey. Yuck." She settled for a tuna fish sandwich.

"Joanna seemed a little put out with me last night," she said when she came to the table. "She thought our . . . decision . . . was some kind of . . . excuse on my part. What do you think?"

"Celibate relationships were kind of trendy a couple of years ago, but personally, I've always preferred those up-front, 'get in my face, jump right on into my bed' affairs."

"Ben!"

He stopped smiling and kissed her, slow and easy, as if he were tasting fine wine. His hand was gentle and caressing on her breast. She leaned against him, aware of a familiar hunger. When her kiss became urgent, he pulled away. "You sure you want to go there?" he said.

"Oh, I know where I want to go, Ben Walker." It surprised her, how easy it would be, how much she wanted to. "Looks like we're going to have to start talking wedding dates pretty soon."

Ben grasped a lock of her hair and wound it around his finger. "You know any judges who will waive the license and the three days and hitch us tonight?"

"Maybe. But they tend to get a little testy when you wake them up after midnight."

"Looks like we'll have to settle for a nightcap."

They kissed again.

He sat on the edge of the cot and sharpened the knife. If he'd had it with him earlier, he could have killed her right there in that bathroom. Not that he wanted to, not yet. He didn't want just her. He wanted all of them. What a joke. The clever homicide detective with the man who was going to kill her just a few feet away and she didn't notice a thing. She didn't even look his way when he came out and sat back down, never even glanced back at him as he ate. Even to her, he was invisible. But soon she would know who he was.

13

The dog was in the kitchen when he let himself in Sunday morning. It looked at him as if expecting some candy, but he had done the last kindness for that dog that he would ever do. There would be no last meal. Everyone was at church, and last Sunday they had been gone until two o'clock. He wasn't sure if they stayed that long every Sunday, and he had considered whether or not to come in for at least ten minutes. The kitchen seemed different today—warmer. He checked. The oven was on. There was a roast inside. And the smells, like a bakery. Two sweet-potato pies were cooling in the pantry. He loved sweet-potato pie. Too bad they hadn't been cut yet. If they had been, he would just slice off another wedge. Tomorrow maybe. He could wait. He had become very good at waiting. Anticipation created its own kind of pleasure.

He had decided that he needed to identify at least three hiding places, one on each floor, just in case he was interrupted or something unexpected occurred. He had to be prepared for every possibility. He turned the light on when he went down to the basement and began looking around. He considered the space behind the sofa, but it was too confining. He'd be trapped if he hid back there. He went into the laundry room, but there weren't any hiding places there. The furnace room seemed like his best bet, primarily because it was the least likely place that anyone would come. It wasn't close to the steps, and there was no exit other than the door. He would have to walk through the rec room to get out, but he was the least confined and the least likely to be discovered if he hid in here. Satisfied, he went to the first floor. Every surface in the living room was covered with a thin layer of dust. Pigs, all of them. They lived like pigs. If he could make it to this room, he could probably sit on the sofa and not be observed.

A sound distracted him. A key! The front door! He crossed the room to the closet and stepped inside. It smelled of cedar and mothballs and he wanted to sneeze but did not. His breath came fast and he could hear his heart thudding in his chest.

"Be right down!" a boy called.

Footsteps ran up the stairs, muffled by the carpet, but heavy because the boy was in a hurry. After a few minutes, footsteps thudded down.

"Got it! Let's go!"

The front door closed. The key turned. The house was quiet again.

At first, he thought of what a close call it had been. Then he realized that it was nothing more than advance preparation. He could be in the house at the same time they were and nobody would know he was here. The dog thought he was a friend and wouldn't give him away. The others felt so secure because the cop lived here that they would probably look right at him and refuse to believe they were in any danger. He wanted to laugh out loud. Stupid, all of them. And their stupidity would keep him invisible, even when he was practically right in their faces.

After the autopsy on the man found at the beach, Marti and Vik knew little more than they had known before. The coroner's office was unable to lift any prints. Forensics was still estimating time of death, although it had been narrowed down to between 10:00 A.M. and 4:00 P.M. last Friday. Variables still had to be factored in, such as weather conditions. They did know the man was approximately forty-five years of age, had cirrhosis of the liver and cancer of the pancreas. According to the medical examiner, he had the lungs of a man who had smoked two packs a day for twenty years. The femur in his left leg had been broken and he had a bridge. They were hoping his dentures would provide a clue to his identity.

Marti felt exhausted. She had napped for a couple of hours, and just before daybreak, she accompanied Vik and three search teams to the DeMarco residence. Knox wasn't there, nor was there any sign that he had been. They did find Ladiya Norris's purse, her jacket, and a suitcase filled with clothing small enough to fit her. Mrs. DeMarco had been brought in for questioning and was being kept in a holding cell until Marti and Vik had the time to talk with her.

"Breakfast?" Vik said.

"Why not."

She drove to a place on Sunrise where they served great Swedish pancakes and waffles. Vik always liked something gooey or syrupy after an autopsy.

"It looks like our Halloween flasher has folded his pumpkin and slipped quietly into the night," Vik said.

"You did have to order that strawberry topping, didn't you?"

"What's the matter, MacAlister, upset stomach?"

"Try exhaustion." She *was* beginning to wish she hadn't ordered scrambled eggs. She wished she wasn't eating at all. "I wish we could put off talking with the DeMarco woman for a couple of hours."

"She's had enough time to think. Besides, she was smart enough to keep her mouth shut until she could retain an attorney. We're not going to get much of anything out of her."

Marti jabbed the eggs with her fork.

"Looks like that fatty layer—"

"Jessenovik!"

"The state's attorney already said he'd go with an accessory charge if we found anything."

"That's not much of a bargaining chip."

Vik poured half a pitcher of strawberry syrup over the syrupy strawberries. He had to use a spoon to eat the pancakes.

* * *

When they got back to the precinct, the desk sergeant motioned them over.

"You're not going to believe this one," he said. "We've got a bomb threat!"

"Where?"

"The college campus. Looks like our little jack-o'-lantern's frustration level got pushed too far and he decided either to scare the hell out of them or just blow 'em up."

Vik looked at Marti and yawned. "Oh well, let us know if anything goes up."

"Just listen for a big bang," the desk sergeant said.

Marti agreed that Vik seemed more alert than she was and should ask the questions. They had to wait half an hour for DeMarco's attorney, an older man with curly gray hair, a long nose, and thick glasses.

"So." The attorney cleared his throat. "Since this is a homicide investigation, my client is prepared to cooperate to the fullest extent possible."

"Why don't you just tell us what you know?" Vik suggested.

Mrs. DeMarco examined her blunt-cut nails and rubbed a cuticle. She took a deep breath. "Knox and my husband were friends, or business associates maybe, I'm not sure. I didn't like Knox; we didn't socialize. I didn't ask any questions. And when my husband died, that was the end of it. The girl showed up on my doorstep Sunday night, out of the blue, suitcase in hand. The only reason I even knew her is because Knox came by the house one day and left her sitting outside in the car. He referred to her as 'the bitch.' That's probably why I let her stay. She said she was pregnant, hooked on drugs, and had to get clean and go home. Said he'd never look for her at my place. Said she would have money to go someplace in a couple of days. I figured if she had managed to break away from him, she should at least have a chance. I went out Monday night. When I came back, she was gone."

Vik's wiry salt-and-pepper eyebrows almost met. "What time did you leave?"

170

"Six-thirty. I go to a seven o'clock church service every Monday night. It was a little before ten when I got back. A group of us go for coffee afterward."

"Did Ladiya Norris say anything about anyone coming, about meeting anyone?"

"She stayed in the guest room. She didn't say anything. I don't even know if she used the phone."

"Do you read the newspapers, Mrs. DeMarco?" Vik asked.

"Of course."

"Then you did know that she was dead."

"And why didn't I come forward? Why? To tell you what? I've already been through this, when my husband died. Do you know any more now than you did before you talked to me? Anything useful? I couldn't tell anyone anything useful then, either. But they asked me the same damned questions over and over, again and again, until I was ready to scream."

"Did you know Knox's wife?" Marti asked.

"I didn't even know he was married. I told you. Since we had no social contact, I assumed it was business, my husband's business, not mine."

"She's right," Vik said as they left the precinct. "She didn't tell us much of anything."

"At least we know why Ladiya was here. And it might be of some comfort to her mother."

"It would be of some comfort to me, MacAlister, if I knew how she got here, why she left that house, how she got hooked up with whoever killed her, and why she went to the lake when she didn't like water. Then there's always—"

"All right!"

A canvass of DeMarco's neighbors didn't turn up anyone who had seen anything.

"Well," Marti said as they sat in the car, "let's talk to our witness again."

"Witness? We don't have a witness."

"Sure we do," she said.

"Not that lying fisherman?"

Lorna, the Irish setter, began barking in the fenced yard as Marti and Vik approached the house. By the time they reached the gate, the fisherman was at the door.

"Settle down, girl. Settle down."

Marti pushed the gate open and stroked the dog between the ears.

Inside, the smell of fish was strong. Marti figured it must be the morning's catch.

"We need to ask you a few more questions about what you saw at the coker plant," Vik said.

"Again? I told you I didn't see anything."

"No, sir," Vik disagreed. "You told us you saw a ghost. Then you said you weren't sure what you saw, a deer maybe, or what looked like something dark. We need a little more information about whatever it was."

"I don't think I have to talk with you two anymore. I think I've said about all I intend to."

"Sorry, sir," Vik said. He was close to smiling. "I have to request your cooperation. This is a homicide investigation."

"The same as it was the last time I talked to you."

"We need to know if you've remembered anything else since then."

"There's nothing else to remember! I've got nothing to add to what I've already said."

"Sir," Marti said. "We have a second homicide victim. We found the body in the approximate area where you said you saw this deer, or ghost, or whatever."

"What? You found what?"

"Another body, sir," Marti said.

"Two bodies? By the old coker plant? There hasn't been one body found there as far back as I can remember, and that's before either of you were born. A few folks who drowned maybe, but nothing like this."

"Well, we've found two homicide victims there now, sir," Vik said. "And within a week."

The fisherman jammed the fingers of both hands into the back pockets of his worn jeans and walked to the window. "Well," he said finally, "I don't know how to tell you this, young man, but I didn't see anything at all. I was just having a little fun, it being Halloween and all. You know, bodies, hearses, ghosts. One thing just seemed to lead to another."

"You didn't see anything?" Vik repeated.

"No, sir, I sure didn't. Not one damned thing."

Vik took out his notebook. "You mind going through the pertinent events of that day again, sir?"

The fisherman faced them. "I didn't go fishing that day. Can't tell you what happened. I didn't see anything. I wasn't even there."

Vik's eyebrows almost met in a fierce scowl. "What do you mean, you weren't there?"

"I wasn't. And that's the truth."

Vik took a step toward him.

The man tried to back away and bumped into the windowsill. He took a step sideways. "Now look here. I didn't mean no harm. I was just pulling your leg a bit, that's all. I thought you knew. I mean, ghosts. Who in the hell would take anyone serious who said they saw ghosts?"

Marti wanted to stick out her tongue at Vik as he gave her a look that said, Didn't I say the same thing?

"Okay, sir," Vik said. "You are now recanting what you told us previously and your current story is that you didn't see anything. Is that correct?"

"That's right."

"Can anyone substantiate where you were and what you were doing that day?"

"No. You'll just have to take my word for it."

"Your word? Do you realize that you could be charged with obstruction of justice by the state's attorney's office?"

"Charged?" he said. He sounded incredulous. "Me? I was just having a little fun."

"Well, it wasn't funny at all," Vik told him. "I'm giving this to the state's attorney. If they decide to press charges, you'll be hearing from them. Meanwhile, if you change your story again, maybe to something the rest of us refer to as the truth, which you probably can't recognize anymore, you had better give me a call right away."

The fisherman's jaw hung open as Vik snapped his notebook shut and walked out. Marti gave the man one final look of disapproval and followed Vik outside.

"See, MacAlister! What did I tell you! Too damned much commercialism, that's what it is. All this hullabaloo over some ridiculous nonholiday dreamed up by the American Dental Association to give business a boost by selling candy. Trick or treat, hah! Witches and damned grinning jack-o'-lanterns everywhere you look. Puts ideas in the heads of empty-headed fools like this one!"

"We did find another body," Marti reminded him. "No matter what he said, or says. I'm sure we wouldn't have ever looked there if he hadn't told us what he did. Besides, how do we know he's telling the truth now?"

"We don't," Vik said. "We don't. About all we can hope is that if he did see something and hasn't told so many lies that he's confused himself, he will tell us what it was."

When they got back to the precinct, Slim and Cowboy were there. It was so quiet in their office that Marti looked from one grim face to the other, wondering what was wrong. They had called the dispatcher. There hadn't been a bomb. Then she saw the package on cowboy's desk. "BOMB" had been printed on brown wrapping paper.

"What's this?" Vik asked. One end of the package was open. Vik looked inside, then took out a square clock with large numerals. Dark smudges showed where the evidence tech had tried to lift prints. "HAHA" was printed on the face, right under a smiling pumpkin with a long tongue.

"They get any prints?" Marti asked. It was hard to keep from laughing. Vik had covered his mouth and was making little snorting sounds.

"Nothing."

"Know what I think?" Vik said. "I think you two have gotten so used to having your perps do everything but cuff themselves, you've gotten lazy. I'd like to see you *solve* something for a change."

The lieutenant was waiting to see them. "We've got another body on our hands?"

"Yes, sir," Vik agreed.

"Seems odd, two bodies at that place. Hard to believe they're not connected."

"It might be easier to get a handle on them now that Halloween is over," Vik said.

The lieutenant raised his eyebrows.

"Well," Vik said, "we've got old Isaac, the wino, sir. Thinks he saw a ghost last week. Then there's Ms. Elizabeth Stiles, sir. She lives in the house where Isaac thinks he saw the ghost, where the Milford murder took place. Ms. Stiles is a witch. She sees ghosts, too. Then there's the fisherman, sir. He saw a ghost down by the lake. Then again, he didn't; said maybe it was a deer. Oh, no. Now that he thinks about it, it wasn't anything at all."

"That many ghosts," the lieutenant said. The corners of his mouth twitched, but he didn't smile. "It must be the time of year." He picked up the hand grenade.

"Anyway," Vik went on, "we know where the Norris girl was staying. We might even know why. As for anything useful, like who killed her or how she got to the beach . . ." He shrugged.

"Tired, aren't you?" the lieutenant said.

"You could say that, sir."

"Grab some shut-eye. A few more hours and you won't be much use to anyone." He dropped the hand grenade on the desk.

Lupe Torres met Marti and Vik near the elevator and went

up with them to their office. She helped herself to some coffee. "We've got something going on at that dope house you told me about one day this week."

"You want me to stay away?" Marti asked.

Lupe straddled a chair. "What's got you over there?"

"Isaac, the wino. He hadn't seen his friend Dare in over a week."

"Dare—skinny dude, dark-skinned, wears sunglasses all the time?"

"That's him. Seems he's got himself a lady friend."

"I haven't seen him around lately either," Lupe agreed. "I don't think that man can walk a block without stopping to talk to someone. There's actually someone out there who will sleep with him?" She thought for a minute. "As far as we're concerned, until the action goes down, it's business as usual. If we reduce our presence on the street, they'll know something is going on." She stood up.

"Oh, and your firecrackers? Gunshots, most likely. I've got a couple of informal reports. Sometimes people call in and say firecrackers because they're afraid to report that someone might be shooting up the neighborhood. I think it's because they think it'll keep them from getting in trouble with the shooter."

Marti drove around looking for Isaac. Maybe Dare would be with him. Then she would be certain everything was okay. She parked and walked to the stump in the clearing and caught herself wishing again that the old place hadn't been torn down. It really was a damned shame. This suited Isaac somehow. It was almost like living in the country. Isaac wasn't an urban kind of person. She returned to the streets he frequented now, and stopped at Dare's watering hole, Queenie's bar. The odors hit her as soon as she walked through the door: spilled beer, cigarette smoke. "Atmosphere," her late husband, Johnny, would have said, tossing off a one-worder the way comics tossed off one-liners. Johnny. She didn't think of him as frequently as she had in the first two years after he died. The urgency to talk to him, to share with him had faded. Now the reminders were subtle. The radio announcer describing a golden oldies show, tomatoes warm from the garden, a chocolate-covered doughnut, the first iris that bloomed in the spring. And the one-worders. And now with each abrupt and unexpected reminder, instead of a sudden rush of pain, she just felt this ache and sometimes, when her eyes teared, a momentary blurriness of vision. What had ever made her think she would get over it? There was no such thing. Last night, with Ben, she'd been ready to get married. When she woke up this morning, she had a vague memory of gunshots and flames crackling. Now she was thinking about Johnny.

As her eyes adjusted to the dimness, she spotted Queenie at one end of the bar. As she looked at the short dark-skinned woman, the word *crone* came to mind, perhaps because of Halloween. Ghosts, witches, bomb threats—what was next?

Queenie saw her standing near the door and grinned. "Afternoon, Officer, something I can help you with?"

The two customers hunched over their drinks at the other end of the bar didn't even look up.

"Have you seen Isaac today?"

"No, now that you mention it." She wiped her brow with the back of her hand. "No. First time since Dare took off that he ain't been in here almost as soon as I opened. 'Course now that Dare's back . . . not that I've seen him today, either. They'll be around, sooner or later. It's Sunday. Ain't too many places for them to go for no liquor."

"Have you seen Dare at all since he . . . came back?"

"Way Isaac tells it, he didn't go nowhere. At least no further than some woman's skirt."

"Which woman? You know?"

"Ain't seen her, neither."

"Do you know her name? Where she lives?"

Queenie hesitated. "Well, now, ma'am, she is a customer."

"Nobody's done anything, Queenie. Isaac told me he hadn't

seen Dare in close to a week. Now he says that Dare has shown up. I just want to check, make sure everything is okay. Nobody is in any kind of trouble."

"Yes, ma'am." From her tone of voice, Marti got the impression that Queenie always thought there was trouble when a cop was involved. "Well, she lives over on Clark. I can't tell you what the number is, but—"

"Seventeen oh two, second floor," one of the men at the bar said without lifting his head. "Everybody knows where she lives, Queenie. That's one thing that ain't never been no secret."

A tall, heavyset woman opened the apartment door when Marti knocked. She was wearing a wig set with rollers, and a short terry-cloth robe. Behind her, the living room was shabby but clean.

"I ain't done nothing," she said when she saw Marti. "Ain't gonna do nothing. Ain't got no record of no kind for doing nothing. I ain't never had nothing to do with the law."

Since the woman obviously knew who she was, Marti didn't bother showing her shield. "Have you seen Isaac or his friend Dare lately?"

"No, can't say as I have. Been laid up with the flu or something. Ain't seen much of nobody for three, four days now at least."

"Dare hasn't been here?"

"Dare?" She laughed. Marti didn't know what the joke was and decided not to ask.

"Dare and I speak in passing. That's about as friendly as we get. For one thing, the man ain't got nothing. For another, he smells."

Marti went to the house where she had last spoken with Isaac and went inside. Blankets were tossed in a heap on the floor. There were some cleaning supplies, a bucket, a mop, and a broom. The place was empty but clean. When she went over to the blankets, she noted the slits right away. It looked as if someone had jabbed them with something sharp. Puzzled, she looked closer. Something razor-sharp. She checked the blankets and the floor for bloodstains but didn't find any. She took one blanket with her anyway, just in case. Then, with her weapon drawn, she checked the rest of the house.

Before she left, she went to the window. The house where Ms. Stiles lived was across the alley and three houses down, but Isaac would have had a clear view of the place where the rosebushes were. The woman was out there now, poking around. What had Isaac seen? She was certain it wasn't a ghost, that it must have been a real live person, the person who had thrown the gun there. Had whoever it was seen Isaac? Troubled, she returned to her car, then changed her mind, walked around to the back of the house and down the alley to the witch's house.

"Well, hello there," Ms. Stiles said. "This place draws you, doesn't it?" She encompassed house and yard with a wave of her arm. "The poor dear has been quite restless since we found that gun. She's wandered every night since. Something is troubling her. I decided to poke around here again."

Marti could see where she had been digging.

"Are you a sound sleeper?" Marti asked. She knew a lot of older people weren't.

"Sleep like a log. Seven hours, whether I need to or not. My mother always said that it is the sleep of the just. I say it's the herbs I add to my tea."

Just her luck.

"So you don't hear things like firecrackers?"

"Oh, those will wake you up."

"Did you hear any last week?"

The woman's eyes narrowed; then she smiled.

"Gunshots," she said. "It happens sometimes around here. When nobody gets hurt, I'm never sure if it's practice or if they're just having fun or what."

"You didn't go to your window?"

"Of course not. I went to my telephone."

"Were you expecting to find a gun when we came out here?"

"I didn't know what you would find. That gun sure wasn't it. I was hoping it would be the knife that killed her. That's why I'm out here digging around."

"Let me know if you find anything else."

"Of course," the woman agreed.

Marti returned to Queenie's place. Queenie was sitting behind the bar with a heavy-duty paper plate heaped with fried catfish and french fries.

"I couldn't find Isaac," Marti said.

Queenie didn't speak, but her eyes narrowed.

"Just what did he say about locating Dare?"

"Oh, just that he'd be showing up pretty soon."

"He hadn't actually seen him?"

Queenie broke off a chunk of fish and dunked it in tartar sauce. She chewed and said nothing.

"I need to know what Isaac said."

"Can't say as I remember."

"Maybe you ought to." Marti leaned toward her with one elbow on the bar.

Queenie switched to the fries.

"Isaac is a friend of mine," Marti said.

"Oh? Friends?"

"You got it."

"Sure thing. And I'm on speaking terms with the President. Come on, what's he done? Stole a bottle of wine from a liquor store?"

Marti felt a quick rush of anger. "Why don't you just tell me what he said."

Queenie's hand paused midway between her plate and her mouth. "No problem," she said.

"Now."

"Yes, ma'am. He's moved, Isaac has. Told me where to send Dare if he came looking for him."

Marti raised her eyebrows when the woman stopped speaking again and took a deep breath. Before she could say anything, Queenie gave her directions.

The garage was falling down. Part of the roof had collapsed. There was nothing and nobody inside. There was nothing to indicate Isaac had been there. Nothing to say he had not. The house was far enough away for the people who lived there to be unaware of a guest. Marti decided against telling them. She would check back later tonight. Maybe Isaac would be here by then. Now that she had discovered the slashed blankets at his last place and had managed to locate his current address, she didn't want anyone to scare him away.

As she turned, she saw a small boy coming toward her. He stopped, adjusted the angle of his cap, turned, and walked away. Marti didn't think he was more than nine or ten, but he was wearing a local gang's colors.

14

When Marti got back to the precinct, Slim and Cowboy had ordered pizza. Marti helped herself to a slice. It was cold, but the microwave oven was in the basement room with the snack machines, and Marti didn't have the energy to make the trip there and back. She peeled the pepperoni off two slices and ate them.

"Any sign of the mad nonbomber?" she asked.

"*Non* as in *nonexistent*," Slim said. "Hell of a waste of time."

Cowboy pulled his hat down over his eyes. "Crowd seemed to be having a good time. Nothing like the threat of imminent annihilation to get the old adrenaline pumping."

"It must be the full moon," Slim said. "We're not having any luck at all."

"Full moon was last week, partner."

"Then the effect hasn't worn off yet."

Vik got out a map. "As far as we know, this guy has just flashed in Lincoln Prairie, right?"

"Since he started?" Slim asked.

"Yes. Since he started."

"Well, let's see," Slim began. "The mall, the nursing home . . . you read the reports, Jessenovik."

"I know, but it isn't my case." He thumbtacked the map to the wall.

Cowboy took his boots off the desk and sat up. "These flasher types aren't usually this much work. It's the rapists that we have to worry about. Ordinarily, these types make it easy."

"Well," Vik said, "this one is not." He put a pushpin at each place the flasher had struck.

"Well," Cowboy drawled, "that tells us one hell of a lot. We already know that when he has gone outside of Lincoln Prairie, it's been to an adjoining town. He also seems to find it challenging to locate an isolated area in a place where there are lots of people. He prefers middle-aged to older women, but he will target someone younger if the other types aren't around. For a while, he was into blondes, but he's become less discriminating over the years."

"There has to be something," Vik said.

"Right, partner, but whatever it is, it's a mystery to me."

"It's as if this one just has to expose himself," Slim said, "no matter who it is, although he does seem to have preferences. For all we know, he could be doing it year-round for gratification, and just going into costume for a week to get some attention."

"What about the areas he hasn't gone to?" Vik asked.

"Yet," Cowboy said. "Give him time."

"Not enough people there, maybe," Slim said.

Vik studied the map. "Look at the areas he avoids. Any pattern?"

"Subdivisions."

"Single-family homes."

"What else?" Vik asked.

They all stared at the map.

Marti had scanned the reports, although perhaps not as thoroughly as Vik.

"We've got two things," she said. "We have no reports of him flashing eight years ago. The next year, he went to that nursing home on Halloween. That year, he started out at strip malls. It didn't go well. One night, he surprised a woman and her friend and they became hysterical and drew a crowd, several of whom saw him. Then he almost got caught the sixth night when the woman began screaming and people ran out of the stores. Then he switched to that nursing home the next night, Halloween. Maybe because it was close to home? It's near a subdivision."

"I don't think so," Cowboy said.

Slim gave her a slow smile. "Maybe you've got something there, Officer, ma'am. Each year, guy has a plan, but no backup. And hey! He did go to nursing homes the next year. Maybe nursing homes were next on his list, so when he couldn't do strip malls anymore, that became plan B."

"But if that's the case," Cowboy said, "wouldn't he have stayed away from his own neighborhood, instead of going to one close to home?"

Slim slapped his hand down on his desk. "Who the hell knows? Who the hell knows anything about this son of a . . . damn."

"Well," Vik said. "The year he didn't show at all and the nursing home are the only breaks in the pattern that we have. I suggest you start looking at known perverts who live anywhere near that nursing home."

"Right, partner," Cowboy said. He didn't sound convinced.

"There's a reason for the nursing home that year," Vik said. "And it's all you've got."

"I suppose this means we have to track everyone down who was interviewed that year and interview them again," Slim said. "Hell, we weren't even working Vice then."

"So much the better," Marti said. "You'll have a fresh perspective."

"Perspective, hell. I prefer quick busts, like last week, when we set up that sting and corralled nineteen johns. All this legwork is for you homicide dicks—cops."

"Tough," Vik said.

"Move on it," Marti agreed.

J.D. took his time looking through the newspaper. He could read real fast, but he didn't always pay much attention to what he was reading. Now he was looking to see if there was anything about Dare or his friend. When he had looked through all of the sections twice without finding anything, he figured both of them must be okay. What did he care anyway? He hadn't done anything but tell his boys where to find them. Now they had promised to let him do some real work. He didn't ask what.

He went through the newspaper one more time and still didn't find anything. Nothing had happened to them. Nobody had done anything to them. They had just scared them off, that's all. This town wouldn't be any worse off with a couple less drunks hanging out on the corner, and especially not a drunk who thought he knew everything. Man didn't even have no home and he was trying to tell him to get out of the gang, keep away from the drug house. Like he'd listen to some old fool who couldn't stay more than five minutes away from a bottle. And telling him not to smoke dope! Man didn't know what he was talking about, acting like he was so smart and letting himself get tricked like that. "Come on, Dare, the lady wants to meet you. You can ride that old garbage truck anytime." And that fool Dare, believing him.

The other one was smarter. He didn't want to have nothing to do with nobody. If he hadn't told Queenie where he was staying, it would have been impossible to follow him around. He would have caught on to that real fast, drinking or not. And both of them were okay. Not that it mattered none to him. No way nothing like that would matter to him one way or another. Even better, he was going to have something even more important to do soon.

J.D. took his math book off the table and took it to his room. If his mother came home and saw it, she would figure he had homework and want him to show it to her. Then they'd argue for half an hour when he lied and said he didn't have none. He had no plans for going to school tomorrow anyway. He was going to be sick. Maybe he should leave the book out. It might keep her attention away from the empty shelf in the freezer until he was in bed. They had cleaned that freezer out again this weekend. His old man would complain about the money the food had cost him from now till next payday. J.D. looked at the clock. If they didn't get home by four, that usually meant they had checked out of the hotel but stuck around for a little more gambling in the casino.

He'd be in bed by the time they got back and they'd be gone to work by the time his alarm went off in the morning. He went into the kitchen and opened a can of ravioli and warmed it in the microwave. Then he folded the newspaper. No telling where Dare and his friend had gone.

Sharon laid back against the pillows and closed her eyes. The water bed gurgled as she moved. Beside her, Phillip snored softly. The television was on, a video playing. Two men and a woman were doing impossible things. Frank had liked to watch porn movies, too. She did not, but here she was, on a Sunday no less, in a motel watching porn flicks with Phillip. Her mother had been right: There were a whole lot of things a woman would do to please a man. But why? She was almost forty, had some financial independence, had what some people used to call a career— why did she have to have a man? There was life without men, and she tried it sometimes, but sooner or later, there had to be a man again. It wasn't sex, it wasn't loneliness, and Lord knows, it wasn't for companionship. She had to walk into the teachers' lounge every few months with that satisfied expression on her face that made everyone look at her with a knowing smile. And the strange thing was, when she was dating, the male teachers at work hummed around like bees, as if her scent or her aura had changed. When she was without a man, they ignored her. It was as if there was some sort of competition going on, and she wasn't the prize unless somebody had already won her. Why did she play these damned games?

Beside her, Phillip stirred. God, she hoped he didn't wake up. She had spent the whole afternoon here, when she should have been home grading papers. When he woke up, he'd be ready to go again. She was ready to leave. Unlike Frank, Phillip told her he loved her more than anything or anyone else in the world. He had asked her to marry him again today. She had promised to think about it. Marti would be getting married sooner or later. Having Phillip around would be better than being alone again. She could tell by the way other women reacted to him that they wanted him. She was the one he had chosen. For the first time, she had found someone who cared more about her than she cared about him. Not that she didn't care. Phillip was a good man in many ways. She would never marry for love again, not unless she was the one who was loved.

Phillip was not like Frank, no matter what her mother had said. She would not keep choosing the same kind of man, keep making the same kind of mistake over and over again. Momma had to be wrong about something, just once. Phillip was nothing like Frank. He rolled over. Without opening his eyes, he smiled, said "Ummm," and began caressing her breasts.

Marti went through her in basket again, read through all her notes and reports on Ladiya. Her friend who worked at the hospital had finally come through. Ladiya had been treated at a different hospital for each injury she sustained. There was a pattern of abuse, and indications that Ladiya wanted to leave the man who was beating her. Real nice guy, Knox. He saw to it that she got medical attention. It seemed like some kind of ego trip on his part, but no matter now. A year and half, months of emergency rooms and doctor visits, and then we get a corpse.

She would return to Elgin tomorrow, talk with Mrs. Knox again, find out what the woman knew about Ladiya, Knox's house in the city, and whatever Knox had been up to—maybe. The woman couldn't talk. She was his wife, and Knox was still on the loose. Maybe, after the beating he had given her, she would be too afraid to say anything else.

Marti drove out to the lake before going home, past the coker plant. It was dark and the pond was deserted. Nobody was fishing from the breakwater. She trudged through the sand and across the bridge, until she reached the spot where Ladiya's body had been found. It was quiet except for the lapping of the water on the shore and a distant foghorn that sounded at some measured time, even though the night was clear. The wind was brisk and cold, but it felt good against her skin, cleansing somehow, soothing. Why had Ladiya been brought here? Why had she been left out in the open? Why had they waited? Because they had already buried someone here? It seemed impossible that the two deaths were not connected, but without knowing the man's identity, or who had killed him, they couldn't be sure. Did they leave Ladiya in plain sight so that there would be no further searching? Was the man the more important victim of the two? There would be a piece on it in tomorrow's paper, but it was sure to be eclipsed by the bomb scare.

Marti looked at the place where the man's body had been found, across the narrow inlet of water, among the underbrush near the dune—an isolated place. A very unlikely place to go looking for a body. One the average citizen couldn't explore. No stumbling over anything there. Maybe Vik had it backward. Maybe the killer, or killers, knew this place very well.

When Ben dropped the boys off at Marti's house after their trip to Adler Planetarium, Sharon was home and the girls were out. When he came back less than an hour later, Chris's purple Tracker was parked at the curb. The garage door was up and Sharon's station wagon was gone. He wanted to believe that Joanna and Chris couldn't get into too much trouble in such a short time, especially with the boys in the house, but he could still remember being fifteen. As soon as he opened the kitchen door, he smelled burned food. A pot was soaking in the sink. No kids. He listened. The boys were downstairs. Music was playing in another part of the house. Should he call out so Joanna would know he was here, or go looking for them? He began whistling.

Two couples were slow-dancing in the living room. Good thing they were wearing clothes—there was little else separating boy from girl. He resisted a sudden urge to grab both boys by their collars, drag them to the door, and apply a swift kick to the butt as he threw them out.

"Ahemm."

"Ben!" Joanna broke away from Chris. Lisa kept dancing.

Ben went over to the boom box and turned it off.

"Whatcha wanna do that for?" said the tall light-skinned boy holding Lisa. He had a goatee and looked at least eighteen.

Ben walked over to him and extended his hand. "You must be Dante."

Dante was almost a foot taller than Lisa, who was short like her mother, but chubby. Dante held out his hand. Ben gripped it and pumped his arm up and down until the boy winced. "Nice meeting you, man. Nice meeting you." Another squeeze and he let go.

"I suppose you're going to tell," Lisa said. It was probably a good thing she had braces. She had enough metal in her mouth to mint coins with if they ever took it out. It was more than enough to limit the possibilities of kissing. Too bad Joanna didn't need orthodontia.

"And Chris." Ben slapped the other boy on the back and put his arm around his shoulder. "Say, man, how's the Tracker running? You get that short in the ignition fixed?"

Chris nodded. "I think maybe we should get going."

"Oh, no. Stay if you like. Joanna's mother should be here anytime now. I'm sure she'd like to see you."

Chris looked at his watch, then the door. "Oh, no, sir. I . . . ummm . . . we . . . ummm . . . we really have to go."

Chris muttered a quick "See ya" to Joanna and was gone. Dante wasn't in quite as big a hurry. He leaned down to kiss Lisa on the forehead, nodded at Ben, and dipped and bobbed in a "pimp walk" to the door.

"Gee, Ben," Lisa said. "You didn't have to scare them away. We weren't doing anything but dancing."

"You're much prettier when you smile than when you pout."

"Oh Ben!" She cocked her head to one side, gave him a quick smile, and winked. Flirt practice. Better him than Dante.

Joanna followed him into the kitchen and got busy scrubbing the pan.

"What did you burn?"

"Just some vegetables."

"Good."

"Good? They were fresh. Now I've got to use frozen or canned."

He measured out some coffee, and when it was ready, he added half-and-half and sugar. "Join me?" he asked.

Joanna made sugar-free cocoa.

"Tastes better if you top it off with half-and-half and a marshmallow," he said.

"Sure. Some people will do anything to get an early start on clogged arteries." When she sat down, she said, "And you don't have to tell Ma about Chris; I'll do it myself. Not that he'll be back, now that you've caught him here."

Ben chuckled.

"It's not funny."

"You think we're treating you like a kid?"

"No, not really."

"I'm glad you don't think I'm butting in."

"I didn't say that, Ben. You butt in a lot when it comes to Chris." She fidgeted with her napkin, twisting it, then tearing off little pieces.

"Well, I'm spoiling his fun on purpose."

"And that's all you think it is, fun?"

"Yes."

"Ma and Daddy were in love when they were fifteen."

"Probably. Are you?"

She shook her head. "But I like Chris a lot."

"So do I."

"Really?"

"Sure. He's a nice kid."

"And?"

"I was probably a nice kid, too, when I was fifteen."

"And?"

"A few more home visits and both of you are going to get in pretty deep."

She got up and went to the sink. "You think just like everybody else."

"Might be a reason for that. We've all been there."

"Is that why you and Ma . . . ?"

"Yes. Been there, done that, want something that's a little bit more." He made another cup of coffee, then rummaged through the refrigerator, careful to avoid Sharon's hiding places for real cheese, butter, and lunch meat. "My mother sent home a casserole, so we don't have to worry about the vegetables."

"Does it go with fish?"

"Fish? On Sunday? I could have sworn I smelled a nice roast when we came in from church. In fact, now that I think of it, Sharon did say something about pork."

"Fish," Joanna repeated.

He and the boys had stopped to see his parents on the way home and had eaten ham and greens and corn bread. "Didn't you cook fish yesterday?"

"The day before."

"I think it's going to be a hard sell tonight. I'll run out and get something, okay?"

"Sure, with all that pork waiting."

"Pigs get a bad rep. I think it has something to do with the way they like to live."

Joanna fixed another cup of cocoa. When he looked at her, she seemed sad.

"That bad, huh?"

Joanna shook her head. "Probably not. But I'll sure be glad when I'm twenty-one."

Ben chuckled. Joanna giggled, too.

When Marti got home, Ben was there, wearing his "Smokin' Fireman" apron.

"This has to mean something good," she said.

"I stopped by my mom's while I was in the city and she sent back some okra, corn, and tomatoes, so I brought that over. Then there are those sweet-potato pies Sharon made last night, and a pork roast. So, I thought I'd surprise you with dinner. I just need five minutes in the kitchen while the biscuits brown."

Marti sat in the rocking chair by the kitchen window and sipped a hot cup of tea. Something had tripped the sensor light on the corner of the garage. A cat, maybe. Dogs had to be leashed. The boys' bikes were in the driveway. They should have been put away. She hadn't seen the kids since morning. The boys were upstairs. Ben had taken them to the planetarium today. She was almost afraid to ask if they'd had a good time.

"How was your day?"

"The planetarium was a great idea, Marti. It was all old hat to Theo, but it made everything they'd been studying at school come alive for Mike. And Theo loved playing teacher. He knows a lot more about astronomy than I do. We're going to have to do things like that more often, find things that are going on at the museums and whatever that tie in with what they're working on at school."

"You are," she said. "I don't think I'll ever have time."

"Next time we come up with something like that for them to do, we'll try to plan it better, when you have time off."

"For all I accomplished today, I could have gone with you."

Ben came over and pulled up a chair. "I know your work is real hands-on, Marti, and you have to be selective about what you delegate, but things worked pretty well when Lupe Torres was helping out last summer. Maybe you could work out something like that. I'm sure the lieutenant would go along with it. At least often enough to spend a Saturday or Sunday afternoon with the kids when you're working a case."

It was an idea. Not that the city of Lincoln Prairie had enough homicides to support two detective teams, but someone could be brought in to handle routine stuff when they were working a case. If she or Vik got sick, which they rarely did, they usually worked anyway. This way, there would be some kind of backup.

"That's not such a bad idea, Ben. They could always beep me in an emergency." This was man's work, after all, just as Vik had told her when she first arrived. And men had the little woman at home to take care of everything. Well, there was no little woman at her house. Maybe it was time the department began changing a few of the rules to accommodate female officers. She was sure Lieutenant Dirkowitz would be receptive.

Ben served dinner—a thick slice of pork roast and palm-size biscuits with gobs of melting butter.

"And . . ." he said, opening a casserole dish.

Marti took a deep breath, inhaling the scent of the vegetables. "It has been ages since I've had this okra dish. My mother used to make it for me before she moved south." Cooking wasn't one of Sharon or Marti's strong suits, which was one reason Joanna got away with so many of her health-food meals.

Ben laughed. "Even Joanna couldn't find fault with it."

Marti savored every delicious mouthful.

Joanna came down while she was eating. "If I don't find that cat!"

"What did she do now?"

"Ma, I think we're dog people, not cat people. Bigfoot is enough."

"What did the cat do?" Marti asked again. She rather liked Goblin, although she didn't see much of her.

"Nothing."

"Then what's the problem?"

"I can't find her!"

"And?" Marti tried not to sound annoyed.

"Ma, she gets into my stuff, my dirty clothes, my underwear. I think she's got this . . . nest somewhere, and it's made of things that belong to me. But I can't find her. I don't know where she hides."

"Has Theo seen her?" Marti asked.

"Oh, they get along great. She lets him pet her and everything."

"Then why don't you ask him to find out where she sleeps?"

Joanna paused midstep. "Hey, Ma, that's not a bad idea."

"I vote that we keep the cat," Marti said. "She's got Joanna so distracted that she didn't say one word about what I'm eating."

He laid on the army cot with his hands clasped behind his head and looked up at the ceiling. He had been in the house with one of them today and they hadn't even known it. The boy had come within inches of his hiding place, close enough to see him standing in the closet, but he had not. All this time, he had been so careful to be certain that they were away, and it wasn't even important. Nothing could keep him from the completion of his plan. It didn't matter what happened that he couldn't anticipate. Nothing could deter him, and nothing, no matter how haphazard, would prevent him from achieving his goal.

15

The kitchen was a terrible mess when he let himself in on Monday morning. It was much worse than usual. Worse than he had ever seen it before. Breakfast dishes still in the sink. Crumbs and a knife smeared with jelly on the counter by the toaster. Someone had spilled tea or coffee on the stove and hadn't wiped it up. There were two footprints near the door where somebody had stepped on a wet floor and nobody had mopped it again. After an entire weekend at home, you'd think they'd have cleaned the place. Here, it was always just the opposite. He had planned to have a glass of orange juice and some sweet-potato pie, but his hands began to itch. Damn. This happened every time he got anywhere near filth. His mother and stepfather would never have tolerated anything like this. Sloth. One of the seven worst sins. And they were all guilty. He got out of the kitchen before the dog even had time to come in.

He met the dog in the hallway but didn't speak. He hadn't brought any candy today, either. The dog looked at him expectantly and wagged its tail, ready to devour anything that he gave it. "Sorry, boy, but you said no twice. That's one time more often than anyone else ever has." He was planning to give the dog one last meal, if he could get his hands on some strychnine.

His hands wouldn't stop itching. He washed them, poured on peroxide, used an antibacterial cream he found in the medicine chest, but nothing stopped the itching. He had planned to stay longer. He had things to do, but it would have to wait until tomorrow. He couldn't stand being around the filth in the kitchen any longer.

J.D. stood half a block from the school and watched the kids going in. That wasn't for him, not today. He hadn't done his homework. In a few years, he'd be able to ditch school altogether. In the meantime, he had to be careful. Getting suspended might be enough to upset his parents. He'd pretended to be asleep when they came in. He'd listened to his father complain about all the food he and his friends had eaten, listened to his mother say that meant he had stayed in the house, like they told him to if he didn't want to stay with his aunt, and as long as he did one or the other, he wouldn't be getting himself into any trouble. His parents wouldn't confront him with anything if they could figure out a reason not to. That was why he had to be careful with school. He would show up tomorrow with a note saying he'd been sick. If it was only one day, nobody would check. He'd worry about his report card when it got here. He could always talk his way out of that, as long as his grades weren't too bad, and any dummy could do this schoolwork. What he really wanted to do was find out what had happened to Dare and his friend. Not that it was important. He just didn't like not knowing what was going on.

Those two were such stupid old men, and Dare had such dumb ideas. And talk about lies. As if he would believe that Dare had ever done anything in his life beside turn that bottle up. Honor student, army medals. That fool couldn't have even have graduated from high school, not the way he drank. The one thing he couldn't understand about grown folks was why they had to lie to you when they were trying to talk you out of something. The real reason why Dare took off was because he was supposed to bring that medal to show J.D. and he didn't have one. And that was one lie that J.D. wasn't going to let him get away with. When he did catch up with Dare, he was going to make him own up to not telling the truth. Then let him tell somebody what he thought they ought not to do.

Queenie was sweeping out her place. J.D. went over and took

the broom. She looked at him as if she couldn't believe he was being this nice. He wasn't doing it for nothing. "Looks like rain. Been a long time since we had rain," he said.

"Sure has," Queenie agreed. "Week before last."

"We might not have too bad a winter."

"Might not."

"I sure hope that guy—what's his name . . ." He stopped sweeping and pretended to think. "You know, those two that live in that abandoned place over a couple of blocks."

"Who's living there?" Queenie asked.

J.D. thought she knew. "Dare, that's his name. Don't know what his friend's name is, though."

"I ain't seen nare one of them. Ain't seen Dare in over a week now. You ain't seen them, have you?"

"No. I don't even know them that well."

"Didn't seem like you did. I don't imagine homeless folks like them get to know too many people."

"Don't suppose so," J.D. agreed. No matter what Queenie said about not knowing where they lived, if anything had happened to either one of them, she sure would know about that. J.D. swung the broom with enthusiasm. If his mother saw him now, she'd either try to drag him home to clean up his room or complain that he never did nothing like this for her.

Marti and Vik drove back to Elgin first thing Monday morning. Mrs. Knox was out of the Critical Care Unit, but she didn't look any better. When they went into her room, she reached for the call button, then put it down when she saw who it was.

"Can you talk at all?" Marti asked.

She made a slight side-to-side movement with her head.

"If I ask you a few yes/no questions, will you answer?"

Again the movement of her head was conservative, as if even that hurt.

"Has your mother left with your children?"

Marti thought the grimace might be a smile.

"Did you know about Ladiya?"

A nod.

"Did you know she was dead?"

Another nod.

"And pregnant?"

She shook her head slightly.

"Did you know she was in Lincoln Prairie?"

A nod.

"Did she tell you that?"

A no motion.

"Did your husband tell you?"

She nodded.

"Was your husband at home the night of Monday, October twenty-sixth?"

She indicated no.

"Did you see or hear from him at all that day?"

Again a no.

"Does he like to fish?"

Mrs. Knox tried to speak, tried either to smile or grimace, then shook her head.

"Has he beaten you before?"

She nodded again.

"Damnedest thing I've ever seen," Vik said.

Marti stopped at the parking lot exit gate and dropped the token she had been given into the slot.

As the barrier arm went up, Vik said, "She must have known everything, but why would she live like that, and let him live the way he did, and with another woman? I don't understand any of it."

"I don't think anyone does," Marti said. "I think Maslow was on to something, though."

"Who in the hell is Maslow?"

"He came up with a theory that if you're always preoccupied with safety and physical needs, you can't develop self-esteem."

"So people who let people beat up on them don't like themselves?"

"Makes sense," she said. "Why the hell else would you put up with being knocked around if you didn't think you deserved it? That has to be part of it at least."

For a moment, Marti thought of Sharon. No. Not Sharon. Sharon thought too much of herself. She had won awards as a teacher. She did not have low self-esteem. Sharon liked herself. "I wonder where Knox is? He sure has gone to ground."

About all she had gotten out of Mrs. Knox was the admission that her husband wasn't with her when Ladiya Norris was murdered. Now she couldn't alibi him. She couldn't get any sense of facial expression when the woman answered; her face was still so swollen that her eyes were little more than slits. She couldn't speak, so there were no voice inflections. The only emotional response Marti had been able to detect involved questions about her children and fishing. Marti couldn't figure out what the response to fishing meant.

"If Knox's relationship with DeMarco was so businesslike, why would Ladiya go there? Why would Mrs. DeMarco take her in? I didn't get the impression that Mrs. DeMarco was lying, but why would Ladiya go there?"

"And how in the hell did she end up on that beach? It might have been a stone's throw from the DeMarco place, but it sure wasn't easy to access from there."

The most frustrating thing about the case was that even when they seemed to have an answer, there was something about it that didn't make sense.

"My best guess is that it was done without premeditation," Marti said.

"But going to that place had to be premeditated. Why would you go there with someone under this set of circumstances if you didn't plan to kill them?"

Marti thought for a few minutes. "She didn't unpack anything. That at least suggests that she didn't intend to be at the DeMarco place long. She said she was going to go into treatment, and, in effect, she said the same thing in that note to her mother. We'll have to check and see if she had contacted any facilities in the area. I get the impression that he kept her isolated, or she isolated herself. The DeMarco place might have been the last place she thought he would look for her. It makes sense, especially if she had a short list of places to go. And if she was desperate enough . . ."

"But how did he find out she was there?" Vik said. "I don't think Mrs. DeMarco would have told him."

Marti swung onto the Interstate 90 ramp. "She made a good impression on both of us. I hope we're not wrong about her."

"How did Knox find out?" Vik said. "He'd been there before, and he would have had at least a general idea of where the lake was. If he took Sherman Avenue, he would have seen the turnoff to the coker plant. If the area wasn't familiar to him, he might have thought he could just drive down there to reach the water."

"With the intention of throwing her in, maybe?" That did make sense. "Then he finds out it isn't so easy."

"So he smashed her face in instead," Vik said. "There are lot of gaps in this, Marti, the biggest being how he found out she was there, but it's beginning to sound like a possibility. Stop somewhere for coffee."

The autopsy report on their unidentified victim was on Marti's desk when she arrived at the precinct. Information she already knew: no fingerprints, thanks to advanced decomposition; black male; height, five feet seven; weight, 145 pounds; medical condition—the pancreatic cancer was beyond any hope of cure; and cause of death.

"Approximate age forty-five," Vik said. "Dare looks at least fifty, but I bet he's not a day over thirty-five. Alcoholism has a tendency to speed up the aging process."

"And Dare couldn't have weighed more than one hundred twenty." She didn't want the victim to be Dare, for Isaac's sake. She had a quick impression of Dare dipping and swaying as he walked down the street. She couldn't recall seeing him with a cigarette. Their victim had the lungs of a heavy smoker. "How tall do you think Dare is?"

"I never got that close. I'd guess five-nine. You haven't seen Dare or Isaac?"

"Not lately."

Vik tossed the autopsy report in his in basket. "Well, it's back to the missing persons reports. Maybe I'll find something there."

Cowboy yanked open his desk drawer. "Hell no." He took out a can of coffee. "How many people do you know who can remember what happened last week, let alone seven or eight years ago? Especially something stupid like a flasher in a pumpkin suit."

"Besides," Slim said. "Three of the four women he flashed in that nursing home are dead. The other has Alzheimer's. Everybody we talked to got their information secondhand."

"So, you go through the original reports."

"Come on, Jessenovik," Cowboy said, "We've done that already. Twice."

"Do it again."

"I knew there was a reason why I didn't want to be a homicide dick," Cowboy said. "Not enough action, and you have to think too damned much and screw around with too much paperwork."

"There's nothing like a little recreational prostitution," Slim agreed.

Cowboy cracked the joints on his fingers. "Mindless sex and lewd and lascivious cohabitation, fornication. Keeps our arrest record at a decent level, at least half of our perps are embarrassed enough to plead guilty and get the hell out of there, and our court appearances brief."

Slim massaged his temples. "And there's a hell of a lot less paperwork."

Vik pushed his chair back. "Now, the only deviation in his behavior that we know of is the year he switched targets after he almost got caught—when he started going to that nursing home." Vik divided that year's incident reports among them. "Try to remember, guys, we are looking for similarities, something the reports have in common, or something unusual that occurs only once, maybe twice."

"Damn," Cowboy said. "This has got to be the most tedious, boring . . . What do you want to bet some student thinks this is a good prank to play because we'll assume it's the flasher. Anybody could have called in that bomb threat and pulled that fire alarm."

"Stick with the flasher," Vik said. "We don't need a cast of thousands here. If he's not our troublemaker, we'll still have the advantage. Dirty Dirk will be happy again once Mr. Pumpkinhead is caught."

The lieutenant so seldom interjected himself into a case that nobody could argue with that.

"Description?" Vik said.

They each scanned a report.

"Thin."

"Dark hair."

"Blond."

"Stocky."

"Short."

"About six foot three."

Vik's eyebrows arched. "Skip it. Costume?"

"Shiny," Marti said.

"This report mentions shiny, too."

"That's affirmative," Cowboy said.

Slim slapped his reports down on his desk. "Big deal."

When they had exhausted every topic they could think of, they had what appeared in every report: shiny fabric and a long nose.

"Now," Vik said. "The hard part. We are going to take every report of a flasher or exhibitionist for the two years leading up to that Halloween and see how close we can get to the nursing home."

"This assumes that our flasher has a record," Cowboy said. "What if he only does this seven days out of the year and the rest of the time he's a nuclear physicist or something?"

"How many compulsive types do you know who can do anything just seven times a year?" Marti asked.

They came up with nine possibilities. When they pulled their files, three had long noses.

"Okay," Vik said. "This is where we bail out. You can do your own legwork."

"Long noses," Slim said. "Is this how you solve homicides, pulling rabbits out of hats? I've bet on better long shots at the Arlington racetrack."

Cowboy agreed. "Let's just have all of these jokers hauled in and have a pecker lineup. The guy with the birthmark is it."

"Sounds good, partner," Cowboy agreed. "That way, the ones with the long noses can't yell discrimination."

Vik watched as they left, shaking his head. "No wonder those two are so crazy. I'd rather work with stiffs than perverts any day. These weirdos make me feel like taking a shower."

Within two hours the coffee was gone. By then, Marti and Vik knew that Ladiya had missed an appointment last Wednesday at Lincoln Prairie General. She was going to meet with a drug-rehab counselor. They were not able to find out anything about Isaac. It was as if he had appeared out of thin air one day and just stuck around.

Vik picked up something on Dare. "He's a veteran. Good military record, too. He served a year in Vietnam, was awarded a couple of good-conduct medals, and one for bravery. He didn't get kicked out, either. He just didn't reenlist. He's a high school graduate, went to college for a year. How did he end up on the street?"

"Alcohol," Marti said.

"Makes you wish for prohibition," Vik said. "Too bad with all of this we still don't have a clue where in the hell he is. I checked to see if he was in the VA hospital. He's missed two appointments, but that's it. Hey—" He picked up the phone again. When he hung up, he said, "He missed two appointments with oncology."

"Our John Doe had cancer." Marti had a sick feeling in the pit of her stomach. She didn't want the unidentified dead man to be Dare.

Vik called the coroner's office. "They'll get right on it."

Marti tried to ignore the queasiness. "This doesn't bode well for Isaac."

"Sure as hell doesn't. And with two cases on our hands, we've got a lot of work to do. It's time for an action plan."

They agreed that since they seemed closer to closure on the Norris case, it was time to put a little pressure on the fisherman. Some semblance of an honest man could be lurking beneath his facade of petty deception. They had also better bring a little pressure to bear on Ladiya Norris's friend Shenea, just in case there was something else she had chosen not to tell them that they could shake loose. Maybe neither of them knew anything. They had been a lot less than forthcoming, which made it hard to tell. As for John Doe, they didn't know for certain that it was Dare. Even so, they needed to find Isaac.

When they went to see the fisherman again, he was on the back porch cleaning the day's catch. Newspaper was spread on a wooden table and a hose snaked from an old sink. The dog walked with Marti as far as the steps, then turned away. It must not like fish. Smart dog, Marti decided.

"You again." He kept scraping scales off of a large fish. Marti thought it must be a salmon. They looked a lot different filleted and without those big eyes.

"We thought maybe you had remembered something else," Vik said.

"An old liar like me? Of course not." He cut off the head, tails, and fins with a few strokes of a sharp knife.

"The trouble is, sir, that if you really did see anything out there, or anyone, and they saw you, they might think it was important that you didn't tell anyone."

"Important enough to kill me? Come on, Detective, this is Lincoln Prairie, not some fictional TV town."

"Right," Vik said. "I used to think that way, too, until I started working Homicide."

The fisherman filleted the big fish and took the last of the day's catch from his bucket. "Anyone comes around here, young man, and you won't have to worry about him killing anyone anymore."

"I suppose you've got a gun."

"And a license to have it, and I'm a damned good shot. I was in the infantry in World War Two. Go out to the range every week."

There was a rasping noise as he began scaling. "Decent of you to come by and warn me, though. I hadn't given it a thought, to tell the truth."

"Does that mean you did see something, sir?"

"Doesn't mean a damned thing, except that I can take care of myself."

"Yes, sir," Vik said. "Just in case, though . . ." He handed him another card.

"Miserable old coot," Vik said as soon as they cleared the front yard.

He went with her on her rounds to look for Isaac, first the tree stump at the old place, then the garage, then the house.

"I think I'd give up and go to a shelter," he said when she showed him the blankets. "Then again, maybe they were like this when he got them."

Marti hadn't thought of that. It was possible. "He's gone to ground, Vik. You'd think he'd still be here if this wasn't recent. Why else would he disappear?"

"If that is the case, it's a good thing he wasn't asleep when this happened."

Queenie gave them a sour look when they walked into the bar. "What y'all doing?" she asked. "Planning on holding a convention here?" She looked up at Vik. "Don't tell me. You're a friend of Isaac's, too."

Vik's eyebrows met and his eyes became fierce.

"Do you have a problem with that?" he asked.

"No, sir." She gave Marti a sly smile. "It's just that Isaac seems to have found a lot of friends lately. Maybe that's why he's taken to hiding."

"Who?" Marti asked.

"You ain't even the first to ask about him today."

"Who?" Marti repeated.

"Just some kid. I truly don't know his name. Belongs to the gang."

"Which gang?"

"The one that owns this street, that's which one. Y'all thinking about taking the streets back or something? There're those of us who'd sure appreciate it. That is, if you're not all too busy looking after your friends."

"Has Dare turned up yet?"

"Ain't seen hide nor hair of him in over a week. Isaac says he's just been shackin' up with some woman, which is damned hard to believe, but I been watching for him all day. If you see him, tell him he owes me some money for his friend. Always good about paying their tabs, them boys are. Both of 'em. But Isaac? Real tight with his money. Ain't getting up off of nothing as long as Dare will."

Outside, Marti said, "I saw a kid in that alley—a little kid. I don't think he's was as old as Theo. He was wearing gang colors, though."

"Then the older ones might have put him up to asking," Vik said.

"But why would they care about a couple of drunks?"

"Maybe that's what the slash marks are all about. Maybe the gang members have been harassing them. Maybe that's why we can't find Isaac. You know how kids are once they start picking on somebody. If they smell just a hint of weakness, they never let up."

"This was not a good move," Marti said. "Those two should have found another place where they could keep to themselves. I think they might be the only homeless people I know who are that way on purpose."

They drove around the neighborhood a few more times, but Marti didn't see any young boy she recognized.

The lineup for the flasher was on when they returned to the precinct.

"Don't tell me," Vik said to the desk sergeant. "No birthmark, so they had to bring in all the ladies, just to be sure nobody could recognize it."

"No, there was a birthmark."

"There was!" Marti said.

"Sure thing. The witness described it to a tee. Now they're determining how many other women can identify it."

"How are they doing this?" Marti asked. "Do I want to know?"

"Only their you know whats are exposed right now. I think they're going to follow that up with a lineup of all nine suspects, unexposed."

Vik got to the point. "Have they found the costume?"

"Can't say. They did get a search warrant based on the make on the penis."

As they walked to the elevator, Vik shook his head. "None of them was old, Marti. Whatever happened to dirty old men?"

"From the looks of it, they're either starting a lot younger or they were always starting young and we didn't catch them until they were older."

Half an hour later, they watched through a two-way mirror as Slim and Cowboy interrogated the man with the birthmark. He had a ponytail and a long neck to go with his long nose. Marti didn't want to be there. There was something about this kind of human depravity that bothered her in a way that nothing else did. She thought of rape, indecent exposure, molestation, stalking, and similar crimes as acts of terrorism, committed most frequently against woman and children—acts that the perpetrator enjoyed.

The flasher sat in a wooden chair at a small square table, facing one of the putrid pink walls, a shade that was supposed to soothe offenders. His foot wiggled; his hands were in constant motion. He smoothed his hair, twisted the ponytail, stroked his sideburns, tugged at his ears. The pink walls weren't having any effect. This wasn't his first arrest, but with luck, it would be his first conviction. Slim and Cowboy remained standing.

"Come on, man," Slim said, "Seven women identified that birthmark. Your mother told us it was there."

"My mother? You told my mother about this?"

"Sure," Slim said. "While we were searching her house."

"My mother's house? What were you doing there? Why did you go to my house?"

"Hey, man, we got six costumes. Six orange jack-o-lantern's with big mouths for that itty-bitty tongue of yours."

"Oh my God." His voice was trembling. "Did my mother see that, too?"

"She sure did. She wanted to know who made them. The one that opened like an umbrella was real clever."

"Oh my God. This isn't happening. This can't be happening. My mother, oh my God." He looked up. "Is this going to be in the newspaper?"

Slim grinned. "Sure is, man. It'll make the ten o'clock news."

"The neighbors. My poor mother, the neighbors. Oh God."

He put his head down and cried. "Nobody got scared this year. They were even trying to catch me. And they were making fun of me, too. I just wanted them to be scared, that's all. I wanted everyone to stop laughing."

"I don't know how to tell you this, man," Cowboy said. "But they are laughing like hell now. And the whole damned town, and maybe the state and half the country will be laughing this time tomorrow."

The flasher sobbed.

The lieutenant came to their office while they were checking out the costumes.

"So, how did you four like working together?"

Cowboy shook his head. "I didn't like it worth a damn, but I guess it paid off."

"MacAlister and Jessenovik just bring a different set of skills to the game," Dirkowitz said. "The way we're set up, with the detective teams specializing in a specific area, we get faster results, and better arrest records, but most of the cross-training gets done in the lower ranks."

He helped himself to some coffee. "I just came to thank you. Keep this under your hat until the announcement makes the news later on this week, but the First Lady will be in town from Friday until Sunday. The department will be getting a little attention because our crime rates are down and we've got a solid community policing program with the bike patrol and the foot patrols. She's going to do the schoolchildren and senior citizen thing, hospital patient photo-op things, too. All I needed was this jerk wagging his 'tongue' and calling in his little threats for the national news media. I'd give you all a day off if I could. Since I can't, feel free to let me know that I owe you."

Marti knew what she was going to ask for—occasional backup so she could squeeze in a little more time with her kids.

"Right," Slim said when Dirkowitz was out the door. "I can hear myself now. 'Say, man, Lieutenant Dirkowitz, sir, you owe me.' "

"Hell," Vik said. "Homicide dicks do that all the time."

"Like I believe you. Say, man, check it out, the shiny pumpkin costume. It looks like he had to unfold it, then put these little rods in the seams to make it stand out. This old felt one was flat. He must have felt like hot stuff when he figured out that umbrella contraption."

"Poor guy," Cowboy said. "Captured at the top of his game, and by a bunch of women who refused to be afraid. Damned shame when you finally perfect something and the intended victims see that you get taken out of action."

"And his poor mother," Vik said.

"Hell," Slim said. "She might not have known just what he was doing, but she sure wasn't too surprised to find out something was going on."

"And the neighbors were already bringing food while the evidence techs were there," Cowboy added. "She's already talked with the *News-Times*, loves the attention, and ain't upset worth a damn. Some folks are just born to be celebrities."

16

He followed Joanna when she left the house. She was on her bike and didn't seem to be in any hurry. It was easy to keep up. She went to the supermarket. Inside, he thought he would lose her, but with her height, he was able to keep her in sight. It was crowded enough so that he wouldn't stand out at all. She went right to the produce department and selected apples, a bunch of carrots with the tops on, a head of cabbage, tomatoes, and a rutabaga. He picked up a bunch of bananas and put them into his basket. He hated bananas, but they were closest to the rutabagas. He looked right at her as she picked one out. She didn't even know he was there.

Marti and Vik made one more tour of Isaac's haunts without success, then headed for the city. It was almost eight when they left Lincoln Prairie, the average interstate trucker's favorite time to fly the expressways of Chicago. This time when Marti called, she advised Shenea that they were coming. When Shenea objected, Marti told her she would see her in about an hour and that she had better stay put.

"What did they do here?" Vik said. "Two years they worked on this expressway, and what has it done for traffic? You see any difference? I don't."

He was upset about the flasher. So was she. There was a good reason why neither of them worked Vice. There were different kinds of anger: the kind that gave you the resolve and perseverance to solve crimes, and the kind that ate away at you until you were bitter and blighted and blind to the good in the world. Slim and Cowboy had the personalities to deal with criminals like the flasher. Marti and Vik did not.

A sullen-faced Shenea answered the doorbell. She was wearing patent-leather pumps, black stockings, and a red outfit with a short skirt. If she did have someplace to go, Marti hoped she was in a hurry to get this over with. Marti took a seat in the ultra-modern living room and didn't say anything. Vik sat across from her and became engrossed in the multicolored abstract on the wall.

Shenea strode from the doorway to the window and turned to face them with her arms folded. "Well? What is it now? I've got better things to do."

"We just wanted to ask you a few more questions." Marti flipped open her notebook, scanned her notes, and asked half a dozen of the same questions she had asked the last time she was here. She got pretty much the same answers but took her time writing them down.

Shenea exhaled with obvious exasperation and kept checking her watch. "Look, I answered these questions the last time you were here. I've got someplace to go."

"Then tell us what you're holding back," Marti said. "What happened that you're not telling us."

"Why do you keep insisting that I know something?" Shenea almost shouted. "Ladiya is dead! She's dead." Tears sprang to her eyes and she wiped at them with wide, angry gestures. "She's dead, damn her. Why did she have to get mixed up with him?" She sniffled and tried to control the tears.

"You were best friends," Marti said. "I have a best friend, too. Now I'm widowed and she's divorced and we're sharing a house with our kids."

"Well, Ladiya and I won't be doing any of that now, will we? Never. We'll never do anything together again."

"What did Ladiya tell you, Shenea, that she wouldn't tell any-one else?"

Shenea cried quietly for a few minutes, then got up and left the room. Marti could hear water running. When Shenea returned, she was quiet and almost composed. She sat, twisting her hands in her lap. "Ladiya called me. She said she was pregnant and she wanted to get clean and have the baby." She took a deep breath. "Knox didn't want her to. He made arrangements for her to have an abortion. She was scared to death, said she had to go along with it or he'd kill her. I told her she could have another baby, later. She said no, that it was alive and she couldn't kill it. She said she had a plan, that she was running away. She said he'd never find her, but he did."

"What day did she call?"

"Friday, October twenty-third."

"Did she tell you where she was?"

"No."

"Whom she was with?"

"No."

"You knew her as well as anyone. Where did you think she might be? Whom did you think she might be with?"

"I . . . I don't know. I . . . I think she wanted me to tell her to come here. But I couldn't, not with him out there. And look what happened. I would be dead, too, if I had. I would! He would have killed me, too!"

"She was your best friend, and you couldn't offer to help her. I can understand that, given the circumstances. And you're right. If she had come here, you might be dead now, too." Marti waited, giving her time to think. "Ladiya has been dead for a week now. That's a long time, Shenea, too long when you have to find out who did it. The longer you hold out, the longer it takes us to get information, the harder it becomes to find the person who did it. Did she call you again?"

Shenea let out a little half-sob, took a deep breath, and blew her nose. "She didn't tell me where she was, or who was with her. I don't know how I can help you." She seemed composed as she sat with her hands in her lap and her head down.

"When did she call again?"

"Sunday night."

"Did she tell you where she was calling from?"

"No, she said that I shouldn't know, just in case he came looking for her here."

"What did she tell you?"

Shenea took a deep breath. "That she had called Knox's wife. That his wife told her a place to go where he would never look for her. That his wife was going to help her, bring her some money so she could get away from him. That she was checking into the hospital on Wednesday, for drug rehab."

Marti thought of several curse words but didn't say any out loud. Mrs. Knox had told him. Knowing how violent he was, she must have known what would happen. Then she must have made the phone call fingering her husband. At least that part backfired. If Shenea had told them this sooner, they might have been able to prevent all of it. They would have Knox in custody now.

As they were leaving, Shenea said, "It isn't that I didn't want to tell you. I promised that I wouldn't let her mother know, not until she was ready. And now you'll tell her, won't you?"

"Tell her what? That Ladiya was pregnant? That she had left Knox and was going into a rehab program so that she would have a healthy baby and be capable of taking care of her child?"

Shenea looked away. "I wanted to believe that. I really did want to. And I think Ladiya meant it when she said it, but . . . Ladiya . . . you don't know how she was with that man. It was as if she couldn't even think for herself."

Marti put her hands on Shenea's shoulders. "Ladiya is gone now. When she said she was going to get her life together, she meant it. That's all we know. I think that's enough. And I think believing that would ease her mother's pain just a little."

Shenea nodded. "Is it okay if I tell her?"

"I suppose so. But only if you do it right now."

For the first time, Shenea almost smiled.

Slim and Cowboy were still in the office when Marti got back to the precinct. Slim was using the typewriter, an older electric model that had been recycled from some secretary's desk to their office during an upgrade ten years ago. Slim typed so slowly that it might as well have been a manual.

"Damn." He aligned the correction paper and retyped four letters. He wasn't pretending to be a lousy typist just to get someone to do it for him. He really could not type. Marti felt sorry for him, but not sorry enough to volunteer.

Cowboy pushed his hat back and propped his feet on his desk. "You will not believe our flasher's porno collection."

"Do us a favor and don't show us," Vik said. He looked ready to bolt from the room if Cowboy tried.

"And he has a foot fetish. He's got a couple thousand dollars' worth of camera equipment, special lenses, you name it, and what does he do? He takes pictures of women's feet: fat feet, thin feet, bare feet, feet in sandals, high heels, everything but socks and tennis shoes. And the kicker is, his mother knows all about it. She thinks because he's taking pictures of women's feet that he's okay now. She even bought him most of the equipment."

"Cowboy," Vik warned. "It's been a long day."

"Oh, man. I suppose. The amazing thing is he really didn't want to hurt anyone, just get even because they were making fun of him. I kind of feel sorry for him."

Vik's expression suggested that Cowboy must be crazy. "You ever think about your victims?"

"Sure. But he didn't hurt anybody. Those women are all just fine. In fact, he'd better be glad that we caught him before *they* did. Those were some ladies with lynching on their minds. They just might have strung him up."

"Cowboy," Marti said. "You can't believe that everyone is okay?"

"This afternoon, I talked with everyone who's willing to testify," Slim said. "They are not even upset."

That was enough to convince Marti to make a few calls and make sure that counseling was available for anyone who wanted it.

She did not understand how two men who could be so empathetic with a rape victim could be so insensitive to something like this.

"Okay, Marti, I get you. Psychological violence. Sorry. This just

214

seems so minor after you see a woman beaten half to death and sexually assaulted."

"Domestic terrorism," Marti said. "Fear is fear. That's why we're here. So people don't have to live in fear. It's time you two got your butts to a refresher course on assisting victims of sexual assault."

As Vik walked her to her car, he said, "You know, MacAlister, I think I've finally got it figured out. A killer isn't necessarily crazy. He might be, for a moment in time, or all of the time, or not at all. The perps Slim and Cowboy work with, they are nuts, always, even when other people think they are sane. Feet, Marti. Think of it. This guy gets turned on by feet. If I had to go around catching idiots like that all the time, I'd go crazy, too. At least we have enough cases of unpremeditated crime to kind of put a human face on it, but these types who do these same bizarre things over and over, year after year . . . I don't understand. You worked Vice. Do you get it?"

"I worked Vice for less than a week, not to long after I came out of the academy. I was a decoy pretending to be a prostitute. It was the assignment of choice for female uniforms back then."

"Catch anyone?"

"None of the johns who cruised my corner would come closer than rolling down their window and rolling it up. The lieutenant said I projected a hostile attitude, and he moved me to a bunco unit."

On the way home, Marti made a tour of the wooded area where Isaac's house used to be, with no results. She drove down the alley where the garage was and past the street where he'd been staying a few days ago. Nothing. Disappointed, she headed home.

As she turned down her street, still preoccupied with Isaac and Dare, she thought of the priest, Father Corrigan. Maybe he knew something. Maybe he was sheltering Isaac. On impulse, she made a U-turn and went to the rectory. Several lights were on, so she rang the bell.

Father Corrigan opened the door. They were acquainted, but

she hadn't been inside a rectory in quite a while. This one turned out to be in a wonderful old house with wainscoting and polished hardwood floors. Real wood was in the fireplace and smiling cherubs were carved into the corners of the mantel.

"Would you mind coming into the kitchen, Detective Mac? I do some of my best work there."

His work turned out to be calligraphy. "There's something about it, you know, it's something of a tradition. It was always a task for the monks. I find it quite soothing." He handed her a greeting card. St. Francis, in a typical pose with a bird on his hand, was embossed in gold on the front. The priest had inscribed a biblical verse. "The cards are made by Poor Clares. I do the inscriptions and send them back. They sell them by mail order and use the money to help fund a soup kitchen."

Marti thought the work probably sold for half of what it was worth.

"You've not come to look at this, though, have you now? It's Isaac you must be looking for. Or has something happened to him?"

His second question answered hers. "You haven't seen him in the past day or two, have you?"

"No. But he told me he couldn't find Dare. Is Isaac missing now, too?"

Marti nodded. She felt more disappointed than she thought she would, and much more apprehensive. "I'm not sure what's going on with those two, but I would feel much better if I could find out where Isaac is. If you hear from him, please let me know. I know about the secrecy thing, but just call and say hi and I'll know."

The old priest smiled. "My dear young lady, you know much less about the 'secrecy thing' than you think you do. The phone call would not be tantamount to violating it. And if it was, I have made so many exceptions to so many rules in my lifetime that the good Lord will either hold me accountable for another or overlook it. If I see or hear from Isaac, I will certainly call."

Marti had a cup of tea and a scone with orange marmalade before she went home.

He walked for a long time in a quiet part of town, along nearly deserted streets lit by porch lights and streetlights. He was too elated to sleep. What a wonderful day this had been. Shopping with Joanna. Just the two of them, standing so close, touching. It was going to be so wonderful—that brief moment when they were together. She was a wonderful light that would shine brightly while he held her and glow until he extinguished the flame.

17

As soon as he let himself in Tuesday morning and saw that the kitchen had been cleaned, he went to the refrigerator to see what Joanna had done with the vegetables. He found a large bowl filled with soup. He put it on the counter and removed the lid. Poking around with a fork, he identified the carrots, rutabaga, cabbage, and tomatoes they had purchased together last night. He spooned some into a bowl and put it in the microwave to heat. He wasn't a big soup eater, especially if there was no meat, but this soup was special. Joanna had made it for him. It tasted much better than he expected. Whatever seasonings she had used had enhanced the flavor of the vegetables. It was the first meal she had ever cooked for him. In all probability, it would also be the last. He washed the bowl and spoon and returned them to the cabinet and drawer.

Upstairs, everything was neater than usual in the kids' rooms. Sharon's room was its usual mess. The cop must have taken the pile of suits and slacks and blouses that had been accumulating on the chair in her room to the cleaners. He went to the closet. The locked box had not been moved. Every cop had a backup gun and he was certain this was where she kept hers. He pulled a chair over and climbed on it to get a better look at the box without touching it. It was made like a strongbox and had a keyhole, not a padlock, and it was covered with dust. Didn't she ever clean her backup, or practice with it? Where did she keep the key? Even if she kept one key with her, she would have at least one spare.

He put on a pair of latex gloves and searched the room, one small area at a time, careful to observe how everything was placed before he moved anything, careful to put everything back the same way. This was a cop's room. She was such a consistent slob that the disorder had become for her what order was to most other people. He would bet she could put her hands on just about anything in here. He could not find the key. He looked around the room, certain he hadn't missed anything. Next, he checked the walls for anything that felt different and the floor for loose places in the carpet. He had turned the drawers upside down when he went through them. The furniture was old, the bureau and night-stand on legs and not flush to the floor. He looked underneath and behind them without finding anything but rolls of dust. Wherever the key was, it was not in this room. Too bad. He would love to kill her with her own gun.

He went downstairs and flipped through the mail that had been left on the table by the front door. Sharon had gotten another parking ticket. Her Visa bill hadn't been opened, but based on past bills that he had perused, the card was maxed out and the payment overdue. He pocketed the telephone bill, not that they ever called anyplace interesting. He'd check that out later, see how often the cop had called her mother in Arkansas, how often Sharon called her ex-husband at his job in Chicago.

The dog watched him as he went to the basement but didn't come near him. "You, too, big boy," he promised. "You, too."

He turned on the computer and browsed everyone's files. Nothing had changed. Those first few days, all of this had been interesting, different, new. Now he was bored by the sameness of this house, and the predictability of those who lived here. He turned off the computer. It was time. He had discovered one flaw in his plan. He did not know what they did when they were here in the evening. He had some idea of when they went to bed from watching the lights at their windows, but he didn't know what their nightly routine was, or even if they had a routine. He couldn't kill them without knowing everything. He couldn't risk being surprised or making a mistake. He had decided to spend at least one evening with them, perhaps two. It still required a little more planning, but he should be ready for a run-through by tomorrow morning. By tomorrow night, he would be their invisible guest.

Marti and Vik found out about the raid on the drug house at roll call. The Narcotics Unit had timed it right and confiscated a major drug shipment as well as a cache of arms. She was pleased to hear about both, but it didn't make any difference one way or the other as far as her cases were concerned. Maybe living in that neighborhood would be easier for Isaac now, if Isaac was still living.

"Nothing from the coroner's office yet on our John Doe?" she asked.

"They've contacted the VA hospital and requested X rays and dental records. It shouldn't take long. The VA always cooperates."

Marti threw half a cup of cold coffee into the pot holding the spider plant and made a fresh cup. "As much as I would prefer that this John Doe be a stranger from another town, we do have to establish identity." She decided to start with an easy out and called Dare's relatives. They had been so hostile when she called to see if they would file a missing persons' report, she thought they might hang up if she called again. The second time, she lucked out. Dare's mother and father refused to come to the telephone, but Marti spoke with an aunt, who said the police should come over.

"It sure sounds odd hearing Dare called George Washington." Marti stood up and reached for her jacket. "Let's go. Someone will talk to us, the aunt, if nobody else."

The address turned out to be a two-story Victorian six and half blocks from the place where Dare and Isaac had been staying. It was a street of older homes, a few in need of painting, but none in disrepair. The yard was tidy and fenced in. A big older-model Chevy was in the driveway. There was a BEWARE OF DOG sign posted on the gate, but no sign of an animal. A heavyset woman opened the door. She had light skin, several chins, and wore glasses with thick lenses.

"Are you the officer I just talked to?" She was the aunt. Marti recognized her voice. "Why, I had no idea you were one of us," she said to Marti, giving Vik a look that clearly indicated he was not "one of us."

"We'd like to speak with—"

"Yes, I'm sure you would. Trouble is, they don't want to talk with you."

"Ma'am, this is no longer a case of a missing person. It's now a possible homicide."

"A what?"

Marti hoped she could shock the woman into being more co-operative.

"We found a body at the beach, ma'am. A black male, approximate age, forty-five. We can't figure out who he is. The problem is decomposition."

The woman's eyes widened.

"He's been dead close to a week, ma'am, and we're having a hard time making an identification. Forensics is working on it, but—"

The aunt gasped.

"We haven't been able to locate Dare and now a friend of Dare's has gone missing, as well. . . ."

"Dear Lord in heaven. You just come right on in." She hesitated and looked at Vik. "Both of you."

The front door opened on a small living room with furniture that wasn't so much mismatched as it was eclectic. It reminded Marti of the house that belonged to her maiden aunt—the one who had never married—with Grandmother's sideboard and a cousin's coffee table and a deceased great-aunt's favorite chair.

"Now, Zetta," Dare's aunt said, "you just hush up before you even open your mouth. These folks got a dead man on their hands and they're trying to figure out who it is."

Zetta was sitting near an electric heater with a blanket over her legs and a walker beside her chair. The muscles on the right side of her face sagged. Marti looked at her hands, considered the lack of wrinkles and the sparseness of gray hair, and estimated that she

221

was probably close to sixty. Although she wasn't more than half the size of the woman who opened the door, there was a close resemblance. There was no sign of Dare's father, but a thin layer of smoke above what appeared to be a new leather recliner suggested he might have been sitting there just a few minutes before.

"Are you Dare's mother, ma'am?"

"Birthed eleven children, I did." Her speech was slurred, but Marti didn't have any problem understanding what she said. "Ain't had nare a one by that name."

"Zetta! You know they're talking about George Washington, and he sure enough is your child."

"Don't know no such thing."

"Zetta, we talking life and death now. This ain't about not allowing no liquor in the house or not letting George Washington come home until he's sober. We talking life and death, and we gonna help these officers, now." She looked at Vik again. "Both of them."

"What you mean, life and death?"

"I mean they found a body down by the lake and they thinking it might be our George."

If Dare's mother's face could have turned ashen, it would have. Instead, it became a dusky kind of gray.

"What you saying, girl? Ain't nothing wrong with George Washington that getting saved won't cure. He's just off drunk somewhere."

"Lord knows, I hope that's true, but we best be talking to these police officers right now so we can all find out."

"Thomas Jefferson," Dare's mother called. Her voice was weak and trembly. "Thomas Jefferson, you be coming in here, now."

Marti expected to see Dare's father, but Thomas Jefferson turned out to be a middle-aged man who looked a lot like Dare.

"Thomas Jefferson is Zetta's oldest." She spoke with pride. "He's older than George Washington by a year. Named for our daddy, he was. Been to college, he has, went right out to the College of Lake County and got himself a certificate in electrical repair." She leaned toward him and said in a quiet voice, "We know you been seeing your brother."

Dare's mother leaned forward. "The only reason . . ." She wagged her finger at Marti. "The only reason that boy ain't been allowed to come in my house is because I won't have nothing in here pertaining to the devil. And that means that liquor he be drinking and that weed he be smoking. Ain't none of my children but him turned out willful and disobedient. I got grands coming up now. I ain't allowing that one bad apple to spoil the barrelful. 'Cast out the devil from among you. Who is my kin? He who believes in and relies on the Word of God.' "

"Yes, ma'am," Marti said. It was something she understood. Some called it "tough love" now, but this went deeper than that. The quotes from Scripture were not exact, but this woman's decision to exclude her son was based on a complete conviction in the literal translation of the Bible. Marti could still remember a neighbor woman like her.

"Thomas Jefferson." Zetta pointed to her firstborn son. "You tell this officer here whatever you be knowing about your brother."

"I ain't seen him now in about a couple of weeks."

"What was he wearing the last time you saw him?" Marti asked.

"He was clean, ma'am. He had on some jeans and a turtleneck, and they were clean. He needed a winter coat, and I tried to get him to go with me to get one, but he said he'd have one before the month was out. Independent, he was. I let him be."

"Did you talk about anything else? Was he worried about anything? Frightened?"

"Who, George Washington? I've never seen him when he wasn't in a good mood."

"You ain't never seen him when he was sober," his mother said.

"You could be right about that, Momma. There was one thing, though. He said his stomach was giving him a lot of trouble. Said he had been to the VA hospital to see what was wrong. He wouldn't tell me what it was."

"VA hospital?" Marti said.

"Yes, ma'am. He was in the service for a while, and he got discharged on a seventy percent disability."

"Seventy percent drinking."

"Yes, Momma. More than likely. 'Course, he did get them medals. Anyhow, maybe that's where he is."

"We need to know if he wears dentures," Marti said.

"He got his teeth knocked out in Saint Louis. He might have gotten them then. First time I saw him after he got back, he was joking about his teeth not being his."

Thomas Jefferson also confirmed that Dare's left leg had been broken. He described several scars and birthmarks, but it wasn't possible to make an identification based on that.

Dare's mother held her chin high and watched them leave. If their John Doe was Dare, she would accept it with the conviction of the righteous. Unlike Ladiya's mother, there would be no second guessing or what if's or if only's.

"I wonder if she named one Herbert Hoover," Vik said as they walked to the car.

"Theodore or Franklin Roosevelt is a better bet. I'll let the coroner's office know about this when we get back."

Marti conducted another unsuccessful search for Isaac. When she returned to the precinct, there was a message to call a doctor. The name wasn't familiar.

They didn't put her on hold when she returned his call.

"Are you the officer who talked with Mrs. DeMarco?"

"Yes."

"Good. I've only got a minute, but I wanted to tell you this myself. I live across the street from her, three houses down. I went home for lunch last Monday after surgery. It was a little early to go to the office. And I saw this car kind of cruising around, moving slowly. It didn't belong to anyone in the neighborhood, so I reported it to you people. I don't know if you keep records of routine calls, and I never heard back. You might want to check."

His description matched Knox's car. Marti put in a request to have the phone records checked. Then she began making the

224

same telephone inquiries to the law-enforcement agencies and hospitals and morgues for Isaac that she had made for Dare, once again without results.

"That shouldn't surprise you," Vik said. "The man's indigent. And most of the time he smells. Bad. People have been avoiding him for years and he's been avoiding them. He has to be good at it by now."

"I don't like the way he disappeared, Vik. It isn't like he packed up and left."

"Street people are somewhat mobile, Marti. It isn't like they have to hire a mover or anything. And when your mode of transportation is your feet, you have to acquire the habit of packing light."

"If he had, Queenie sure would know."

"Maybe she does."

"I don't think so."

"Maybe," Vik conceded. "But Isaac is not your average citizen. We don't know if he has any relatives or where they are if he does. We don't know anything about Isaac at all." That said, Vik picked up the telephone and helped her make the calls. They had been at it for about half an hour when Lupe Torres came in.

"Congratulations!" Marti said.

Lupe sprawled in a chair with her legs stretched out and her arms folded across her chest. She looked exhausted, but she jiggled her foot, still wired from the action. "Thanks, but we got the info on the shipment from a snitch. How's the search for Isaac coming along?"

"Nothing."

"And Dare?"

Marti couldn't answer.

"It looks like he might be our John Doe," Vik said.

Lupe began toying with a lock of hair. "There was something I wanted you to take a look at."

"What?"

"Fragments of sunglasses, splattered with blood. The lab has a stat order to see if the blood type matches your male victim's."

Marti said, "Sunglasses? Dare wore them year-round."

"He's the first person I thought of, too."

"Lupe, you've worked that beat for a couple of years now. You've seen a lot more of Isaac and Dare since they moved there than I have. I wouldn't know a friend of theirs if I tripped over him. Do you know of anyone?"

"Every time I saw Dare, he was talking to somebody. I might have seen Isaac twice. If I did, he was alone. There're a couple of guys sharing a place not too far from theirs. I can't say I've seen them with Dare, but odds are they knew him."

"Maybe we should take a ride, ask around. Maybe somebody saw something."

When Marti walked into Queenie's again, this time with Lupe, and her eyes adjusted to the dimness, she could tell by the expression on Queenie's face that the woman was not glad to see them.

"Mmhmm," Queenie said. "Another friend of Isaac's?"

Lupe tilted her cap back and let her hand rest on her baton. Marti gathered that she and Queenie were not on good terms.

"I expected you'd be back, Officer Neighborhood Watch. What is it this time?"

"We're not looking for minors," Lupe said.

"Seen Isaac?" Marti asked.

"No, I ain't seen him."

Marti knew there was no way he could go this long without a drink. She couldn't think of another place where he could get one, and his check didn't come until tomorrow. "Then I don't suppose you've seen Dare, either?"

"Ain't seen nare one of them. I sure was expecting to see Isaac by now, though."

"Can you remember what Dare was wearing the last time you saw him?"

"You've got to be kidding."

"Give it a try, Queenie."

"I ain't got to. I'd have a hard time telling you what I was wearing the last time I saw him. Hell, I'd have a hard time telling you what either of us was wearing the last time I saw you. I'm color-blind. They tell me everything I see is some shade of gray and blue. I can tell you what he was drinking. House whiskey with a draft beer chaser. Isaac prefers wine."

"Have you seen that kid around?" Marti asked.

"What kid?"

Marti gave her a hard stare. No doubt Queenie was afraid.

"The little kid wearing the gang colors."

"That one? The one you're suppose to be protecting us from? What's the matter? You can't find him? Well then, I ain't seen him, neither."

Marti handed her a card. "Call me if you do."

"Sure thing."

Marti didn't think she would, but sometimes people surprised her.

Another sweep of the neighborhood turned up nothing. No Isaac, no kid.

"Makes them twitchy," Lupe said, "having a drug raid go down. You never know who your friends are until they get locked up. There're always some who will try to sing their way out. You'll want to question them."

"Not yet. You're holding them all without charging them for twenty-four hours, aren't you?

"Damned straight. And we timed it so they might miss court in the morning and we could buy a little more time before the judge set bail."

"Good. We need a lot more than we've got now. Better to wait than let them know how much or, in this case, how little we know. Right now, they think they're just looking at drug-related charges. How tight is your case?"

"We sat on this for almost four months. Knew what was going on. It wasn't until the snitch gave us the date, though, that we had what we needed to go in. We've got them. The only way they'll get away with any of it is with a plea. At least half of them are looking at some serious time."

As they drove, Lupe watched out the window. These streets

were usually busy until bad weather hit. Today, everything was quiet. There wasn't a gang color to be seen. Even the young children were inside.

"Try this house," Lupe said as they approached what looked like an empty wood-framed building that was partially boarded up. "I've seen Dare with a guy who lives here, if he's at home."

Marti marveled at how easily both she and Lupe had come to call these abandoned and dilapidated buildings someone's home.

Lupe knocked, and after a few minutes, they heard noises inside. There was a hole drilled into the plywood that covered part of the door. Someone was looking out at them. Marti put her hand in her purse, closed it around the grip of her Beretta, and stood to one side. After a moment, the door opened with a soft squeak.

"Say, man," Lupe said.

He held up both hands. "We ain't done nothing, Officer Torres."

"I know that. You know you're straight with me. I was just wondering if you'd seen Dare lately, or his friend Isaac."

The man's right hand shook as if from a palsy as he scratched his beard with his left hand. "I think I did. Let me think on it for a minute." He seemed slow, almost retarded. "I could have. I wonder, when did we cook them mountain oysters? He ate some of them with us."

"Isaac or Dare?"

He gave her a blank look.

"Who was here eating mountain oysters?" Lupe asked.

He frowned. "Isaac, I think."

"What are mountain oysters, man?"

He grinned. All of his top teeth were missing and half of the bottom ones. "Hog nuts, ma'am."

Lupe made a face. "Did it rain the day he was here?"

"No, he came by after the rain."

That was still within range of when Isaac had last seen Dare.

"Drizzle, was it kind of drizzly?"

"Umm . . . It . . . it was after that."

The weather been misty one day after Dare went missing, so it could have been Isaac.

"Can you remember what Dare was wearing the last time you saw him?"

The man gave her another near-toothless grin. "Had him some jeans on and a black shirt like this one." He was wearing a green turtleneck. "Keep you warm."

"You seem sure about that."

"We went to Sally's together. I got these pants, too." He looked down at his paint-stained khakis. The frayed cuffs didn't quite reach the top of his tennis shoes. "They let us have it free on account of they was going to throw it away."

Lupe took something out of her pocket and gave it to him. "You take care of yourself."

"Yes, ma'am, Officer. Sure was nice talking to you."

"What did you give him?" Marti asked as they got into the car.

"A food voucher. Community foot patrol has a small discretionary fund that citizens and businesses can contribute to. It makes it a lot easier to walk a beat when you can do something, even if it isn't much. Looks like your male victim might be Dare."

"We're pretty sure he is. Just waiting for the coroner's office to make it official."

"Marti, there's something you need to know about Dare. He was my snitch."

"What?"

"I didn't recruit him. He came to *me*. Talked about that drug house being a bad place with so many kids going in there. Said he'd find out whatever I needed to know. He called me on a Thursday night, two weeks ago, told me when this shipment was coming in."

"And he's been missing since that Friday."

"And we might have found his sunglasses in there. I'm sorry about not being able to tell you."

"No. That's all right. My husband was a narc. I know the drill."

"Marti, if Isaac knew about the shipment, too . . ."

"Don't even think it," Marti said.

They met Vik at the drug house for a quick tour. It was a two-story brick bungalow, with close-cropped grass and no flowers, trees, or bushes in the yard. Shades were pulled down at each window. The door had been busted off its hinges and was not yet secured. Inside, the foyer was paneled with oak. Slots had been cut into the door to accommodate the exchange of drugs and money, and metal plates protected the locks.

"We think we might have someone here who thinks on one cylinder," Lupe said. "All of this up front, and we accessed the interior through the back door—with one hit. When the door went down, we were right in the kitchen."

This place was nothing like the ramshackle, roach-infested drug houses Marti had seen in Chicago. People lived here, and lived quite well. There was wall-to-wall carpeting throughout, an intercom system, a spacious kitchen and dining area, a family room with a large-screen TV.

"Come in here," Lupe said. She led them into a small den with a computer. "Check this out." She accessed a program and pulled up a listing of names and addresses. "Some of the names we recognize as dealers and gang bangers. We could be sitting on a gold mine, and this idiot didn't even make it hard for us. Not a single password. Turn on the computer go to the list named 'Addresses,' and print it."

The paneled basement had bright overhead lighting. One area was set up like an assembly line, with two long tables pushed together and stools on each side.

"They packaged the shit down here," Lupe said. "We've got a whole shipment, partially packaged. This is where they were when we came in. Nobody guarding upstairs, nothing. And no plan. The guns were locked in that closet, except for the ones kept upstairs for when they were open for business."

"I wonder why they felt so safe here," Marti said. "The only ones they protected themselves against were their customers."

"Well, except for us, that's where their biggest threat was.

Everyone involved in this operation was related. That's why we couldn't get anyone inside. Maybe they were a close-knit family. Obviously, they thought they were too clever to get caught."

"Where did you find the fragments from the sunglasses?"

Lupe led them to a small windowless corner room. On two sides, the brick foundation was exposed. The floor was concrete.

"Those stains are blood," Lupe said.

"I'll admit that Isaac was antisocial and Dare was nosy, and they didn't do much of anything besides drink, but they didn't cause any trouble," Vik said when they returned to the precinct.

"I don't know where else to look for Isaac."

"Let's not go to the coker plant. Three bodies there would be stretching it."

He had a stack of reports on his desk.

"What have you got?"

"A transcript of the doctor's call. Same description of the car. A report from the beat cop. No sign of the car when he got there. That places Knox at the scene."

Vik called the state's attorney office and relayed the additional information.

"We've got a warrant out for Knox. State police and the sheriff's department are working on locating him. Everything's progressing at the usual speed—slow motion." He picked up the reports again. "Nothing much from Forensics. The gun we found at the wi—at Ms. Stiles's had been fired recently. Reported stolen four years ago during a burglary downstate. We have no casings for comparison checks. So much for that. The coroner's office says someone is working on what they got at the drug house as we speak. Lab work on the blood samples shouldn't take long. If we can match the sample on the fragments of sunglasses with the victim's blood, establish who the victim is, get some evidence to support a motive, and identify opportunity—"

"Come on, Jessenovik. Let's not linger on the weaknesses in this case."

"Well, we can start talking to these guys about murder, then. With eleven of them under arrest, somebody is bound to turn state's evidence."

The coroner's office called with a positive ID on the John Doe.

"It's Dare," Marti said. "God help Isaac."

J.D. went right home after school. He would have hung out for a while if it wasn't for this morning's raid, but now everyone was lying low. He didn't know too much about what had happened, or who had been arrested, but the word had been passed at recess: Keep off the streets for a few days. If it wasn't for him telling about Dare and then telling them where Dare's friend was, twice, he would be mad because he couldn't hang out. As it was, he didn't want the cops looking at him, looking for him, or looking anyplace where he was. In fact, he'd like to leave town for a few days, maybe even a month.

He thought these dudes were so cool, so smart. How could they have been so stupid to sell to a cop? Even he knew better than that. Anyone could spot a cop. When he was in charge of things, dumb stuff like that wouldn't happen anymore. He was way too smart for that.

Nobody was there when he got home. His parents always told him to look after his little brother, and if he didn't find out where the little dude was, they'd yell at him. But neither of them needed anybody looking after them. They knew how to take care of themselves. The old man didn't even bother telling them when to come in anymore. If he did, he'd have to stay home to make sure they came in. Tonight was one of Ma's bingo nights, so Dad wouldn't even bother to show up before ten.

J.D. went into the kitchen. There weren't any clean glasses, so he rinsed one out. It would sure be nice if his mother would clean this place up. The kitchen was supposed to be his job, but he couldn't be bothered anymore, no matter how much she yelled. The worse thing that could happen was that his father would hit him. He didn't intend to put up with that too much longer. If he dropped the old dude once, he'd leave him alone. J.D. read the note telling him what to fix for supper and crumpled it up. Steak, he decided after looking through the packages in the freezer. He didn't take one out for his brother. Little dude could fix whatever he wanted.

It was so quiet, he turned on the TV in the kitchen as well as the ones in the family room and his bedroom. He hated coming home. Better to be anyplace else. Except for today. And tomorrow. What was he going to do? He didn't know what had happened to Dare and his friend. He didn't want to care what had happened to them. He didn't care about either one of them at all. But he had told. It hadn't seemed like much at the time, letting them know Dare was hanging real close to that booth at Queenie's while they was talking with them dudes with the funny accents, that lots of times Dare pretended to be asleep when he wasn't just so he could eavesdrop. He thought telling them might be enough so he could get something important to do. But since Dare and Isaac weren't around anymore, there must have been more to it than he knew. And that meant they had tricked him, telling him it was no big thing. No, they hadn't tricked him. Two drunks weren't a big thing, not to them. And he shouldn't let it be important to him. Except that the cops were looking for Dare's friend. And the cops had raided their main house this morning. The one place that was supposed to be safe.

The news came on and J.D. flipped to a channel that was showing cartoons. He wanted to join the gang to have fun, to have someone to hang out with. They hadn't asked him to join; he had asked in. He thought it would be exciting, being a gang member, and sometimes it was. He wanted to show them how smart he was, what he could do, and he had. What if he had done too much, got himself into so much trouble that he would go to jail? Everyone who had been arrested and in jail had to brag, but the things they were bragging about were scary. Just listening to them, he had known he was going to be careful. And now look at him. Three months in the gang and he might be in big trouble. J.D. stared at the cartoon. The cat was trying to get the damned bird again. When would that fool cat figure out that he wasn't going to win?

"It's hard to believe," Vik said. He was reading through some reports from the coroner's office and looking at faxes sent in by the VA hospital.

"That the government responded so quickly? It was the call to our congressman's office."

"No, not that. Dare and Isaac in the military. Who would ever associate either of them with cleanliness, order, and discipline? I can't even imagine them sleeping in a real bed, or using deodorant, or being clean-shaven. Can you imagine either of them being disciplined enough to get up at six in the morning, brush their teeth, get dressed, and go marching?"

"No." Just as she couldn't imagine them living in a real house. It was impossible to think of them as anything but benign, terminally drunk indigents. For all that she liked them, Isaac was just that. And Dare—she had just found out his real name a couple of days ago.

Vik organized the reports and put them into folders. "I don't think we're ready to talk with these guys about Dare yet."

"Why not?"

"Well, the blood sample matches, so we can tie him to the house. We even have a motive, but we can't connect Dare to anyone specific. All they have to do is deny knowing anything and stick to it. The state's attorney's office won't make a move with what we've got now, unless they're in search of something to barter with, and I think Dare's life was worth more than that. As dumb as these guys are, they might luck up and get lawyers smart enough to explain all this to them in a way that they can understand."

Marti put a call in to Lupe. She was going to find Isaac dead or alive. He was worth something, too. She gave Lupe the scant description she had of the boy in the alley and got the answer she expected. Lupe had no idea who it could be.

"But," Lupe said, "if he's as young as you think he is, and wearing gang colors, and if you think he's talked with Isaac or Dare, maybe I can pick up something. The trouble is, it could take days."

"Keep him in mind," Marti said.

Vik was drumming his fingers on the desk.

"If you don't stop that, Jessenovik . . ."

He did, then muttered something in Polish. "Damn. We can't find Knox, we can't find Isaac, and we can't get enough to talk to these jerks about Dare."

"Don't forget the ghosts."

Vik ran his fingers through his hair. "The witch, and the kid, the ghosts, the fisherman."

"We're going to have to track down that kid. Hell, I just got a glimpse of him. If we could just find Isaac."

"Alive." Vik shook his head. "Whatever else he was, he was harmless. I wonder how long he and Isaac had been on the streets together?"

"They were an odd match," Marti said. "For all that we connect them, how often did we actually see them together? They each kind of went their own way."

"But they looked out for each other," Vik said. "Up front, Dare seemed to do most of the taking care of, but those kind of relationships are seldom what they seem to be on the surface. Isaac gave Dare something he didn't have."

"A brother, maybe," Marti said. "A family."

The telephone interrupted.

"Our local Joe Trout wants to see us," Marti said.

"The fisherman?"

"You got it."

Vik reached for his coat.

The fisherman was in the front yard, playing Frisbee with the dog. When the dog saw them standing at the gate, she interrupted her game and ran to Marti, tail wagging.

"Good girl," Marti said, running her hand over her soft, silky red hair. "Good girl."

The fisherman came to the fence. "What do I have to do to get rid of you for good?"

"Is that why you called?" Marti asked.

"You could start with the truth," Vik said.

The fisherman took off a Cubs baseball cap and scratched his head.

"I've talked with the state's attorney's office," Vik said.

Marti knew it was a lie.

"They want to hit you with an obstruction of justice charge. I'm willing to suggest that they drop the whole thing if you just tell me the truth. If you can remember what that is."

The fisherman put his cap back on his head and stared in the direction of the setting sun.

"You got someone lined up to take care of the dog?" Vik asked.

"Why?"

"When they bring you in, you'll be locked up for twenty-four hours before you can make bail."

"And they call this a free country." His hand went to the bill of the hat and gave it a tug. He swore under his breath. "Land of the free. Home of the brave. It's a damned lie, all of it. If a man don't want to see nothing, he shouldn't have to. I told you, I didn't see no ghost."

"We know what you didn't see, sir," Vik said. "What we want to know is what you did see."

The fisherman shoved his hands into his pockets, muttered something else about a free country, and stared off into the distance.

"Road down past the old coker is real rutted," he said finally. "It ain't even a road really. Damned mud hole when it rains. So I'm going down there real slow. 'Fore sunup, it was. I could see a flashlight bobbing, but it wasn't nowhere near where I told you the ghost was. It was somewhere near the footbridge. I wasn't close to it. I could just make it out. I was still a bit away, by the old coker. Next thing, I hear an engine rev and a car comes tearing out of there, going too fast for road conditions, and the head-lights bouncing up and down. Me, I pulled into the parking lot at the coker plant, doused my lights, acted like I belonged there. They were so hell-bent on getting out of there, I don't think they paid no attention to me, least I hope not. I was kind of curious about the light and all, but once you found that girl's body, I didn't want to have nothing more to do with it."

Marti looked at Vik. His chin dipped just a little. She agreed. This had the ring of truth.

"What kind of car?" Vik asked.

"Can't say. Small. Made like a box. Too noisy to be new. Bad muffler. Not exactly a clunker. Small engine, too."

Marti thought for a minute before it hit her. He could be de-scribing the Ford Escort she saw parked in Knox's driveway.

"What color?"

"Can't say. Dark, though, whatever it was. Oh, and a stick shift."

"How could you tell?"

"I just know. That's all I ever drive."

"Anything else?"

"Something odd about the left headlight. It was on, but . . . funny angle, maybe. I don't know."

"Sir," Vik said. "Why didn't you just tell us this in the first place?"

The fisherman looked Vik in the eye. "Free country," he said. "I didn't want to get involved."

Marti called in the information about the car and told them to have somebody check Knox's driveway. Then she drove over to the rectory and told Father Corrigan about Dare. He hadn't seen Isaac, either. Their next stop was to Elizabeth Stiles.

As they sat in her tiny living room in the light of at least twenty candles, Marti wondered if they had interrupted something. The woman neither extinguished the candles nor turned on the lights. A dish of dried leaves sat in the center of the table, a pattern of rose petals surrounding it. Or maybe Marti was imagining a pat-tern.

Vik shifted, cleared his throat, shifted again. He leaned forward and clasped his hands. He was getting twitchy, and Marti was ready to leave herself.

"You arrested those people in that house," the woman said.

Marti didn't think Vik wanted to do the talking. "Yes, ma'am," she said.

"I've dug all around the rosebush, but I haven't found a thing. I was so hoping that was why her spirit was disturbed. For the past two nights, she has come as far as the second-floor landing and wept. Usually, she just wanders around a few nights a month."

"Did you see anything unusual at that house in the past couple of weeks?"

"No."

"What about the night . . . that friend of ours thought he saw a ghost?"

"No. Nothing. Everything was the same as always. It was a very quiet house except for all the comings and goings. They spent a lot of time in the basement, I think. At least the lights down there were always on all night."

"But you don't remember seeing anyone in the alley?"

"No."

"Did you hear anything unusual?"

"Well, that was one of the nights when the gunshots went off, but you already know that."

Gunshots, both nights. Their witch was going to have to come in and make a statement, but the timing was bad. Now that the Halloween flasher had been arrested, Cowboy and Slim were no longer the butt of every joke at the precinct. If the witch came in and said anything about this ghost while she was there, Marti and Vik would be the laughingstock for days.

As they were leaving, Ms. Stiles said, "The child you seek wanders alone."

"Thank you," Marti said. "Can you tell me anything else?"

"He looks for what is not there. Someone else must give him what he needs."

Vik pushed Marti aside and went down the outside stairs ahead of her. He locked the doors as soon as they were in the car. "She didn't know that, MacAlister. She didn't know that we're looking for a kid."

Marti was quite certain that she did.

Father Corrigan unlocked the rear door to the church and reached for a light switch as he went inside. It was an old church, one of the first Catholic churches to be built in Lincoln Prairie. Of all the churches he had been assigned to over the years, this was his favorite. Here he could remember the smells of long ago, beeswax and incense. He inhaled deeply. Perhaps there was just a whiff of the old days in the air; perhaps it was his imagination. It didn't matter. The incantations came: *Dominos vobiscum,* the old Latin. Every time he prayed aloud in English in his mind, he translated it to the Latin that he loved.

"I shall dwell in the house of the Lord forever," he said softly in Latin.

From the altar, he could see the steady light of the votive candles. No beeswax now. Electricity. Put in a coin, flick the switch, and the tiny bulb came on. No flickering flames, no risk of fire, not that he had ever heard of a candle setting a church on fire. Funny how the light changed things. With candles, the statues seemed almost lifelike. Now they were just plaster. Now he had to find a place very deep inside when he prayed. Sometimes the memories were more real than this moment; sometimes they just flitted away and he was left with electric candles, English, and an empty censer, because the ritual so seldom called for incense. At least there was still the miracle of the wine and the bread to bid him to come here each morning.

He went to room behind the altar where the wine was stored and pulled a case from the cupboard. He checked the bottles at the back, and yes, four were empty. He smiled and hummed as he began looking for Isaac. The choir loft, he thought. There was no choir here anymore, just the organist who played at the ten o'-clock Mass and the soloist who came in for funerals and weddings. In the loft, the odor of incense and melting candles was stronger, and closer to the vaulted ceiling, he could see the cracks and the places where water was beginning to seep in. They would have to have a new roof soon, but keeping the school open was more important. There was no longer a way to do both. God would make a way.

"Isaac," he whispered. "Isaac, it's me." There was no answer, but he walked around the organ to a spot that could not be seen if the loft and church were filled.

"Isaac." The priest sat on the floor beside him. Isaac smelled awful. Father Corrigan smiled. Hundreds of years ago when holy men never bathed, this was the odor of sanctity. "The lady police officer came looking for you. I was hoping that you were in here somewhere. I can see that you've had enough to drink, but have you eaten?"

Isaac nodded. Father Corrigan could see that he wasn't drunk. In fact, he looked close to sober. There was just a slight trembling in his hands. "Keeping yourself together you are, that's good." He picked up a half-empty bottle of altar wine. "What bad things does this drive away? For me, it was not being worthy. I was never good enough, Isaac, never good enough. And I'm still not, nor will I ever be." He sighed, no longer longing for perfection, just accepting the reality that he would never attain it.

"I will always sing just a little off-key, my homilies are regrettably forgettable, and, beyond feeding the hungry and helping to shelter and clothe the homeless, I will never make much of a contribution to social justice. Ten minutes after I'm in the ground, I'll be forgotten, or those who do remember me will remember the days when, like you, I was drunk. 'Remember when he got vested for Mass and passed out in the sacristy,' they'll say, and that more than once. Ah, but I never missed a wedding, baptism, or funeral, and I was more sober than drunk for them all, a little fortification maybe, but never downright drunk."

He put his arm about Isaac's shoulder. Isaac didn't flinch or pull away.

"We have shared a few things together, Isaac. A sunny day, a reasonably good meal. But it's a sad thing now that I must tell you." Isaac stiffened, then leaned into him. "It's your friend Dare, I'm afraid. The dear Lord has called Dare to Himself, but very quickly and before he knew there was pain."

Isaac remained still beside him.

"Like brothers you were, I could see. You were family in a world too often without any family at all. You'll be like half of yourself now without him, and there's not much to be done about that. There is a time to mourn. It can be a healing thing."

Isaac didn't react in any way. He sat there more like stone than flesh and blood. Isaac, who "never saw nothing," said nothing now.

"Would you like me to leave you to yourself for a while?" Father Corrigan asked, although he had no intention of leaving.

After a while, Isaac said, "The dreams. They'll come now. Ain't no way I'll be able to keep them away."

"What do you dream of, Isaac?"

The priest had often listened to other men's nightmares. It was one of the few things he was good at.

"The water," Isaac said. "I dream of the water. I dream of the woman who goes to the water and screams."

In the calmness of Isaac's voice, he could hear the distance between the words and the pain. He held Isaac closer and Isaac did not pull away.

"And why does the woman come to the water and scream?"

"Because the water has taken her children away. Both of her sons and her baby girl. All what she had is gone."

"And you were there when it happened?"

Isaac shuddered. "The rains were gone. The sun came out. I say, 'Let's go fishing.' The others, they want to play. But we were eating pinto beans and corn bread for so many days while it rained that I said, No, we bring Momma some fish."

He shuddered again.

"It's all right, Isaac."

"They fell in, my brothers just younger than me and my baby sister. I watch the water take them away. I run and hide two, three days. When they find me, I say I don't know what happened. I don't know they gone fishing. I say I don't see nothing. And they whip me, my mother, then my grandmother, then my aunt. But still I tell them I never see nothing. Still, to this day, they never believe me."

His shoulders heaved. "I didn't try to pull them out. And I didn't drown. I didn't do not one thing right, same as always." His whole body shook as he cried.

When Marti and Vik arrived at the rectory, Father Corrigan led them to the church. Vik had asked if Marti wanted to go alone, but Isaac had grown on him, too. Isaac would sense that. It might make it easier for him to tell them whatever he knew.

"He's up in the choir loft," the priest said. "In a safe place."

The space between the pews in the loft was cramped. Isaac was huddled in a corner on the floor. The priest sat down on the floor beside him. Vik and Marti sat just a little farther away, on a pew.

"Isaac, when was the last time you saw Dare?" she asked.

"That Friday morning. Early. I didn't see him really. I heard him go out."

"Did he say anything about where he was going?"

"To see about getting some work."

"What did you talk about that Thursday?"

"Nothing special."

"Nothing special to him, Isaac," Marti said. "It could mean something to us."

"Was a drug house right nearby. We was talking about moving. Dare didn't want to. He liked being around folks, Dare did. He said there wasn't any need for us to leave, that the dope sellers wouldn't be there much longer, that we was going to have a neighborhood that was safe for the kids. He and I needed to get used to being around people."

Marti listened in amazement. This was more than she had heard Isaac say at one time in the three years that she had known him. She looked closer. He seemed like the same man. Not sober, but not as drunk as he usually was.

"What did you talk about the day before that?" she asked.

He thought for a minute, then shrugged. "Same thing, most likely, or just about. Dare's stomach was acting up again. I wanted him to go get some medicine for it. He said he had an appointment with the doctor and he'd be all right until then."

"Anything else?"

"No. Not that I can think of."

Marti and Vik exchanged glances.

"Why are you hiding here, Isaac?" she asked.

When Isaac didn't answer, she said, "We saw those blankets where you were staying. And found out about the garage you moved to. It wasn't much of a place."

There was still no response. "You didn't stay at that garage for too long, either."

"She told you, didn't she?" he said.

"Queenie? I did have to coax her into it."

"I bet. Looks like she told someone else, too."

"Oh?"

"I think maybe whoever done Dare in is looking for me."

"Do you know who they were? Why they did Dare in?"

"I ain't never known Dare to be in no kind of trouble. Dare liked everybody. Folks seemed to like him. If he had gotten himself into something, he would get himself out of it. He wouldn't have got me mixed up in it."

"Isaac, Dare's stomach hurt because he had cancer. He knew that he did, and that there wasn't anything they could do to help him."

Isaac seemed to be thinking. "Ain't so bad then, is it," he said, "him leaving here quick and all." He spoke just above a whisper. "Not bad for him at all." He turned away, but not before Marti saw the tears begin streaming down his face.

There was a curbside fight in progress when Marti and Vik went back to Queenie's. Two men swung wildly, and as Marti watched, neither one landed a punch. The only other person watching, another man, went inside.

"Want to call this one in?" Marti asked Vik.

"Nah." He cupped his hands around his mouth and called, "The left, man. Lead with your left." Neither man paid any attention. Neither landed a blow.

Inside, there was a boxing match on the small-screen TV perched on a platform that jutted from the wall.

"See," Vik said. "That's what I mean. The power of suggestion. As far as I'm concerned, they could ban Halloween next year."

They stood at the bar. Queenie looked at them, then looked away. Business was better than usual, maybe fifteen patrons, and she kept up a steady conversation with three or four of them. Marti decided that just standing there ought to be enough to make Queenie so nervous that she'd come over and talk to them, and she was right.

"Now what?" the dark-skinned old woman demanded.

Vik leaned over the bar. "We need to talk to you in private."

"Private? Ain't no private here."

"Ma'am, we wouldn't want any of your customers to repeat what we're about to say. It could get you into some trouble."

Queenie looked from one of them to the other.

"Oh, just ask her right here, Vik," Marti said. "I don't see anyone wearing gang colors."

Queenie looked around, too. Then she came from behind the counter and motioned them to a narrow hallway that led to the bathrooms. The sour smell of disinfectant and urine was almost enough to make Marti's eyes water. Queenie must not have been able to stomach it, either. She unlocked a third door and left it open just long enough to turn on the light and motion the detectives inside.

She faced them with her hands on her hips. "What you two be wanting here now? Tell me what you want so's you can get on out of here and let me go about my work. I ain't minding nobody's business but my own. I don't understand why you all got to be messing with me all the time."

"There's no way we'd come here more than once if we didn't have to," Vik told her. "Maybe if you just told us what we need to know."

"Which is?"

Marti took a step closer, and Queenie was forced to tilt her head back to look up at Marti. "You knew where Isaac was staying. Who did you tell?"

"Ain't told nobody," Queenie said. "Not a soul."

Marti was familiar with that self-righteous tone of voice.

"Then who overheard him telling you?"

Queenie seemed surprised. Marti must have gotten it right on the first guess.

"Who heard him talking to you?" Marti demanded.

"Nobody, far as I know."

Vik began to inspect the room. "Hey, Marti, these look like mice droppings to you?" He looked around the unopened boxes of liquor stacked in one corner. "Damn, a roach. We'd better get the Health Department inspector in here first thing in the morning."

"Wasn't nobody I know," Queenie said.

Vik took a carton of cigarettes from a shelf, ripped something off, and said, "No tax sticker. How much time do the feds give you for that?"

"Wasn't nobody listening," Queenie said. "Wasn't nobody around except for some kid."

"That kid?" Marti asked.

"What kid?"

"The kid we've talked about before?"

Queenie's lower lip jutted out again. "I suppose."

"What?"

"I suppose it could have been him."

"What's his name?"

"How do I know?"

"Jeez, Marti," Vik said. "There're no smoke alarms or a sprinkler system in here."

"Don't know his name," Queenie said. "Calls himself J.D. or R.T. or M.B. or something."

Marti took that down. Queenie's description of the boy sounded close enough to the kid she had spotted in the alley.

Lupe Torres met them outside Queenie's about fifteen minutes later.

"What are you two doing, scaring business away?"

"I hope so," Vik said.

Lupe glanced around. "It looks like this morning's raid and the cold weather have gotten everyone lying low. We'll have to knock on a few doors."

They went to several houses and a couple of apartments. Lupe spoke too low for anyone but the occupants to hear what she said, but came away each time shaking her head. "We really need to get to this kid," she said. "I'm out here advertising that we're looking for him. If he did tell someone something he shouldn't have and he wasn't on their hit list, he could be real soon."

They drove around and talked to a couple of beat cops; then Lupe made a few calls.

"A kid using initials rings a bell with a few people, but they don't think he's local. I've got the names of two kids he might have been seen with."

Lupe took them to a house about eight blocks west. In that short distance, there was a significant change in the neighborhood. There were bungalows and ranches and a couple of two-flat dwellings, and new fenced-in bilevels had just been built on two corners.

"It's nice to see that they're building this place up again," Vik said. "Nice area now that the bar and liquor store are gone."

"Now if there was just a way to control this element," Lupe said. She pulled up in front of one of the larger brick ranch houses. The garage door was open, but no lights were on. The tips of two cigarettes glowed in the darkness and Marti could make out two people sitting on lawn chairs.

Lupe unsnapped her holster and kept her hand on her grip. Marti and Vik did the same. As the three of them approached, one of the shadows started to rise.

"No need to get up, gentlemen," Lupe said. "Just stay right where you are."

As they got closer, Lupe said. "No fast moves, either. Just sit there and speak when you're spoken to."

Teenagers, both of them.

"Yes, sir, Officer Torres, ma'am," one of them said with just a hint of sarcasm.

Lupe was in front of them in two long strides. "And watch your mouth as well as your attitude. We can talk wherever you want to, and I've got all night."

"Yes, ma'am." The sarcasm was gone.

"Where does J.D. live?"

"Who?"

"You're pissing me off, Lopez. You know the drill. Answer the question or I take you in."

"The kid lives over a block. White house with green trim."

Lupe leaned over until her face was about an inch from the boy's. She stared at him until he looked away. "I told you about recruiting these little kids. This ain't the big city, man. These streets are mine, not yours. I can watch you and I can find you whenever I want to. You better keep cool."

"He asked in," the kid said. "We didn't invite him."

"Then the next time, just say no."

As they walked to the car, Lupe shook her head. "The next indictment that comes down for anything gang- or drug-related and I'll see to it that a station adjustment puts their names on it."

Vik came close to smiling. "Isn't that something like harassment?"

"I'm not their mother," Lupe said. "When I specifically tell them to do or not do something, I expect them to listen. Those two will stay on my list until they learn that."

Marti started the car.

"The people in this neighborhood think they've escaped gangs," Lupe said. "They think the problem is over there." She waved her hand eastward, in the general direction of the drug house. "I think it has something to do with keeping your grass cut and the lids on your garbage cans. It gives them a false sense of security, but nobody is safe."

The next ranch house they stopped at was also well kept. Large white and green flowerpots lined the walk. Brown stems were all that remained of the flowers that had been planted there. Lights were on in almost every room of the house. As they neared the door, Marti heard a hum, which, as they got closer, she could distinguish as voices. A boy of about ten answered the bell without checking to see who it was. Marti recognized him and he recognized her. Lupe intervened with her foot before he could close the door.

"We'd like to speak with your parents," Lupe said.

"They're not home."

Lupe checked her watch. "Where are they?"

"How should I know?"

"Did they leave a phone number or address where they are?"

"What for? I'm not no baby."

"Are you here alone?" Lupe asked.

"Of course I am."

"How old are you?"

"I'll be eleven in May."

Before Lupe could say anything else, a car pulled into the driveway. The garage door went up and a BMW drove inside. A tall man in a jogging suit emerged a few moments later.

"What is this? Some kind of complaint?" He spoke to Lupe, who was in uniform.

"Is this your son, sir?" Lupe asked.

"Yes, he is."

"This is Detective MacAlister and that's Detective Jessenovik. They are homicide detectives. I'm Officer Torres, neighborhood foot patrol, Gangs and Narcotics liaison."

"Homicide? Drugs? Gangs? What does any of that have to do with my son? J.D. is only ten years old."

"That's what we'd like to find out, sir."

He looked from one of them to the other, and then at his son. The boy had taken several steps back from the open front door.

"Maybe we'd better go inside."

He led them past the living room, which looked like something out of a magazine, to a family room with two sofas and a large-screen TV.

"Turn that off, J.D. Is the one in the kitchen on? Turn that off, too."

"What is your name, sir?" Marti asked.

"Laurence. Alex Laurence."

"Mr. Laurence, could you tell me why J.D. was in an alley between Fourth Street and Eureka late Sunday afternoon?

"That can't be true. He's not allowed in that neighborhood."

"Are you saying that he was at home?"

"Umm . . . yes."

"Was there an adult in the house with him?"

"I . . . um . . ." The man shook his head. "J.D. was here alone that weekend. He was supposed to stay with my sister, but he didn't. My wife and I were in Wisconsin."

Marti let that one go, certain that Lupe would follow up on it, with Mr. Laurence and with DCFS if necessary. "So you don't know where he was."

"I guess not." He turned to the boy. "Were you in that alley, J.D.?"

The boy continued to look at his tennis shoes.

"J.D., answer me." He raised his voice. "Now!"

"I was home."

Mr. Laurence turned to Marti. "The boy says he was home."

"I observed him in that alley, Mr. Laurence. And I want to know why he was there."

"Are you lying to me, J.D.?"

The boy shrugged his shoulders.

"May I speak with him?" Marti asked.

"Why not?"

Marti went over to the boy. "Why don't we sit over here?" She led him to a chair with a hassock and let him sit in the chair.

"How well did you know Dare?"

Another shrug.

250

"Why were you looking for his friend Isaac in the alley last Sunday?"

Same response.

"J.D . . ." his father began.

Marti motioned Mr. Laurence to be quiet.

"J.D., we have a problem. We have a very serious problem. Dare is dead. Someone has tried to kill his friend Isaac. We think you know something about that."

The boy shook his head.

"Sometimes, when younger boys join gangs, the older boys take advantage of them, get them to do things to show how big they are. Sometimes the younger boys want the older ones to know that they're brave."

"Gangs!" the father interjected. The boy jumped. Marti motioned to his father again.

"Something bad happened to Dare."

The boy gripped the arms of the chair.

"Once the word is out that we've been talking to you, something bad could happen to you, too. In order to prevent that, I need to know what happened between you and Dare."

He began twisting his T-shirt. "All I did was tell them Dare was listening when the men with accents were in Queenie's talking."

"When were the men at Queenie's?"

"A week ago Thursday."

"Who did you tell?"

"Sky Pop."

Marti looked at Lupe and she nodded.

"Were you and Dare friends?"

"Not exactly."

Marti waited.

"He was a liar, that's what. He was just a damned liar."

Marti gave the father a warning glance before he could speak.

"What did he lie to you about?"

J.D folded his arms and looked down at the floor. "He just lied to me, that's all."

"About what?"

"Being in the army and having a medal. He was just an old drunk, that's all, and I don't care what happened to him."

"He *was* in the army," Marti said.

"You lie!"

"No. And he did have a medal." Dare's brother had mentioned that. "Do you want to see it? His family has it."

"What family?"

"He had ten brothers and sisters. He was next to the oldest."

"Dare was just a smelly old drunk. If he had a family, how come he was living in that house?"

"Maybe because he wanted to. I don't know."

The boy's lower lip trembled. Tears filled his eyes and spilled down his cheeks. He wiped them away with the back of his hand.

"Do you know what happened to Dare?" Marti asked.

"No. I did like Sky Pop told me. Told Dare to meet in the alley behind the drug house. He was always asking questions about that place. Always telling me to stay away. I told him there wasn't nothing wrong going on in there. Said I would meet him and take him in so's he could see."

"But you didn't meet him?"

"No."

"Who did?"

"I don't know. Sky Pop was supposed to. Sky Pop said he'd let the old dude in. It looked just like a regular house except for the basement, and the front door. That's why he had to go around back."

"What did you tell them about Isaac, J.D.?"

"Dare's friend?"

"Yes."

"Just that he was asking if anyone had seen Dare."

"You've got one damned big mouth, boy," the father began. "I—" Marti looked at him and he shut up.

J.D. smirked. "Then I found out where he was for them. I told him I'd seen Dare and then I waited until he went to Queenie's. And I listened while he told Queenie where Dare could find him."

He seemed to be proud of that. An "old child," her mother would have said, meaning one that was too settled in his habits to change.

"Isaac could have been killed, too."

"But he wasn't?"

"No."

"That's good."

To Marti's relief, the boy didn't seem disappointed that Isaac was alive. And he did cry when she asked about Dare. Maybe someone could still reach him.

Marti turned her collar up and put on her scarf as they left J.D.'s house. The wind must have caused the temperature to drop ten degrees while they were inside. "Who is this Sky Pop?" she asked when they were in the car.

"Travon Gordon," Lupe said. "Thirty-four. He's our local friendly gang recruiter, sort of a big daddy to a lot of the kids around here."

"And loved and respected by them all," Vik said. "I hope his name is on the list of those you arrested this morning and we don't have to go looking for him. We're not having much luck finding people right now."

"We got him this time. Until now, he's always been the one who gets away with everything."

"Just because Sky Pop is the person J.D. tattled to about Dare doesn't mean he's the one who took Dare out," Vik said. "Sky Pop could have relayed that information to someone else."

"Don't burst my bubble, Jessenovik," Lupe said. "Do you know how badly I want Sky Pop off the streets? He's the biggest single obstacle to our neighborhood program with the kids—literally as well as figuratively."

Marti didn't ask what she meant.

When they got back to the precinct, Marti scanned Sky Pop's rap sheet. Other than petty crimes as a teenager and in his early twenties, there were only a few traffic tickets. He had been a known member of his gang since he was fifteen. According to Lupe, Sky

Pop was a recruiter. He brought in new members and trained them to break into houses, steal cars, use weapons, sell drugs, whatever. Otherwise, he was soft-spoken, well mannered, and attended a sanctified church with his eighty-seven-year-old grandmother most Sundays. Lupe said he got the nickname because he was addicted to heroin when he was born. His grandparents had brought him home from the hospital and raised him. There was some brain damage, but he was mechanically inclined and could do almost anything with his hands. There was no indication that Sky Pop did drugs.

As she poured a cup of coffee, Marti considered adding a teaspoon of instant to Cowboy's already-potent brew. Her eyes burned as she scanned a few other reports, and every bone and muscle from the waist up ached. She knew she wasn't getting enough exercise.

A call came in. The public defender was here. They could talk with Sky Pop.

"He would have talked to us without a lawyer," Vik said.

"I know," Marti said. "Maybe I'm just too tired to be ruthless. I got a case thrown out once because the perp was mildly mentally challenged. The defense raised a lot of questions about competence. This way, we cover our butts."

The lawyer asked to meet with them first.

"Kareem." Marti held out her hand. Kareem Shabazz had been with the public defender's office six years, a lot longer than most attorneys stayed. He was six foot six, with a bald head and thin frame. She thought he looked like a black Ichabod Crane.

"I'm not letting this guy roll over on this one, MacAlister. Don't think that because he's got some mental disabilities you can take advantage."

"Sit down, Kareem," she offered, sitting herself. "I'm tired."

"You look like you haven't had any sleep in three or four days." He sat across from her and next to Vik. "I'm pretty damned sure that Sky Pop's friends will let him take the fall for this, to the extent of perjury or anything else that will save their asses. I don't intend to let that happen."

"And if he did it?"

Kareem shrugged.

"You've talked with him, Kareem."

"Right, sister. And now it's your turn."

Sky Pop was huge. He stood at least six feet and Marti guessed his weight at three hundred pounds, give or take. His thighs hung over the chair. He was wearing a short-sleeved shirt, and his upper arms were as large as hams. He seemed to take up most of the space in the room and Marti felt uncomfortably confined. She hoped that the pink color of the walls, which was supposed to calm suspects but never seemed to, would be effective this time.

She stared at him until his Adam's apple bobbed a couple of times, then straddled a chair.

"We hear you arranged a meeting with a friend of ours, a man called Dare."

Sky Pop folded his arms and smiled. "Where'd you hear that, ma'am?" His voice was a higher pitch than Marti expected from someone his size.

"Let's just say we have our sources."

Kareem raised his eyebrows. She wasn't saying anything about J.D., at least not yet.

"Not to be disrespectful, ma'am, but I don't know nobody named Dare."

He was too calm, too polite, as if he could anticipate the questions on this one, and knew the right answers. As if he was guilty as hell.

"Well, Sky Pop, I hope you're right. I hope you don't know my friend. The kids in the neighborhood all seem to like you. They really seem to look up to you."

He smiled. "They're my little buddies. I look out for them. Teach them how to look after themselves. Tell them we're family, that we got to help one another."

"And they look up to you. You must be like a brother to them."

He smiled, nodded. "It's like I'm their uncle, even their daddy for some of them who don't have one."

Kareem stared at Marti. His eyebrows were furrowed. He leaned forward and touched the tips of his fingers to his chin. She hoped he thought she was just playing good cop to gain Sky Pop's confidence. She had better not make any mistakes.

"You've been looking out for them for years now, haven't you?"

"Long enough for some of them to have kids."

"You were a family, weren't you? Did it upset you that Dare wanted to change that?"

Sky Boy's eyes narrowed. His jaw tightened. He clenched his fists and slammed one on the table so hard that the table bounced. "Nobody talks to my kids."

"Sky Pop," Kareem said. "Settle down. Calm down, now. Don't let them get to you."

Sky Pop rose from the chair. Rolls of fat shook as he towered over Marti. "Nobody tries to take my kids from me. We is family, them and me." He jabbed his chest with his finger. "I protect them from everyone. I keep them safe. I see that they eat and have decent shoes on their feet and warm coats. I take care of them. Me."

The anger left him all at once and he sat down. "Who else you think is gonna look out for them? Their daddies? Where are they? Their mommas? They out running the streets or doing drugs. Who's gonna look out for them? Some half-drunk, half-witted fool who ain't even got no home?"

"Sky Pop!" Kareem said. "Shut up! Now!"

Sky Pop sat with one hand cradling his head. His shoulders shook. He was crying. "Who's gonna take care of them now? You close up that house, where they gonna go when they come home from school and ain't nobody home and the doors locked? You don't understand. Don't none of you understand. You so busy getting to the adults, you ain't got time to figure out what happens to the kids. We got kids staying at that house who ain't got no momma or poppa. Their folks are dead or in jail. I wouldn't let nobody hurt them kids, least of all some damned worthless drunk."

"Sky Pop, did you kill Dare?"

Sky Pop sniffed. He wiped his face with one arm. He looked at her. "I took that trifflin' son of a bitch to that basement and I blew his brains out. Nobody messes with my kids."

Marti leaned forward. "What did you do with the gun?"

"Sky Pop!" Kareem said. "Would you please listen to me!"

"Oh, man, just shut up." He looked at Marti. "It's somewhere in the bushes at the old witch's house."

Kareem groaned. "Damn!"

"Why the beach?"

"MacAlister!"

She didn't even pause to look at Kareem.

"Didn't seem like no place anyone would ever look for him. Would have thrown him in the water if the place hadn't changed so much. Thought I was lost for a while. Damned shame he got the chance to call y'all and let you know when that delivery was coming. I beat the hell out of him and all the while he swore he hadn't told nobody. I didn't think nobody could take a whipping like that and keep lying."

After the guards took Sky Pop away, Kareem said, "I knew where that was going. If I could have stopped him, I would have. He did give me a damned good defense."

"That guy's a one-man crime wave," Vik said. "He puts kids who are trained to commit crimes on the street faster than we can apprehend them." He walked ahead of Marti.

"Kareem," Marti said. "Sky Pop did have a point. While you're looking out for his rights, do you think you could spare five or ten minutes to give some thought to helping those kids?"

She left him standing there with nothing to say.

He took the padlock off of the footlocker and removed the blanket folded on top. He wouldn't need the knife tomorrow, but maybe, since they would be at home while he was there, he should take a gun. But which one, the .38 Special? No. It might not stop her with the first hit. The .357 Magnum? Damned near the same weapon as the .38, but if she was wearing a bulletproof vest, this one had enough firepower to penetrate. Maybe the Colt

.45. Reliable. Or he could go with one of the other .38s, the Diamondback or the Commando. He decided on the Wesson Pistol Pac. He could use a barrel that made it easy to conceal, then toss that one and switch to another barrel and there would be no way to link the weapon to the dead cop.

20

The cat was there when he went into the kitchen Wednesday morning. How long would it take for them to notice it was missing if he killed it now and threw it in the garbage?

"Here, kitty, kitty."

Instead of coming closer, it hissed and backed away.

"Stupid cat." Maybe it still remembered he had thrown it across the room.

He stamped his foot and the cat arched its back.

The dog padded in, looked from him to the cat, then sat, putting himself between them. After all he had done for him, the dog was siding with the cat.

"You, too, big boy," he promised. "You, too."

The dog didn't follow him into the basement.

He went right to the small room where the furnace and the water heater were. He would be here for the rest of the day and at least part of the evening. As they went about doing whatever it was that they did every night, he could determine if there were any weaknesses in his plan, anything that needed to be changed. He would pinpoint the best time to kill each of them. Once everyone was in bed, he would leave, whether the cop had come home yet or not.

He opened the small sports bag he had brought with him and arranged items inside: the bottle that would serve as his bathroom should the need arise while they were home, the chocolate candy bars—although he routinely practiced going a day or two without food—the flashlight, inflatable cushion, bottled water, and, yes, the gun. He had come prepared for everything. This was the final step in his plan. Tomorrow night, they would all die.

Marti felt exhausted. She and Vik had been up most of the night. It had taken several hours to complete their reports and by the time she got home, she was too wired to get to sleep. Vik missed roll call, came in late, and looked more rested than she felt. For some reason, that annoyed her.

"That Ford Escort in Knox's driveway has been impounded," she said. "The fisherman's description matches the condition of the headlight. They found sand in the carpet. Right now they're checking for trace elements to match those found on Norris. The car is registered to his wife, so they're getting her prints for purposes of elimination."

Vik yawned and rubbed his eyes. The bags under his eyes were darker than usual. Maybe he hadn't had as much sleep as she thought.

"This Norris case just bugs the hell out of me," he said. "Bad enough when the locals kill one another, without having someone just happen to come here and end up dead."

"I don't know what else to do with this one," Marti said. "I think we've got all the pieces. With that sighting of his car in the neighborhood, even if it wasn't at night when the doctor saw it, we've got opportunity. We've got motive. All we need now is Knox."

"You don't suppose he's done something clever, MacAlister, like check into a hospital or something?"

"Not under his own name. It's not that hard to go to ground. I wish it was easier to talk to his wife. There might be a lot that she would tell us if she could."

"The way they lived, she in Elgin, he in the city, she might not know much."

Father Corrigan called Marti a little after eleven to tell her that Isaac had just signed himself into an alcohol-rehab program.

"Yes!" Marti did a little dance around the office.

"Want to tell me what we're celebrating?" Vik said.

When she told him, Vik broke into the biggest smile she had ever seen.

The next call was from the hospital in Elgin, asking why the officers had taken Mrs. Knox away. When Marti called the Elgin police, they had no idea what she was talking about. They had printed the woman, but that was all. She called the hospital again to make absolutely certain Mrs. Knox was gone, then talked to the Elgin cop again.

"Now what?" Vik said.

"It looks like Knox might have gone to the hospital after all—to get his wife. They've got an APB out on Knox and both houses are being watched."

"Will anybody in Chicago actually watch the house?"

"On this one, they will. It looks like a hostage situation and the man is wanted for murder."

He sat without moving, something he had practiced many times. The boys were in the next room, playing a game. The television or the VCR was on. The noise and the chatter were almost more than he could take. If he had been near the box that controlled the electrical circuits, he'd trip one. Anything for a few minutes of quiet. The boys giggled. Their laughter escalated until he thought the walls were going to vibrate. Damn but he hated kids. He ought to slit their throats tomorrow night. He would if it wasn't so messy. By the time their laughter subsided, he had a headache. Tomorrow, tomorrow, tomorrow, he thought, keeping time with the pounding in his head.

By four o'clock, Marti was ready to give up on ever finding either of the Knoxes. Nobody had a clue where Knox could have taken his wife. When the call came in from Chicago, not even the thought of fighting rush-hour traffic could dampen her relief.

"They've got him?" Vik said.

"A uniform spotted the car parked in an alley behind a motel.

Mrs. Knox is back in the hospital. They don't think she'll make it this time. She's in a coma."

It took two hours for Marti and Vik to reach the Chicago city limits and another twenty to get to the precinct on the North Side. This interrogation room was painted white, and the walls were clean. Knox was sitting on a metal bench bolted to the floor. One of his legs was crossed over the other and one foot was doing a jig. He was wearing a T-shirt and jeans. His clothes were stained with blood. His skin glistened with sweat, even though he wasn't exerting any energy, except for the foot.

"Company," said Riley, the Chicago cop, as the three of them squeezed into the room. It wasn't much bigger than a closet. "Mr. Knox, I'd like you meet Detective MacAlister, now of Lincoln Prairie, formerly of the Chicago force. She works Homicide, used to work out of Shakespeare, Wentworth, and Central."

Knox looked at her and smirked.

"This is her partner, Detective Jessenovik. They'd like to have a few words with you."

Vik was looking at Riley as if he'd been expecting a rubber hose and a few moves out of a movie. "Detectives, we did determine that this was a custodial interrogation and Mr. Knox has been Mirandized. His attorney is in Key Biscayne. Mr. Knox has agreed to entertain a few questions while an associate of said attorney is en route."

"Mr. Knox, I'm not going waste your time or mine," Marti said. She had to stifle a yawn. "We are going to charge you with the murder of Ladiya Norris. We have sufficient evidence to do so. If you have anything to say, please feel free to wait until your attorney arrives and make any statements through him. Otherwise, see you in court."

Knox wasn't smirking as she stood and prepared to leave.

"Hey, I didn't kill her. Why are trying to pin this on me?"

Riley smiled. "Where have I heard that before?"

He looked at his wrist, unable to make out the numerals on the face of his watch, and wondered what time it was. Good thing he had this run-through tonight. He'd have to find a watch with luminous numbers tomorrow. Sharon was home. There had been a lot of door closing and yelling when she came in. She had been shopping and brought ice cream home. A treat? For what? They had done nothing to deserve it. She was a bad parent. The children were bad. They were allowed to watch television. They did not have to speak in a quiet tone of voice. They were allowed to jump on the furniture. They didn't even have to pick up their clothes or clean their rooms. When they came in from school, they did not do their homework. There was no quiet place where they could sit and reflect on their imperfections when they did not meet their parents' expectations. There was no rod of chastisement when they missed a spot on the floor or added a sum incorrectly. They were bad children, being raised by bad parents. They all deserved to die.

Knox's lawyer looked like he was just out of college. He was young and blond, had a cowlick and an earnest expression. They met in a slightly larger room. The table was long enough for six chairs. Marti felt less claustrophobic.

"Mr. Kirkwood," Riley said, giving the lawyer a broad smile and winking. "I'm quite certain that even though your father is out of town, his allowing you to represent the firm indicates that he has complete confidence in your ability to handle this matter before us."

Junior blushed and shifted in his chair.

"Now, I have been in conference with my colleagues from the north suburbs, and since we have an airtight case against your client, we see no need for this discussion. However, out of deference to your father, whom we do see a great deal of, we will entertain whatever you might have to say."

Junior cleared his throat. "We want to make a deal."

"A deal, Mr. Kirkwood?" Riley seemed mildly astonished.

Kirkwood looked confused, as if he'd said something he shouldn't. "He'll tell you what really happened if you'll reduce the charges for beating his wife."

"Kirkwood, we're talking homicide."

"No, we're not. Well, yes, we are, but my client can explain that."

Riley leaned forward. "Does your client want to explain now?"

Riley seemed disappointed. He'd wanted to haggle over this one a bit. That was always fun when all the aces were in your hand, something that couldn't happen often enough.

Riley picked up the phone and made a call to ask about Mrs. Knox's condition. "Sorry, Kirkwood," he said when he hung up. "Mrs. Knox has passed on. So we're talking two counts of murder here."

Marti thought of the battered woman she had visited at the hospital and the three children she had never met, and she felt saddened by the children's loss.

"What are you giving us?" Riley asked.

"What do you want?"

"Knox," Riley said. "Something that's within his capacity as financial adviser."

Lawyer and detective looked at each other for a moment. There was just the slightest nod of agreement.

Marti couldn't believe it. Junior didn't seem to know what he was giving away, or what he would get in return. Riley had just talked him into giving up whatever illegal activities Knox was involved in, and based on this discussion, she could assume there were some. He'd agreed to suggest a lesser charge than murder one on the wife, something that was up to the state's attorney. The Norris case was out of Riley's jurisdiction. He wasn't speaking for Marti.

"You can have Knox," Kirkwood said.

Riley smiled. "So, give him to me."

"Let me confer with my client."

When they returned to the interrogation room, Knox said, "I get some kind of immunity here?"

"I ask them not to charge you with murder one if your story is entertaining enough," Riley said.

"My wife killed her."

"Come on, man," Riley said. "Cut me some slack here. You've at least got to tell the truth."

"I'm not lying. The bitch . . . my wife . . . oh shit. Ladiya was pregnant. She got that way on purpose. She wanted to keep it, I said no. She took off. That was all I knew. Then my wife called me, said Ladiya had talked to her, was going to cause lots of trouble because of my little business ventures. And she told me where she was. I went looking for her, but I didn't kill her. When I found out she was dead, I knew it wasn't me, and I knew it couldn't be anyone else besides that bitch. After I whipped her ass for a while, she admitted it."

"I'd call that duress," Marti said.

"Hell, I don't care what you call it. I'm just telling you what went down. Then, when she made those phone calls, I could see she was setting me up, so I got her the hell out of there and whipped her ass again. No bitch does me like that."

"Mr. Knox," Marti said. "Please be advised that we have so much physical evidence that we will know within a very short time exactly who did what."

"Good. Then you can clear me of the charge and I can get my ass out of here."

Riley rubbed his chin. Knox wouldn't be going anywhere for a long time.

"Might take a few days," Kirkwood said. "And you still have to make a statement about your other activities. We'll go over that before you do."

The lawyer and Knox both nodded. Lawyer and client stood up and shook hands. Junior seemed relieved that it was over. Riley gave him a hearty pat on the back. "Your old man would be proud," he said. "Next time I see him, I'll tell him you handled this like a pro."

As they walked down the hall, Riley turned to Marti and Vik. "Before we start patting one another on the back, Kirkwood senior just handed you Knox on a silver platter, for whatever the reason. Either he wants to make a killing defending Knox or his client is

266

getting too hot to handle and he wants to get rid of him. Maybe he's got another client who wants Knox out, or he can get a bigger client if he gets rid of Knox, who knows. I checked. Kirkwood senior is not in Key Biscayne. He is in his Lake Shore Drive apartment on the Gold Coast with the redhead of the month. Junior came in and did his dirty work like a good little boy. Junior is a lot slicker than that. He'll probably outlawyer his father one of these days."

He tried to listen as Joanna talked to a friend on the phone, but after what seemed like an hour, the snatches of conversation he managed to overhear were both disjointed and inconsequential. She couldn't possibly be saying the things he thought he was hearing, some nonsense about kissing Chris, something else about a party. Joanna wouldn't waste this much time on the phone discussing something so trivial. Besides, he had seen the look in her eyes when he brushed past her in the school hall and touched her hair. He had seen the way her lips parted in invitation while they were shopping together. Joanna had to be discussing someone else's boyfriend, because Joanna was saving herself for him. She laughed, exuberant with anticipation. Soon, he promised. Soon.

Before she left the Chicago precinct, Marti drank several cups of coffee. It tasted like someone had boiled rubber and she tried not to gag. By the time she pulled into traffic, her eyes were so wide-open, she didn't think she could blink. She might have to run a few laps to wind down so she could get to sleep, not that she'd be heading home anytime soon.

"I hope this is the last case of ours that Riley is ever involved in," Vik said. "That man's not a cop; he's a politician."

There were half a dozen reports and several faxes in Marti's in basket when she got to her desk, and a few phone messages, as well. "Looks like all hell broke loose while we were gone."

"If we've got another stiff on our hands, I'm going home sick."

"Jessenovik, give me a break."

He picked up his copy of the reports.

Marti checked her phone messages. Nothing from home, two calls from Elgin, one from Jamaica, West Indies. "They must have notified Mrs. Knox's mother. That was fast."

"What the hell," Vik said. "Take a look at this report, the one from the forensics lab. None of the prints in the Escort match Knox's. They found Ladiya's, Mrs. Knox's, and some that are probably from the kids."

Marti scanned the report. "Sand in the tread of Mrs. Knox's tennis shoes match that at the beach and in the car. Her bloody jacket was in the garbage."

"I'll be damned," Vik said. "It looks like Knox wasn't lying."

Marti put in a call to Riley. "He says not to worry," she told Vik. "He's got what he wants on Knox's job connections—mostly gangs and drugs—and he's got no intentions of discussing anything less than murder one with anybody."

Marti thought of Mrs. Knox again. Would they have been able to prove premeditation? Or had she killed Ladiya on impulse?

She put in a call to Jamaica.

"I am going up there to bring her home," Mrs. Knox's mother said. "She wanted to leave these islands so badly, but the only time she was happy was while she was here."

"Did she tell you anything about what happened?"

"No. Only that she had not known she was so angry."

The boys were in bed by the time Marti got home. She sat in the driveway for a few minutes, too tired to get out of the car and too tired to pull into the garage. The caffeine kick had worn off. She had tried to boost it with Mello Yello while she wrote out her notes, but she felt so tired, she ached. The cold air hit her as soon as she opened the car door, but that wasn't even a jolt. Even her purse felt too heavy to carry, weighed down by her gun.

She went in through the back door. Sharon and Joanna were in the kitchen. Sharon was grading papers. Joanna was peeling vegetables.

"More soup?" Marti asked. The last batch wasn't bad, but she didn't see any reason to make it a habit. "A little meat this time would be a nice change."

"You're tired," Joanna said.

"And you're up late."

"She's grouchy," Sharon amended.

Marti hung her jacket over a doorknob, put her purse on the floor beside the rocking chair, and sat down.

"There is something to be said for catching a few hours' sleep every now and then," Sharon said. "There are those of us who manage to get seven or eight hours, at one time, in one night."

Joanna brought her a cup of tea. "When you're ready, I'll run water for a bath. I've got some papaya and aloe bath oil with vitamin E. You need to relax so you can get to sleep."

"Sounds nice," Marti said, and closed her eyes.

She awakened to the sounds of Joanna chopping carrots and Sharon sharpening a pencil. That wasn't what woke her up, though. She looked around. The cat was backing away from the basement door, its back arched. Someone was down there. Marti groped for her purse. She kept her hand out of sight as she pulled out her gun.

"Where are the boys?" she asked.

"Upstairs, sleeping," Sharon said without looking up.

Joanna put down the knife and went to the cabinet near the basement door.

The cat hissed.

"What's the matter with her?" Joanna asked.

Before anyone could answer, the basement door opened.

Marti raised her weapon and trained it on the man who stood there. He had a gun, too. He was looking at Marti, but one hand aimed the gun at Joanna while he grabbed her with the other.

Joanna did not resist.

Marti made eye contact with Joanna. She seemed calm. When she moved, the man twisted her arm. She moved again, winced, said nothing.

The man stared at Marti. A smile twitched at the corners of his mouth.

"Marti . . ." Sharon said.

Marti glanced at her, gave a slight shake of her head. She wanted to hold his attention.

"I think you'd better put that gun down," he said.

"You know I can't do that."

"Sure you can—I've got your daughter."

Joanna shifted again. Marti looked at the way she was standing. There was something about her feet. . . . Good girl, she thought, and held up one hand.

"I think we need to stop for a minute before things get out of hand and talk about this."

"Oh, sure, right. Come on, give me a break. I know the drill."

She didn't doubt that. And she didn't have any time. She brought down her hand.

Joanna screamed. He yelled. His gun fell to the floor. Marti jumped up and kicked it away. He was doubled over, holding his groin.

"Good girl," she said.

Joanna grabbed the phone. "Officer needs assistance!" she said. "Officer needs assistance! Now!"

He groaned and tried to straighten up.

"Don't move," Marti warned. "Do not move."

Sharon circled the room, cast-iron skillet in hand. "You son of a bitch," she said. "It's you."

"Who is he?" Marti asked, motioning to her to stay away.

"Phillip, goddamn it. Mr. Wonderful."

They sat at the kitchen table while the evidence techs went over the house. Sharon was pale and quiet. Joanna was wired on adrenaline, darting from the chair to the stove, over to the refrigerator, and then to the basement door. She wasn't upset. She hadn't been afraid.

"If it hadn't been for the cat, Ma, if you hadn't noticed the cat . . . If he had gotten a chance to come out of there with that gun . . . He must have been down there while I was. He must have been listening to me on the phone. How did you know what I was trying to do?"

"You weren't trying to pull away from him. Then I looked down at your feet. I could see you were in position to knee him. Where did you learn that? In that gym class last year?"

"It was more than just one class, Ma. A cop came in and taught us self-defense. A lady from LaCasa came in and told us about preventing date rape.

"It was wild," Joanna said. "As soon as he grabbed me it was like the light was brighter, sounds were louder. I wasn't afraid or anything. I knew you wouldn't let him hurt me, and I knew I could defend myself, too. And when you looked at me and put your hand up, I knew just what you wanted me to do. It was like telepathy or something. It was awesome."

"It was all my fault," Sharon said.

Marti said nothing. She didn't disagree.

Sharon clasped her hands behind her neck and sat with her head down. "He looked so different with that ponytail attached to his cap, and the way he was dressed in those faded old jeans. I didn't even recognize him at first. Phillip drove a Jaguar and he dressed in three-piece suits and took me to expensive places. This man wasn't Phillip. But he was. I should have known."

"This is the guy you knew in Atlanta?"

"Phillip and Frank," Sharon said. Her voice sounded wistful. "I thought it was so wonderful having two men pursue me. I can't tell you how many times I kicked myself for choosing Frank, how many times I wished I had picked Phillip instead. He lived in this elegant old house. There was a fountain in the yard and stables that they used as garages. They drank from crystal goblets and had china that had been in the family for years and a real silver tea service." She sighed. "His parents were just so strange. I think they were the reason why I chose Frank."

Marti wondered why Sharon had felt she had to marry either of them. "How were they strange?"

"They were so . . . proper. As beautiful as everything was, I hated being in that house. The way they looked at me, the way they looked at him—it was as if there was nothing about either of us that they approved of, and he was their son. And that house, everything seemed arranged with such precision. She threw out a vase of flowers one day because one rose had wilted. And the day she found a spot on the carpet—my God, I thought she was going to go into apoplexy."

That didn't sound like enough to make anyone crazy.

"And there was that sister of his. Little Miss Perfect. If Phillip did everything wrong, then she did everything right. Of course, she was the child they had together. Phillip was just his mother's bastard son."

Sharon's face became softer. She sighed. "Poor Phillip, his whole life was so tragic."

Marti wanted to shake her. Tragic, hell. Not as tragic as it would have been if someone in this house had been harmed.

"He was engaged right out of high school. The poor girl died so tragically."

"How?"

"Oh, some kind of boating accident, just the two of them. He was devastated. Then his parents died. He was in Atlanta then. And as mean as they were to him, he was just inconsolable."

"How did they die?"

"Nobody is sure. It was some kind of freak accident involving their car. One of those unsolved accidents."

This is beginning to sound interesting, Marti thought.

"Then there was his sister."

"What happened to her?"

"Nothing. She got all the money. Oh, it was just control of Phillip's share, although he got less than she did. She got to parcel it out."

"Is she still around?"

"Of course. And it's a good thing for him. Would you believe that when she dies, all of that money goes to the Humane Society?"

"Good Lord," Marti said. "Do you have any idea why he would do something like this?"

"Well, the poor man, Marti. After all he's been through, I guess when I turned down his proposal, it was just one rejection too many. Lord knows, I didn't mean to be the one to send him over the edge."

From Sharon's tone of voice, Marti suspected just the opposite. She leaned back. This was someone she didn't know. This Sharon was a complete stranger. As for Phillip, she'd see to it that someone took another look at those death investigations. It wouldn't surprise her if they found a few more bodies in Phillip's past. She shuddered. How could Sharon have brought this man into their lives? How could she have been so careless, so stupid? She could be dead now. They all could.

There was a knock on the kitchen door and Ben came in. He looked from Marti to Sharon. "I was on a call. Are you all right?"

Marti wanted to say no, but she nodded her head.

Ben moved toward her and she stepped into his arms. The house didn't feel right anymore, not when a stranger had lain in wait here, waiting to kill.

"Where are the kids?"

"The boys slept through everything. Lisa was supposed to be on a field trip with her French club, but it seems that she's off somewhere with Dante. She doesn't even know anything has happened. Joanna's upstairs taking a long, hot soak. You should have seen her. She was great."

After Marti explained what had happened, Ben said. "She's just like her mother—and her father. She'd make a good cop."

"She'll have to see someone, talk it out, but I hope it wasn't too traumatic for her. Do you suppose having two parents so involved with violence that it's different to her somehow?"

"I think you've got the right idea about her seeing a professional. Maybe you should go, too. And Sharon." He stroked her hair. "Are you sure you're okay?"

"No," she admitted. "Some crazy man invaded my home, came into a place where I thought my children were safe. No, I'm not okay. I want to go out and buy six guard dogs, have a security system installed, put up a chain-link fence with barbed wire, and then sit down and cry because I don't feel safe here anymore. I really need a place to feel safe."

And she did cry, because so much had been lost.

He sat in the cell, in jail, and all because of a woman. Everything that had happened to him was because of a woman. And all of this was because of Joanna. They were all so stupid when they questioned him. Why was he after the cop? Why was he after Sharon? Because they were there. He didn't care about the cop when he went in there. He didn't know there was a cop at first. It didn't matter. Did he target Sharon? Did he target Joanna? He targeted a woman. Would he go after them again? Maybe. Or the next time, it might be somebody else.